Project Alpha

Bronco Lane

Bronco Lane.

HAYLOFT

First published 2004

Hayloft Publishing Ltd, Kirkby Stephen,
Cumbria, CA17 4DJ

tel: (017683) 42300
fax. (017683) 41568
e-mail: books@hayloft.org.uk
web: www.hayloft.org.uk

ISBN 1 904524 21 4

A catalogue record for this book is available
from the British Library

Produced, printed and bound in the EU
Jacket photograph of author courtesy of *Soldier* magazine

It is not the critic who counts - not the man who points out how the strong man stumbles, or where the doer of deeds could have done them better. The credit belongs to the man who is actually in the arena... who strives... who spends himself... and who at worst, if he fails, at least he fails while daring, so that his place shall never be with those cold and timid souls, who know neither victory nor defeat

Theodore Roosevelt

Also by Bronco Lane:

Military Mountaineering, A History of Services Mountaineering, 1945-2000 (Hayloft Publishing Ltd)

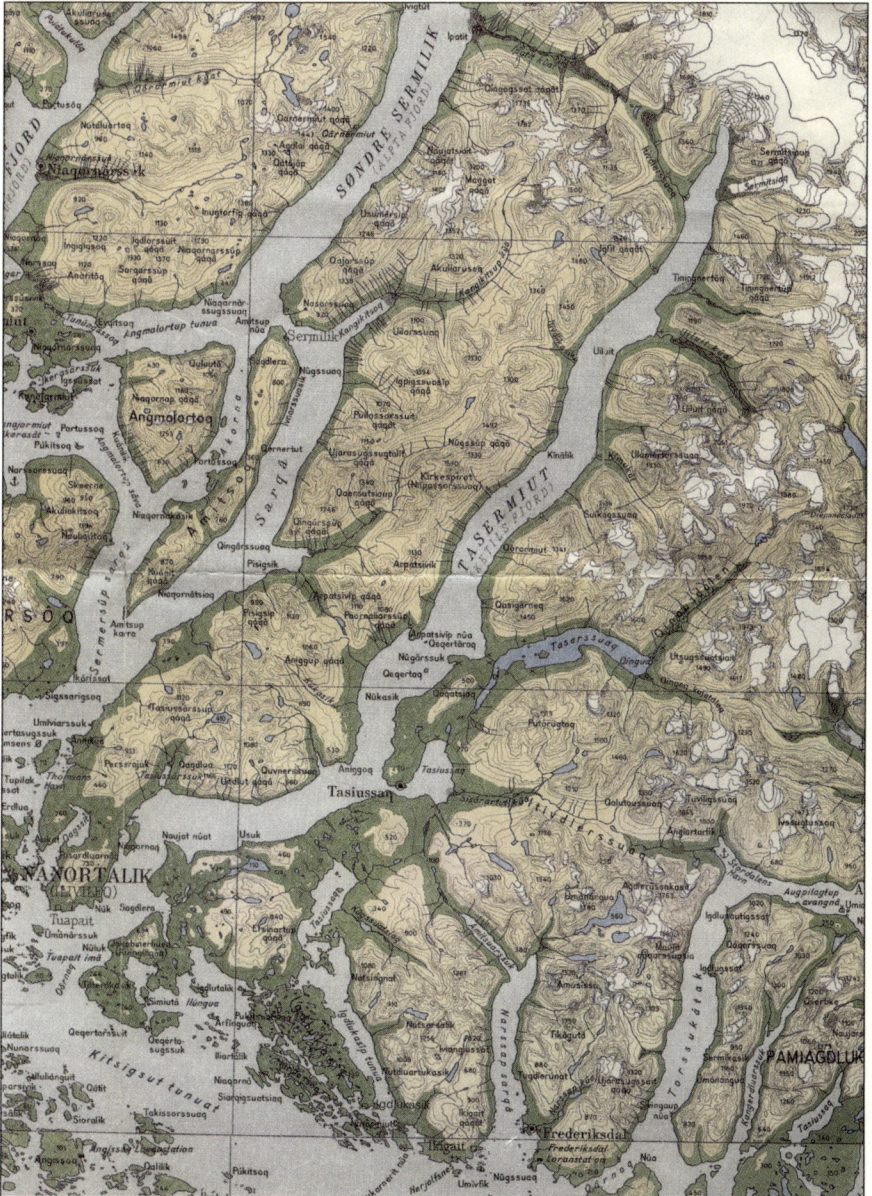

Greenland map courtesy of Tage Schjøtt, 1992.

CHAPTER 1

'Ladies and Gentlemen. Welcome to Aberdeen, where the weather is cold, clear and windy.' The cabin steward continued 'on behalf of the Captain, may I thank you for flying......'

In Business Class, Henry Todd was already up and out of his seat, clasping his coat, brief case and suit bag, ready for the door to open and steps to be positioned.

'Have a nice day,' smiled the lithe air stewardess as he manoeuvred past her down the steps. Taking a lung full of clear crisp Highland air, he mused how great it was to be back, after what - three or was it four years? Inside the arrival hall he waved, having caught sight of Barney, his Texas Oil colleague and friend of twenty years.

'Good to see you,' smiled Barney extending his hand.

'Barney! Whatever you're on old pal, I want some of it!' laughed Henry, as they swung outside and sauntered into the car park. Settling into Barney's BMW car they quickly drove west out of Aberdeen, following the River Dee in the mid-morning sunlight.

Spending the next hour chatting and catching up on events, they turned sharply into the sign-posted drive of Lochnagar View, their home for the next couple of days. This was a secluded Edwardian granite shooting lodge on the outskirts of Ballater, five hundred yards off the main road and shielded from view by fir and larch plantations. Barney had been busy since the previous day, opening up the place, lighting log fires and stocking up both larder and cellar.

'Why don't you let me unpack and freshen up,' Henry suggested, 'that should still give me time to run over a few points before Alan and Pete turn up.'

Later, as they made themselves comfortable in the leather chairs, sipping mugs of freshly brewed coffee, Henry looked hard at Barney and asked, 'You're probably wondering why I asked to meet you here before the rest of the team?' Not waiting for a reply, Henry continued, 'In this neck of the woods you're the only one I know and trust. Project Alpha is of such importance to Texas Oil - if we get it right - we can retire wealthy - get it wrong and we'll be lucky to get a week's wages in lieu of notice.'

'You're way ahead of me Henry!' Barney replied, 'all I've heard is that we may be doing something joint with the Norwegians in Svalbad.'

Henry quickly consoling his old friend went on, 'Great, let's keep it like that. All I want is for the others to familiarise 'Kevin' with the seismic recording apparatus and GPS he'll be taking - without any nosy parker asking bone questions.' Lowering his voice Henry continued, 'It would appear that one of our competitors may have a high level source in place, maybe even in the Houston main office.'

Barney, keeping direct eye contact replied, 'You know the risks he'll be taking - I don't - ah! Here come the others.'

Clambering out of a Land Rover Discovery, two confident and burly individuals, in their late thirties clattered to the porch, let themselves in and strode over. Greetings and introductions were quickly made and hand shakes exchanged. Like oil men the world over, Alan and Pete were used to the unusual and fully expected to excel in whatever area of expertise was required.

Quickly settling around the roaring log fire, clutching fresh coffee mugs, they turned as Henry stood and said, 'Gentlemen thanks for your attention and now for the explanation you rightly deserve as to why Barney has got us together here and not at the Aberdeen Office. As you know I am the vice president of exploration and we are embarking on a delicate joint project with the Norwegians. To keep it at a low profile, I have taken the small precaution for us to live here in relative isolation - Barney will go into the details - but all I ask is that you give the best detailed instruction possible to 'Kevin', who arrives later this afternoon.'

Henry went on, 'The next two days are all we have to ensure he is suitably qualified to operate the various instruments. It goes without saying that an ongoing discretion in the matter is essential. I'll be staying tonight and then head back to London on tomorrow's shuttle. Barney will organise and run everything here. Hopefully his cooking has improved since we last shared a shack in Alaska! Finally - could I repeat how important it is to Texas Oil's future that no word of Kevin's preparation leaks out, ever!'

Henry then took a chair whilst Barney briefed them on Kevin's training and familiarisation for the next 48 hours. The next morning Barney took Henry to the airport, conscious of his tension as they drove along the picturesque A93 into Aberdeen. Turning to face him, Henry asked bluntly, 'How does Kevin strike you?'

Barney carefully considered his answer and replied, 'Competent, pleasant, easy going and potentially a real mean nasty bastard.' Henry laughed and crackled, 'That's as good a CV as I've ever heard and one I know he'd be happy with.'

Later as they said their goodbyes, Henry playfully dug Barney in the ribs and declared, 'It's been great meeting up again pal. Hope the rest of the time goes OK. And I look forward to your up-date call at home in two nights time. Regards to Helen and the kids!'

The 737 quickly climbed to cruising altitude and wrestling with the food tray, Henry mused that Barney's character assessment of Kevin alone had been worth the effort of setting up the discreet rendezvous at Ballater. He was due to have lunch with Kevin later in the week and mentally rehearsed how he'd obtain his assessment of the others in the lodge, before he casually revealed Barney's opinion of him.

As the captain talked of their descent path and weather at Heathrow, Henry ran through the main features of Project Alpha which had started seemingly a lifetime ago. In fact it had only been the previous week when he was quietly summoned to the chief executive's suite in Texas Oil's Houston tower headquarters.

Ray Watkins, known to all as RW, was everything an oil mogul was expected to be - mid-fifties, fit, independent, wiry, ruthless, politically focused, well travelled with a strong maverick streak. He'd spent most of his working life in the oil industry and judging by the pile of dead animal trophies littering his suite, it had given him the opportunity of wiping out most of the world's exotic creatures.

What he so casually voiced, as they lounged in his conference area, was almost a conspiracy against the human race.

'Henry,' he murmured, 'we have it from a usually reliable contact that the Danes may have found geographical evidence of oil in potentially massive quantities on the southern tip of Greenland. Far in excess of what the Brits are holding out for in the Falkland Isles and much closer to the main northern markets of Europe, Canada and the USA.

'Trouble is they are already rich enough not to need the stuff for a while. Whilst they didn't mind off shore exploration, like we did a few years ago off the west coast in the Fylla area, they are dead set against any inland exploration and exploitation because of concern about interfering with local Native rights. We cannot allow some Eskimo seal hunters to get in the way of progress and hold the rest of us to ransom!'

Standing up he continued, 'I'm doing what I can through Washington, but what I need to know before I ask for a return on Texas Oil's financial backing and demand Presidential pressure - simply - is it true? The Danes have flatly refused to co-operate with anyone and have strongly declined to allow access for ground exploration. So we will have to do this one covertly. I would like you to think about it over-night and call in late tomorrow afternoon with some proposals I can mull over.'

Henry took his leave and rode the lift back down to the lesser mortals' zone. He quickly booked in with Debbie, his long term personal assistant, who'd slowly followed him up the promotion ladder. She had proved to be more valuable as an asset, friend and ally than anyone else in Texas Oil.

Quickly gathering his jacket and briefcase, he said, 'Debs - I have an urgent study to complete for RW and will not be available for anyone, war, famine or disaster until after lunch tomorrow. Please give Catherine my love and explain that I will not be home tonight - as I am on a pressing project.' Tapping his waistband he continued, 'I'm on my bleeper and I only want calling if RW needs to get in touch. See you tomorrow 'bout 11 - bye.'

Debbie was well used to Henry's non-corporate way of operating when under time pressures and made it a point of honour that she would shield him mercilessly on occasions like this. She knew he would drive out to a one-horse township, book into a small motel and then submerge himself into the problem - feeding and drinking on anything to hand until he had a solution. He would then reduce it down to its bare essentials on a small piece of note card, before slipping into a deep sleep for the rest of the available time - sweeping back in; relaxed, shaven, animated and bursting with energy half an hour before the appointed time.

Regrettably over the years Henry had never made a pass at her, pondered Debbie. She'd been married once to Phil, a roustabout, who discovered he was more attracted to Asian girls and left. Fortunately, her job gave security and the emptiness of an erratic love life looked to be filled by Jake Norris, a recent acquisition and nine years younger than her 44 years.

They'd met on the aircraft en-route to her annual autumn holiday in Maine and shared a bottle of wine to combat the tedium. During the next three days they saw a lot of each other for walks, lunch and then dinner twice. Debbie was besotted with the attention and willingly shared her bed for the remainder of the week and whenever Jake was in town. He had an interest in Nesco, an oil service industry concern, providing everything a giant like Texas Oil needed. He was due in Houston again soon and Debbie was already planning the detail of their few days together.

'We'll call this one Project Alpha,' stated Ray Watkins, when the next day Henry strolled leisurely into his office suite.

'Take a seat. Want some coffee? What have you got for me?'

Henry declined coffee and reading from his note card, looked directly at the other man as he quietly voiced, 'RW we have two options. One - go in completely covert and risk complete or part compromise from the presence of the sea assets we would need to get in and out successfully. Or, two, cover the whole thing with open normality, such as an adventure tourist or mountaineering party - I would imagine we could quickly train someone suitable to take whatever seismic recordings and location shots needed, whilst using the expedition as natural cover. I favour this option as it leaves the first one available should it backfire, which cannot be said for the reverse.'

Ray stared at him for a full minute before answering, 'It's now 28th April and I need a firm answer by the end of July - in three months time. It's got to be completely deniable right along the line, with any money spent being cash straight from your pocket, or however you can fix it with accounts. But no cheques! Questions? Good - well go for it Henry! Keep me informed of whatever you come up with. I'll tell Jill you have constant access to me whenever you need it. Good luck and keep your powder dry!'

Immediately afterwards Henry had been on the phone to UK, successfully making contact with Kevin Roach, fortunately catching him at home pottering around the garden. Gillian - Kevin's long suffering wife of 24 years sounded pleased to hear him and they quickly decided it had been much too long since she and Catherine had visited each other.

'Kevin - I need to see you urgently tomorrow,' Henry announced, 'I can get on a flight tonight and be in Heathrow for 8am. Can we meet?'

'Not a problem mate,' replied an intrigued Kevin, 'what's bubbling?'

Chuckling gently Henry responded, 'Let's just say it's something I know you will find interesting and it will pay the boys' school fees for a couple of years. The only clue I'll give is that you should dig out your muklet boots and wind proofs and it is north not south.'

Laughing and with a controlled excitement Kevin declared, 'In that case I shall definitely be there - will you be stopping with us or what?'

'That would be a great idea,' replied Henry. 'It will give us plenty of time to quietly chat things through and sort out any immediate problems - I'll send my arrival details later and look forward to meeting you in the morning.'

'Well I'll be a wrestler's Jock Strap,' ruminated Kevin, putting the phone down. Going into the kitchen he automatically flipped on the kettle and prepared two mugs of coffee as Gillian turned from the pantry and smilingly enquired, 'And who's suddenly become indispensable?' A reminder of a recent discussion they'd had about his life style since retiring after 30 years service with the Royal Marines.

'What ever he wants doing it's a paying job,' pondered Kevin. 'It's something in the Arctic or such like and probably involves a bit of lurking. It will be best to put him up here for a couple of days and we can thrash it out quietly.'

'OK,' answered Gillian, 'but do please remember it's Simon's birthday on Saturday and he wants to have some of his mates over.'

'Oomph,' snorted Kevin, 'yards of fart sacks and unwashed feet - OK pet - I'll make sure the business is over before then and he is on his way back to Houston.'

Funny old world mused Kevin as he heard the fax machine clattering away in the office upstairs. His memory flipped back five years to the first meeting with Henry at McGill University in Aberdeen.

They had worked together in a syndicate during an oil industry offshore security seminar. Kevin had wangled an invitation onto the conference as he was due to retire soon and wanted to put out feelers for any employment in his second innings. They found working together relaxing, discovering they both shared similar views about politicians, drinking Scotch whisky and playing golf.

Over the next few years, they exchanged Christmas and birthday cards. Kevin once had them both over to stay, during one of Henry's working visits - when the girls had got on great and the two boys were mesmerised with Henry's accent and accounts of life in the world of oil exploration.

He had really won them over with an account of how one winter he had lost a couple of toes to frostbite. Kevin had quietly ascertained it had really been his own fault and booze was involved, but did not let this influence the boy's picture of Uncle Henry. No Sir! He even wore the funny boots Americans preferred and it was sometimes difficult to remember his British parentage.

Picking up Henry the next day at Heathrow, they were well on their way heading west, down the M4 before Kevin broached the subject. Henry had already decided to give him the full details of what he had been asked to organise, working on the principle that unless Kevin knew the whole story, he couldn't contribute fully.

Accepting the responsibility, Kevin's mind immediately started working overtime and he began throwing out initial thoughts with a lucidity bred from a lifetime spent analysing combat situations, then making speedy appreciations of all the possibilities. Henry relaxed as they cruised along, listening to Kevin quickly list the key factors for consideration and congratulating himself on having made the best choice to put the field project together.

'Tasermiut Fjord Southern Greenland eh! Well I cannot say I've heard of it or the area' said Kevin, 'but it may be on one of my maps at home - won't be long now and we can have a look. Straight off the top of my head, it would seem that I could probably put together one of three options. A naturalist photography jaunt if it is a region that contains something unique - a canoe or cross-country ski expedition, say coast to coast. Maybe a mountaineering trip if it's an area of virgin peaks - and there are hundreds of them in Greenland.

'The outdoor season is pretty short whatever you're doing, but we should be able to fit something into the time frame you want. Fortunately I was in Greenland a couple of years back and know the score with getting permits and the like.'

'What were you doing there?' inquired Henry. By now they were on the exit slip road so Kevin waited until he had picked up the A429 to Malmesbury before answering.

'I was base camp manager for a large commercial outfit in an area called Sweizerland, which is bloody enormous and full of unclimbed mountains. Arctic Challenge Expeditions - the company that put it together had George Merryweather as the climbing leader with a three to one client ratio,' Kevin laughed.

'Even I was pressed into service - looking after two Canadian matrons who were determined to bag themselves a virgin peak. In fact we managed three.' He chuckled at the recollection. 'They were game birds I can tell you - quite a handful - metaphorically of course!'

'What else have you been up to since then?' Henry asked, conscious they were now close to Kevin's country cottage near Rodbourne.

'I have an involvement with Aces High, a Bristol based management training company - mainly for clients wanting a team building event. That is a lot of fun, as well as being quite demanding,' Kevin replied.

'I've also put together a history of mountaineering by Royal Marines in the 20th century. It's been a real joy digging out from the old boys who did what to whom and why? It's finished and I'm now doing the rounds to source a sympathetic publisher which is as hard as finding a virgin in a brothel!'

Henry laughingly retorted, 'Seems as if you've kept the promise you made when you retired from the Royals that second innings are for enjoyment!'

'Here we are then - La Bivouac Roach' proclaimed Kevin, as they swung into the driveway of a thatched character cottage.

Gillian was at the door and giving Henry a welcome hug, led the way inside, saying, 'The boys will be sorry to have missed you Henry - as they don't get home from school until Friday night.'

Reaching into the outside pocket of his suit bag, Henry produced two small packets and, passing them to Gillian, replied, 'Perhaps these new CDs will help. I'm told they are quite the business.'

'What a thoughtful one you are,' Gillian stated and after enquiring about Catherine's health, led him off to the guest room, mothering him mercilessly.

When he'd unpacked and rejoined them, Kevin was bent over his Greenland maps spread out on the floor.

'Here we go,' he exclaimed, 'Tasermiut Fjord, just north of Kap Faval at the southern tip and running in from Nanortalik - which looks like a small township, probably given over to fishing, sealing and taking the odd whale. The fjord is about 60-70 miles long and heads straight to the central icecap. Looking at the relief colouring, I would guess it'd be flanked by mountains. What height and difficulty I cannot say until I've dug a bit more.'

'How will you go about that?' asked Henry.

'Four ports of call,' replied Kevin. 'Firstly the internet, then Stanford's Map Shop near Leicester Square - followed by a trawl in the

Alpine Club Library and finally a look in the Map Room at the Royal Geographical Society. By this time tomorrow we should have a much better idea of what approach to use.'

'How will you go about getting into the area - which ever choice is taken?' Henry queried.

'Rather depends on what's used to service Nanortalik,' said Kevin. 'Could be coastal steamer, small fixed wing, or by helicopter. Either way they will have some Government representation there, as it is the single largest employer in Greenland.'

'Do they have a Police Force and what have you?' Henry queried.

'Not in the same way we are used to - but every Government employee, whether customs, park ranger, teacher or medical aide will have a greater sense of responsibility and higher status than expected as in their particular patch they are the Government. The Danish Armed Forces have a few small teams dotted about - mainly communications and liaison with Uncle Sam. Other than that it's pretty well live and let live - with the main infrastructure being manned by ex-pat Danes, or of Danish descent.

'The locals, or Inuit, have all but forgotten the old ways and their traditions of hunting and fishing - such has been their transformation over the last 25 years. There is a realisation that more must be done to help assimilate them into the modern age, yet still remain Inuit - and this is beginning to happen through youth education.'

Kevin added, 'A lot of the older generation have been lost to alcohol, welfare dependence and suicide, but right-minded folk are trying hard to reverse that trend.'

'Right you two,' called Gillian 'lunch is served and no more business talk until it's over. Tell me Henry all about last year's holiday in Bermuda - it's probably the nearest I'll ever get to going there.'

Later as the two men walked along a local bridle path, Henry suggested that the next day they split the outstanding chores - Kevin going to Stanfords, Alpine Club and the RGS, whilst he called in at Texas Oil's office in West London to make the arrangements with his Aberdeen contacts, for Kevin's technical familiarisation.

'In which case I suggest we drive into Swindon tomorrow morning and catch the 8.30 to Paddington,' said Kevin. 'We could then meet up again in the Paddington Hilton foyer - say about 3.45 - before the evening rush starts.'

'Yes I'll go with that,' replied Henry as they briskly swung along getting long needed air into lungs.

Their conversation over the next hour or so concentrated on a 'current state of play' for the global energy industry and how the events of 9/11 had brought into focus the political agenda being played out. Henry remarked that the potential of oil reserves in the Caspian Sea and the former Soviet states north of Afghanistan was so enormous, it was driving the super powers' strategy, as they positioned themselves to gain influence in the area from where it was likely to be shipped. Henry remarked that he thought some of it was going to have to go through Afghanistan and Pakistan to the Indian Ocean, principally as there were also known quantities in Afghanistan. The fragile peace in the area could easily erupt into conflict, as the various factions jostled for supremacy with America, Russia and China all having a vested interest in the outcome both there and elsewhere in the Middle East.

Henry reminisced, 'Remember when we were told the eviction of the Argies from the Falklands in '82 was to protect the rights of the 1200 Falklanders? I don't remember anything being said then about the potential reserves of oil, both off-shore and probably in Antarctica.'

'Yes I do recall that a few years later the Government announced exploration drilling licences were up for grabs,' chuckled Kevin. 'This time I'm out of harm's way, they would really have to be pushed to resurrect this old soldier.'

'I agree,' replied Henry. 'But it does give you some idea of why Project Alpha suddenly takes on such an importance.'

That evening, following a relaxed early supper, Henry succumbed to jetlag and went sleepily to his room, whilst Kevin mulled over the options with Gillian.

'What I don't want is for anyone to suffer either physically or professionally. Best bet will be to keep it tighter than the proverbial duck's bum. Whatever team goes shouldn't know anything. That way they can always honestly plead total ignorance.'

Gillian studied him quietly and with her usual feminine logic softly replied, 'If you weren't doing it they would only get someone else who may be a right cowboy. I would rather you went than have any regrets later.'

Placing his arm around her and gently pulling her towards him, he nuzzled her throat and teasingly whispered, 'All you're thinking about is the post trip honeymoon. Then I'll swear - for at least three days of warmth, food, beds and you - never to go away again. Until the next time that is!'

Tenderly teasing her earlobe with his tongue, he urged, 'Perhaps we should have something on account?'

The next afternoon Kevin was the first to return to Paddington and selecting a corner table in the hotel foyer, he ordered them both tea.

'Hi pal! How did you get on?' enquired Henry, as he arrived minutes later.

'Very well indeed. I have 1:250,000 map coverage of the complete area from Stanford's and at the Alpine Club, I found a recent account by a very successful Swiss-German expedition that climbed a peak called Ketil,' replied Kevin and with a growing excitement went on. 'It's a colossal granite face of 6,000 feet that rears straight up out of the Tasermiut Fjord. It took them three weeks to climb, using siege tactics and they more or less fixed-roped it to the top. Other accounts of the area talk of unclimbed domes, with faces reminiscent of Yosemite. Finally, the township where Tasermiut Fjord meets the sea - Nanortalik - is linked by helicopter and ferry to the internal airhead at Narsarsuaq. I also have contact details for Eric Larsen the parks and tourism official who covers the patch.'

Henry turned and in a quiet voice remarked, 'I've had a productive time at the office. I had to book in with the operational guys - who'd been told by Houston that I was around. They bought my tale of building liaison with the Norwegians and gave me a secure office to make the preparations with Aberdeen. A fellow up there who I have known for a while, called Barney, is putting it together and will give you a call soon with a rendezvous and timings, etc. I should think it will take a couple of days. I've made a booking back to Houston on tonight's flight and will see you again after the work with Barney. How does that sound?'

'Pretty good!' Kevin responded, 'I suggest that between now and then I make more general enquires and get a feel for what may be possible. One question - you mentioned how sensitive this is and how we must play it down - how does that leave us for money to cover whatever expenses we occur?'

'Yes I'm sorry,' said Henry, 'I really didn't make myself very clear did I? We cannot afford traceable links with the scheme, other than cash to yourself, which we will vehemently deny ever took place. There's no way Texas Oil can be seen to be in any way involved.'

Kevin was quiet for a few moments then replied, 'OK I now have it loud and clear. By the time we meet next week I shall hopefully have a solution.'

'You're a star,' Henry smiled and checking his watch gestured, 'I think it's time I made the Heathrow Express. I'll just collect my suit bag from the luggage hall and get on my way.'

As they said goodbye outside, Kevin proposed, 'When we next meet you can take me for lunch at the best Indian restaurant in town. It's on the west side and fairly convenient for both of us.'

Shaking hands as he boarded Henry laughed in reply, 'You're on! See you soon.'

CHAPTER 2

Whilst returning home, Kevin's thoughts dwelt on the very first occasion he'd visited Greenland and the High Arctic. Thirty years back his very first mountaineering expedition had taken him to Axel Heiburg Island. That had been in the summer of 1972, when twelve service climbers led by John Muston had visited for a six-week exploration.

Lying at 80 degrees north latitude adjacent to the frozen polar icecap, it is the size of Wales and was unexplored except for its southern section. Heavily glaciated, with unclimbed mountains reaching 7,000 feet, it was an ideal location for a fairly novice team, bent on some serious exploration.

They had staged first by RAF C130 aircraft through the USAF base at Thule, Northwest Greenland. The base was a relic of the Direct Early Warning (DEW) Line set up across the High Arctic and Greenland to monitor any ballistic missile threats from the Soviet Union. Following an unbelievable night of luxury in the Officers' Club, they then flew on to Resolute Bay on Cornwallis Island, Canada, to rendezvous with a De Havilland Twin Otter, the workhorse of the High Arctic.

Flown by bush pilots who are recognised mavericks of the skies, they were in great demand at the time as Canada opened up its North West Territories (NWT). At one stage Resolute became the busiest airport in the world, recording more take off and landings in a single 24-hour period (of Twin Otters and other small aircraft) than anywhere else. The flights were supporting small and isolated field exploration teams prospecting for minerals and petroleum throughout the NWT.

The plan was that a Twin Otter would shuttle their party forward in the almost permanent daylight, complete with some tentage, food, fuel and climbing kit, and land them on a makeshift strip on the tundra by the Middle Glacier snout. Once there, Kevin and Noel Dilly would carry on up the glacier for about ten miles and set up a parachute drop zone, onto which the RAF C130 would mount an airdrop from Resolute Bay the next day. Thus they put the team and all their stores for six weeks directly into the area for exploration. Kevin smiled to himself, remembering that critical day working with Noel, whom he knew only by reputation, not having met him before flying out from the UK.

Noel was definitely one of life's characters and was a medical professor at a London teaching hospital and part-time a doctor in the Royal Navy Voluntary Reserve. He was an accomplished mountaineer and had participated in previous service expeditions to the Himalya and East Greenland.

Ten hours hard work found them skiing across to an identified rock feature in the centre of the glacier. The surface was smooth and glaring white with a wonderful crust of new snow. There were no signs of crevasses and for convenience they'd decided to travel un-roped. Kevin was taking a turn in the lead, breaking trail when the next thing he knew he was making a rapid, screaming descent into the dark, icy tomb of an unseen crevasse.

Fortunately his skis jammed about twenty feet down and controlling a total panic he shouted to Noel. Luckily, their only climbing rope was in Noel's rucsac. He quickly set up a firm stanchion using his skis and poles buried in the snow. Lowering the rope down there followed an age with Noel first pulling and then Kevin scrambling in the dark oppressive crevasse, before he reached a position where he could see daylight.

With Noel loudly exhorting him to use self-help, as he did not have any strength left to haul any more, Kevin in a sheer frenzy got to the surface, spending twenty minutes gasping for breath on the crevasse edge.

Gingerly feeling their way over the glacier, the pair found a safe area and made camp for the night. They then brewed innumerable mugs of hot sweet tea before Kevin had recovered and steadied his shattered nerves sufficiently to sleep.

The next morning, in fine weather and demonstrating their ace flying skills, the RAF C130 crew circled to make beacon and visual contact, before performing two run-ins. Each time they dispatched a heavy drop platform with their stores, safely suspended by parachutes, which landed accurately onto the area designated, alongside their large red fluorescent marker panel. Waggling their wings in farewell the C130 departed, leaving the pair below totally exhilarated at a job well done, having turned a disaster into triumph - alone.

'Airdrop Camp' became their focal point for the next six weeks, as in three teams of four climbers, they explored and climbed virgin peaks to their hearts content, staging through the camp every couple of weeks to haul away new supplies of food and fuel on their individual sledges.

Kevin and Noel continued to work as a pair, with Kevin the eager apprentice to Noel's experienced tutelage. With Noel as leader the team that consisted of Kevin, Terry Lane and Ken Scaife, climbed 33 virgin peaks, traversing uncharted ice fields and glaciers.

As it was almost 24 daylight in the short, but intense Arctic summer, with very soft snow conditions during the 'normal daytime', Noel suggested that they reverse the clock, moving and climbing during the colder hours of the 'normal night' on better, less dangerous and certainly less tiring snow conditions. They agreed whole-heartedly to this, spending an idyllic time with mainly good weather conditions.

On their final day, they left 'Airdrop Camp' for the last time, setting off down the glacier to the snout and a rendezvous with the rest of the team for a lift out by Twin Otter the following day. An hour later found them in an active area of deep and wide crevasses, which Kevin as lead man was crossing using suitable ice bridges. This meant taking a zigzag route through, with Noel safeguarding him across each new bridge and then he'd reciprocate.

Ken and Terry followed. Turning uphill after crossing a bridge, Kevin looked over and to his abject horror could not see the second pair. Shouting like a demented idiot to gain Noel's attention, they both then made their way speedily back to where the pair had fallen off an ice bridge into a deep crevasse.

Quickly setting by a stanchion with ice screws, they threw down a climbing rope where they could hear low groans. Kevin quickly said he would abseil down to lend assistance, to which Noel reminded him that he was both the doctor and team leader, therefore if anyone were going down it would be him.

Accepting this logic, Kevin set up and double-checked the safety ropes, whilst Noel quickly readied his climbing and medical equipment before slithering off down. After what seemed like an age, but probably was a couple of hours, Noel shouted up that he was making his ascent and using jumar-ascending clamps arrived at the surface incoherent, totally exhausted and cut by icicles.

Hauling him out the last few feet, Kevin dragged a semi-unconscious Noel to safety and bundled him into a sleeping bag. Firing up a stove, he quickly made a hot drink and got the now hypothermic Noel to force it down his throat. Hallucinating with fatigue and cold, Noel spluttered out that he had found Terry with an injured shoulder and in shock about a hundred feet down, had wrapped a tent round him and tied him off to the safety line. Un-roped he'd then continued climbing down another sixty feet to find Ken buried head first at the bottom of the crevasse, showing no sign of life. By now Noel realised he was quite close to becoming a casualty himself, so had made it up to the surface, checking as he passed that Terry was still conscious.

Whilst Noel recovered in the sleeping bag, Kevin started to haul Terry out, using the jumar-haulage clamp secured to the ice screws to hold the small six inch gain after each yank. An hour of this got him a little closer to the surface, the momentum picking up a little with Noel gamely joining in.

By now, Kevin could communicate directly with Terry, telling him in no uncertain terms that if he wanted to live, he would need to kick-in his crampons at each haul. With a huge effort they continued for two more hours, slowly but surely encouraging Terry to hold his weight with his crampons after each snatch of the rope. Crying with pain they continued, until with a tremendous cry of anguish, Terry at last finally appeared ashen, bloody and totally exhausted.

Whilst Noel checked him over to ascertain his full injuries, Kevin hurriedly made them all a hot drink and put up a tent. Once this was erected Noel continued his examination inside and, after making Terry comfortable, they reviewed the situation. With no communications to the remainder of the team it was a self-help situation.

Neither Noel nor Kevin felt strong enough to safely sledge Terry the five miles down the crevassed glacier to the others at base camp. Looking at the various options, they considered it unwise for either Noel or Kevin to descend alone through the crevasses. Deciding that they would make Terry comfortable inside his sleeping bag, with plenty of fluids available and safe in the tent, both would descend as quickly as possible to raise the alarm.

Hiding Terry's boots just in case he decided to follow them, Noel and Kevin made best speed down the glacier. The innumerable ice bridges to cross and then lower down the appearance of knee deep surface water vindicated their difficult decision. Only an hour from base camp, succumbing to total exhaustion, Noel wordlessly slumped to his knees and groaning quietly, keeled over to one side.

A distraught Kevin reached over to pull his face clear of the snow. thinking, 'I am in a right pickle! Ken's dead, Terry's wounded and now Noel's collapsed.'

Desperate times call for desperate measures he decided, heaving Noel into a position where he could rest against a rock. Delving into his jacket pocket, he pulled out a Mars Bar and quickly unwrapping it, ordered Noel to eat it all, NOW! Fortunately Noel did, giving an immediate rise in his blood sugar levels.

With Drill Sergeant shouts Kevin got him to his feet and together they lurched the last twenty minutes to base camp, their final obstacle being a waist deep fast flowing river. The now alerted members of the team scrambled from their tents as incoherently they blurted out their sad news before collapsing exhausted into sleeping bags. The remainder of the team immediately made best speed to the site of the accident and having rescued Terry conducted a burial service in memory of Ken.

Some months later Kevin heard that John had persuaded the relevant Canadian authorities to adopt the name 'Scaife Glacier' in his memory, for the place where he died and was subsequently buried.

CHAPTER 3

It was a week before Kevin and Henry kept their lunch date at the Bombay Brasserie, close by Gloucester Road Tube Station. The sense of the grandeur associated with the British Raj, made it an ideal choice to enjoy both a good meal, not too spicy, and the opportunity to exchange a quick update.

'So how was Barney's session?' asked Henry as they nursed a Kingfisher beer in the bar.

'Very interesting, professional and fun,' replied Kevin. 'I was doing it in my sleep before the session was out and feel very confident I can handle it efficiently on the ground come the day.'

'Excellent,' said Henry. 'Now tell me what scheme you have dreamt up to get in there.'

Kevin hunched forward and lowering his voice quietly ran through the preferred option. Henry listened without interrupting and as they were called to their table, calmly stated, 'So everything then hinges on George Merryweather's relationship with his patron - this French guy, Richard d'Ilsey! What do we know about him?'

Pausing to order and confirm their intention to stick with Kingfisher, Kevin then quickly and concisely listed what he knew of Richard.

'He's about 58, in fairly good health, a recognised French Anglophile, present wife Camilla is number three. Father was strongly rumoured to have made his pile with Tolz; the Nazi forced labour outfit. Therefore he has never felt quite at home in his country of birth.

'Various estimates of personal wealth indicate somewhere in the region of £250m. His interest in mountaineering stems from an introduction he received at school near Geneva from Jean Mardour the physical education master, who also happened to be an Alpine Guide. He regards his sponsorship for exploration of virgin mountains as a very private and personal pleasure, demanding anonymity for his contributions.

'He first met George Merryweather in 1990 at a private dinner organised by Camilla, in celebration of Richard receiving a gong endorsed by the Royal Geographical Society. This was in acknowledgement of his contribution to the furtherance of human knowledge.

'Richard has patronised George before - first for a trip to the Pamirs and also to explore the British Empire Range on the northern tip of Ellesmere Island in the Canadian Arctic. I do believe George also had a short fling with Camilla before she married D'Ilsey.

'Other than that he now lives a fairly reclusive life with a London house in Mayfair, a mansion on a country estate somewhere near Winchester and an isolated retreat outside Mallaig in the North West Highlands.'

'He sounds just the job for this scheme,' Henry acknowledged. 'What do you know about George Merryweather?'

Taking a deep breath Kevin continued, 'I first met him twenty years ago in the Tour Rouge bivouac hut near Chamonix - that's in the French Alps below Mont Blanc. I was with Jim Simpson, a mate from the Royals. George was going solo and we were both planning to climb the Aiguille du Grepon East Face route - an Alpine classic. George was really beginning to make a name for himself doing routes solo, really fast, so that even the French Alpinists were in awe of him.

'Well to cut a long story short, we both set off early the next day, with George naturally in front, as he was going faster than we were. We'd been going for about three hours and were making good progress when we arrived at a major feature of the climb - known as Le niche des Amis.

'It was about 7.30 am and I was in the lead, moving together with Jim, as we completed an easy section of monster holds, with masses of sound rock and natural protection. Arriving at the large ledge we found George slumped semi-conscious in a corner, with a bashed in helmet and blood running down his face. Obviously he had been hit by a falling rock from above.'

The memories flooded back as a now animated Kevin quickly explained, 'Remembering to leave his helmet on we treated him for shock and gently checked him over to ensure nothing else life threatening had occurred. We sat him up and after a short time he accepted sips of hot orange juice and nibbled at a fudge bar which seemed to perk him up. So we decided to get him down to the hut unaided. After resting for half an hour and stocking up on our food and drink intake, we started escorting him down.

'Firstly, we would fix an abseil line and whilst one of us descended that, the other would lower George just above him, so that he could guide his feet. It's a slow process but pretty safe and luckily George continued

26

to improve and fend more for himself as the morning progressed - not so fortunate was our luck with the weather.'

Pausing to eat his excellent Lamb Tikka, Kevin continued, 'As we made the third or fourth abseil the bright day began to take on a definite dullness with a drop in temperature and a cold wind strengthened to strong gusts. On the next changeover Jim made a quiet remark to the effect he'd be glad when we get down off this one. A typical understatement of our somewhat precarious position!

'By early afternoon light flurries of snow developed, adding even more urgency to our descent. The horizon had turned an ominous dark indigo colour and I mentally worked out how much daylight we had left to reach the bivouac hut.

'Fortunately, George maintained a steady progress and tried to increase his descent rate - despite our pleas to take it easy. With only three rope lengths to go, and to remind us of our vulnerability, we were assailed by the full blast of a nasty, howling storm.

'Visibility dropped to almost zero, as we each maintained a deliberate downward movement. I can only describe it as each withdrawing into a survival cocoon - very aware of the other two - but unable to draw any strength from them. Prayers were being muttered to an assortment of Gods that we would make the hut.'

Sipping his Kingfisher Kevin quietly continued, 'At one stage we were delayed by a jammed rope that Jim somehow managed to clear, when suddenly out of the wildness we could see the hut which we finally made - battered, freezing cold but still intact - just as darkness came.

'Exhausted, we spent the night warming up before returning the next morning to Chamonix - once there we took George to have an X-ray and to be checked out.

'His helmet had absorbed most of the damage and within a couple of days he was fit again. He was that chuffed he took us for a meal at the Bar National - where even Maurice the owner bought us a round.

'We went on to have a great trip, finishing with a traverse of the Matterhorn from Cervinia to Zermatt, before heading back to Arbroath, our base with the Royal Marine Mountain and Arctic Warfare Cadre.

'I have followed George's rising fame - which I reckon he owes to Jim and I for keeping what brains he had encased in the helmet.'

Henry smiled and remarked, 'I am sure I have heard a bit about him -

didn't *Time* do a feature on him last year? Hasn't he written a recent best-seller - something about classic mountain stories?'

Kevin replied, 'Yes, he has put together some original mountaineering tales and photography.' And taking a second coffee refill he observed, 'That was the best Naan bread I've tasted.'

Agreeing that it was good, Henry then inquired, 'Do you have any idea of George and D'Ilsey's current whereabouts?'

'I know George is at home in the Peak District, near Sheffield - he's just finishing a biography of John Hunt, and a trip he'd planned to Ladakh in India this summer has been postponed because of some border tension. So he could be available if we move quickly enough. He will know how to get in touch with D'Ilsey - or probably more likely with Camilla,' said Kevin.

'Let me chat to him about Ketil and see his reaction. My guess is that he may well be ready for something that is not at altitude for a change, yet is still a challenge and the first alpine style free climb, with say two others, would certainly be that!'

'OK,' Henry agreed, 'Let's compare notes again once you've done that and have his reaction. Use my home phone to save going through the office switchboard and we'll refer to George as Peter and D'Ilsey as Paul - any idea of a time frame before you can get back in touch?'

Kevin quickly said, 'Either way I'll call within a week.'

The next morning saw Kevin heading north-west towards Snowdonia. He'd phoned George's wife Phoebe, who explained that George, was spending a couple of days in Llanberis Pass and could be contacted at the Vaynol Arms. Traffic on the M54 and A5 was flowing well, so by mid-afternoon he pulled over into a small car park below the Gromlech boulder in Llanberis Pass and gazed up at the magnificent curtain of rock looming above.

Two climbers were attempting a classic route known ghoulishly as 'Cemetery Gates'. Brightly coloured clothing and equipment gave the first indication of their presence, before snatched shouts could be heard, echoing off the walls. Drinking in the clear mountain air Kevin leaned against the car's hot engine and observed the small figures slowly inch up the climb.

Watching them took his mind back twenty years when he too had wrestled with its mysteries, once having stood triumphant on the top, following a fierce battle of the mind with a balance of upper body strength, speed, agility and confidence.

'Right now I would be pushed to bloody lead Rib and Slab,' he muttered, referring to a climb graded far less difficult just down the pass.

Spending a further thirty minutes absorbing the unique atmosphere he began humming *The Travelling People* as content with the world he drove the last mile to Nant Peris and the Vaynol Arms, home for the night.

A few hours later found him nursing a pint in the bar, reading his newspaper, as a couple of local shepherds, studiously ignoring him, chatted away in Welsh. He had confirmed with Gwyn the landlord that George had booked in and was expected back that evening. Preceded by a burst of laughter he strode into the bar, ordered drinks before looking around and spotting Kevin, George moved across and, gripping his hand exclaimed, 'Well I'll be a, Kevin you old bugger. How are you?'

'Good mate, alive and keeping out of trouble,' Kevin replied, conscious of the magnetism that George exuded as he laughingly cried, 'Come and meet Rick Schofield a friend of mine - we've just had a great day over at Tremadoc. Rick meet an old mate, Kevin Roach, who once brought me down the Grepon with a hole in my head.'

They in turn shook hands and Kevin asked them both, 'Had a good day?'

'You bet!' replied Rick. 'We did two routes on Vector Buttress that I've long fancied and the weather was excellent.'

George laughingly interjected, 'What he really means to say is that he dragged me kicking and screaming up two 'extremes' before I won a reprieve by promising to buy him a 'Special' at Eric's Caff,' grinned George, before continuing, 'Rick has to head back north tonight once I get a meal into him.'

Later that evening, following a sumptuous roast lamb banquet, Rick sped off up the pass into the night, whilst they nursed a whisky night-cap in front of the fire.

'What do you fancy doing tomorrow youth?' enquired George.

'How about kicking off with Crackstone Rib and then if the weather is good have a look at Sabre Cut?' replied Kevin, as downing his drink he chuckled, 'It's months since I've climbed and I would like to ease back in quietly.'

'Sounds good to me,' replied George. 'I've got to hit the road about three o'clock, as I have to be in London tomorrow night for a breakfast meeting early the next day with my literary agent - so we should be able to squeeze them in.'

'How's the new one going? John Hunt isn't it?' Kevin asked.

'Fascinating!' answered George. 'There has been enough material for two books, as he was one of the few who successfully bridged the gap from the pre-war gentlemen's club attitude and moved it to where UK mountaineering is today - egalitarian and open to all. I've more or less finished it now and just agreeing what pictures should be used.'

'Sounds good, and I'll meet you at breakfast, about seven? And then we can give it a go,' Kevin said - moving towards the stairs.

'Gottcha pal,' agreed George, 'see you in the morning.'

George led easily up the first pitch of Crack-stone Rib the next morning. The weather was again dry, sunny with a gentle breeze and upon reaching the first belay stance Kevin gave out a wild rebel yell in elation at their situation, so close to nature it defies adequate description.

'Want to lead through?' George queried.

'You bet mate. I'll just relieve you of a few slings and krabs,' replied Kevin.

Moving delicately past, he swung up the seemingly blank fold in the rock face, fingertips sweeping and gripping into the small cracks to gain balance, allowing his toes to take the full body weight on the rock nubs and wrinkles. Creating a series of rhythmic moves would open the route's defences. Twenty feet on he discovered an inch wide crack, where he was able to introduce a climber's mechanical safety device, known simply as a 'Friend'.

This worked on a cam principal and when clipped onto a climbing rope by a short nylon sling and 'karrabiner' - also known as a 'krab' and 'snap link'- it would provide 'running protection' should he fall off. George securely attached to the rock face on the belay stance, carefully paid out the climbing rope. Keeping a watchful eye on Kevin's progress, he was ready to lock out the rope should Kevin peel off the route, or fall due to a rock accidentally hitting him from above.

The 9mm nylon climbing rope, 90 metres in length was used doubled, so that a single line could be clipped into each point of protection, giving good safety protection without rope drag for the lead climber.

Besides being a safety asset, the rope also symbolised their commitment to work as a team, totally reliant upon each other. Once Kevin had reached the top of the pitch and suitably secured onto another belay stance, he was then able to take in the rope tied to George and safeguard his ascent.

George in turn would repeat climb the route, removing in passing the protection put in place by Kevin, leaving nothing behind. Known as free climbing, in theory they could thus be self-contained for any number of pitches, as the interval between the belay stances were called.

In practise, climbs using this method would normally be over within a day, but on big Alpine walls, or at Yosemite in the USA, they could last for days when climbing is totally dependent upon the weather, plus how much water and food could be hauled up behind.

George soon appeared smiling broadly and saying how good he felt. They sat in safety, coiling the rope and looking out across the valley towards the cloud free and magnificent view that was the Crib Goch Ridge of Snowdon.

'This is living,' remarked George.

'It certainly is,' Kevin replied, pulling out his half litre steel thermos flask and pouring a cup full of hot sweet orange juice. He asked, 'Have you been asked by Arctic Challenge to take anyone up there this year?'

'Unfortunately not,' George sighed. 'It certainly would be nice to go again, as I really enjoyed the last trip, even if some of the clients were a little suspect.'

Kevin laughed as he recollected the occasion when a normally relaxed George had been goaded into a flurry of swearing irascibility by a male client, who had a great affinity for eating food, but no affection to cooking or washing up after.

'Guess that's the down side of a commercial expedition,' ruminated Kevin. 'It would certainly be nice just to go with a few mates and do something really exciting.'

'You bet,' replied George. 'Want some more before we look at Sabre Cut?'

Later, driving home Kevin mulled over the previous 24 hours and its potential success of setting Project Alpha into action. After a most enjoyable, if a somewhat gymnastic ascent of Sabre-Cut, as they rested and recovered at the top, allowing the trembling, over-exerted muscles of calves and biceps to recover, he had again casually mentioned a wish to re-visit Greenland, sometime soon.

George repeated his interest in making a return trip for anything he considered as a worthy project. Introducing the next step would be crucial, so that George perceived it was nothing more than a natural course of events.

Kevin muttered to himself, as if for confirmation, 'I'll drop him a postcard tomorrow, saying how much I enjoyed our short get together and enclose with it a couple of pictures of Ketil to whet his appetite. He may take the bait - but it really depends on what else he has planned.'

The next day, after sending the vital envelope with postcard and photos of Ketil, to George's home near Glossop, he contacted Henry at home in Houston at 7am local time, just as he was leaving for the office and gave a progress up-date.

'Thanks for that old buddy,' replied Henry. 'I'll keep the boss informed and listen out for any developments. My regards to Gillian and the boys.'

CHAPTER 4

Kevin spent the next week restlessly delving deeper into Greenland logistics and trying to identify British climbers with first hand knowledge of the area. Making contact with Jack Baynes, the most current, he spent an interesting half-hour having a general chat about Tasermiut Fjord.

He could easily visualise the wind whipped wave tops crashing against the sides of the boat, as they made progress round yet another headland, to be greeted with yet more unclimbed sheer granite faces reaching for the stormy sky. All this against the dramatic backdrop of the inland Greenland icecap stretching away into the distance.

'There's just so much to do. You're spoilt for choice,' remarked Jack passionately. 'I'll send you a couple of panoramic shots and when you've had them copied, pop them back.'

With this fresh news and stirred by Jack's unbridled fervour, a few evenings later he phoned George, finding him very animated as he queried, 'Where did you get that postcard youth? It had me in stitches I can tell you!'

'An old mate from the Marines is now a commercial artist, with a bent for the comical. He was quite a mountaineer in his day and conjured up 30 climbing situations and had them made into postcards. I'll send you some blanks,' replied Kevin before venturing, 'How did Ketil grab you?'

George whooped and laughingly remarked, 'It looks like it's always been waiting for a first free climb. What have you in mind?'

Consciously keeping his excitement in check, Kevin steadily talked through a basic concept, that George selected two other suitable climbers, whilst he would organise the logistics to get them there, plus maintain the essential safety link whilst the trio free climbed Ketil.

'Sounds good to me mate,' replied George. 'Any idea what it will cost?'

'I have some broad figures and outline planning dates,' Kevin ventured. 'Why don't I put them together and email them to you, so you can have a look and confirm they are OK.'

'That will give me something to talk over with whoever else we take,'

George quickly rejoined. 'I'll get back once I've asked around the lads for another two idiot volunteers! Meanwhile I think any specific info you can gather will be useful.'

Kevin suggested, 'I'll try to make contact with Albert Kurt in Zurich, who led a successful Swiss-German team a couple of years ago. Also Doug Scott had a look, I'm not sure for how long, or what he did. Meanwhile I'll wait for your call.'

Barely able to conceal his excitement he immediately phoned Henry's home number. There was no answer, so he tried the Houston office number and spoke with Debbie. She politely informed him that Henry was in conference for the rest of the day and asked if she could pass a message when changing over the coffee.

'Just let him know that Kevin phoned about a positive conversation he had with Peter,' Kevin said, 'and that I shall be at home for the next 24 hours - should he wish to call.'

'Right I'll do that sir, anything else?' asked Debbie.

'Yes! Another thing - could he look through past American Alpine Club journals and see what they report in the area, especially for any pictures or video.'

Debbie assured him that Henry would get the message and biding him to 'Have a nice day' rang off. As an administrative instinct she immediately contacted the building exchange to have them secure Kevin's phone number and jotted it down in her diary of the day's events. At an early opportunity she slipped Henry a short note on a visit to the conference room, noting his smile and favourable reaction on reading it.

Debbie could hardly wait for the conference to finish, so that she and Henry could depart. Jake would be meeting her later at a quaint, romantic Italian restaurant he had recently discovered. There, they would enjoy a happy meal before returning to her duplex just a little tipsy from the Chianti, for hopefully a wild night of shameless eroticism. She was slightly concerned for him, as Jake had intimated at their last tryst that his boss had started heavy pressure to find out who else was submitting proposals for a service contract in Texas Oil's element of the North Sea's Norwegian sector.

Despite Henry's diligence, she had seen and overheard various references to the Norwegians and had rightly guessed that Kevin's recent call was somehow involved. Perhaps if she continued to casually record anything relating to the mysterious new mission and pass it on to Jake, he could relax enough to make their occasional meetings even more fulfiling for the wanton physical passions he had awoken in her. 'Please hurry up in there' she groaned, wishing Henry to finish really soon.

Back in his office once the conference was over, Henry phoned Kevin as soon as he could. After the initial greetings, Kevin quickly reported that, 'Peter is now picking the other two for a team and has asked me to prepare a broad logistic plan. No mention yet of Paul, but I'm sure that will follow.'

'That's really made my day,' laughed an exultant Henry. 'Do keep in close touch and best regards to the family.'

'Debbie,' Henry asked, 'would you clear me an immediate appointment upstairs with RW - tell Jill it's good news to do with Project Alpha.' That should get me in before he scoots off for a daily round of golf. He deliberated, running over in his mind the main briefing points to communicate.

'Will you require me to wait until after you've seen RW?' Debbie enquired, 'as I have an appointment I'd very much like to keep.'

'No that's fine,' Henry replied. 'You pack in once I'm cleared with Jill and I'll see you in the morning.'

Debbie briskly obtained acquiescence for an immediate interview with RW, passed this on to Henry, who smilingly waved goodbye, as she strode out of the office with a quickening step and the skittish jaunty style of a woman half her age.

Meanwhile in Glossop, UK, George's first call was to get in touch with Hugh Maclean, who was probably the most experienced active British big wall climber. Jane Fletcher, Hugh's partner at their cottage, on Anglesey told him that he had gone to the Lakes and the best bet was to try his mobile, or Rick's place in Penrith.

'Maybe I can kill two birds with one stone,' he thought, dialling the familiar number of the Manchester Outdoor Education Centre, where Rick was a teacher of outdoor pursuits. 'Could I possibly speak with Rick Schofield please. This is George Merryweather calling.'

'I'll just see if he's about,' the centre secretary replied.

'Hello pal - what gives?' chuckled Rick.

'Thought I'd just check up on how our hard earned taxes are being squandered,' George retorted. 'Jane mentioned that Hugh may be with you and I have a proposition that will interest you both. Hello you still there?'

'Yes George I'm here and Hugh is out having a scramble around Skiddaw. What's the poop?' Rick replied.

'How does a month late July to late August in South Greenland sound? The aim will be to make a free route on Ketil in Tasermiut Fjord with Hugh, you, me and Kevin as base man,' explained George.

'That would fit in very nicely mate,' enthused Rick. 'I was going to the Alps, but somehow they fade into insignificance at the mention of Greenland.'

'Marvellous!' George replied, 'could you have a chat with Hugh when he's back and ask him to give me a bell at home.'

'Sure thing George - speak with you later,' Rick answered.

George's next series of calls entailed trying to locate Camilla D'Ilsey. This firstly involved leaving a message on the answer phone at her Chelsea flat and then waiting impatiently until she contacted him. George never tried to communicate direct with Camilla's husband Richard, knowing full well she wished to exercise 'that' control. What the hell, so long as Richard continued to lavish patronage for his expeditions, who could complain!

'Darling - how are you?' breathed Camilla. 'It's an age since we last saw you - what are you up to now?'

'Hi pet,' George smiled a reply, 'I've just completed a biography of Lord Hunt and I am currently looking at making the first free climb of a peak called Ketil in Greenland.'

'That sounds intriguing,' she said, 'do you want a meet with Richard to see if he can help you with this one?'

'Very much please,' George replied, 'whenever it's convenient. I could pop down to town and maybe we could get together?'

'That would be nice,' purred Camilla. 'Why don't I look at both our diaries and let you know?'

'Couldn't be better,' growled George and lowering his voice said, 'I can still remember our frolics in the bath the last time. I promise to bring my rubber duck.'

'Do that darling,' she said breathlessly. 'I'll be in touch soon sweetie - ciao!'

Putting down the phone George could hardly restrain his grin at the ludicrous situation. Not only did he receive patronage from Richard but his wife threw in a frisky romp at her discreet Chelsea flat for good measure. He realised there were possibly some Freudian undertones, but so long as Phoebe did not get hurt - what damage was there? An hour later Camilla phoned back with a possible slot in two days time for a late afternoon meet with Richard and sensuously asked if he would like lunch at her flat first? They could then go their separate ways, meeting again later in Mayfair. George reached for the Sheffield-London train timetable.

Hugh phoned that evening to say he would be available for a trip to Ketil, asking when they could all get together for a pow-wow.

'I'll ring round everyone later in the week and arrange for something here next weekend if possible - say Saturday afternoon,' George replied. 'Then those who want can stay over and try out some local ale.'

'I'll let Rick know that and will keep Saturday clear,' said Hugh.

George's meeting with Richard passed smoothly. He listened attentively; asking a couple of pertinent questions, before offering whatever help George needed for financial support to top up any budget deficit. His only criteria being that within reason, George must first exhaust all other possible avenues of support.

'Making you work hard for it?' he said - with a possible glint in his eye when they shook hands in farewell by the front door. Camilla waved and smiled goodbye from the lounge, without giving the slightest clue to their torrid session earlier in Flood Street. Striding away in search of a cab to King's Cross - he celebrated how once again Lady Luck had dealt him a winning hand to play.

Later, whilst taking a gentle walk to his club Richard D'Ilsey used a public call box to reach a north London number. In short monosyllables he ascertained from 'Alan' that Camilla had indeed entertained George Merryweather for over two hours in her Chelsea flat.

Smiling, as he strode purposefully away, his mind flipped back to the first time he'd utilised Alan Wade's services over twenty years previously when Sophie his first wife had become belligerent and distant. He suspected she'd taken a lover and through a family contact and member of the Security Service, he'd been introduced to Alan a discreet private investigator, who specialised in high profile assignments. Alan quickly confirmed his suspicions and ever since then Richard had kept him on a retainer to undertake similar enquires as required.

More recently, whilst Richard and Camilla were basking in the Caribbean sun on Tobago, he'd gained entry with a copy of her flat key and introduced a voice activated listening device into the bedside light. This was capable of being monitored from 300 yards away, well within the distance of a nearby garage Alan rented, where an automatic recording machine was installed. He was able to interrogate the machine remotely and ascertain the amount of traffic, before making a call to retrieve the tape.

Richard had no problem with her taking a lover, so long as she used the utmost discretion and kept it private. He just wanted to be aware, as he'd long learnt in life that knowledge is power!

CHAPTER 5

'Lads – perhaps if I start the ball rolling you can chip in as things come up,' invited George. The others had arrived at his Glossop cottage on the Saturday as planned. Phoebe had made them a late lunch of soup and sandwiches and they were now gathered around the thick oak dining table, alongside which stood a flip chart easel bearing a southern map of Greenland, with pictures of Tasermiut Fjord and Ketil. George continued, 'Kevin – perhaps you would like to lead us off by describing what you've been able to find out about the area and in particular Ketil.'

Moving over to the map display Kevin quickly orientated them and pointed out Narsarsuaq, the airhead from Europe, Nanortalik settlement at the entrance to Tasermiut Fjord and the location of Ketil on its south side, only a few miles from the permanent inland icecap.

He then described what pertinent climbing information he had already accumulated and its source. Finally, he gave a broad overview of the probable logistical matrix for their movements and arrangements for freight, communications, helicopter emergency response, medical self-help, food, fuel and local resources.

After answering a couple of relevant questions he handed over to George, who rising to his feet thanked Kevin for a lucid brief before going on to ask that they each take on a specific responsibility.

'If Kevin can continue with logistic co-ordination, especially move-ment of freight and ourselves to base camp, plus food, medical, comms and the budget – any problems with that Kevin?' he asked.

On seeing his negative head shake George had a quick sip of water and continued, 'I shall concentrate on liaison for any diplomatic clearances, fund raising and public relations.

'Hugh would you take on a really detailed study of the actual climb-ing problems? What special gear we will need and photography issues.

'Rick could you decide on our equipment requirements, source and purchase them and arrange with Kevin centralisation for packing and dis-patch?'

'Am I right in thinking Kevin that the freight will need to be in Copenhagen by the 20th June – to ensure a sea move to reach Nanortalik by the 20th July?'

Kevin nodded an affirmative and speaking across to Rick reminded him that every report had spoken of the torment provided by the virulent Arctic mosquitoes and gnats in the short summer.

'Could I suggest we take a bee keeper hat each and some of those battery operated widgets that you have at barbecues which attract and grill the beasties.'

They continued in a similar vein for the rest of the afternoon, until Hugh and Rick both started making a move to their respective homes. With cries of farewell and last minute reminders of keeping in touch, they drove away, leaving George and Kevin to quietly decide their forthcoming priorities and trying to identify future problem areas.

George explained, 'My benefactor has said he will top up any budget deficit, provided that I have fully explored every source available to us. This is his usual method and with the tight time frame left, I'll have to discount some of the more obvious as too long term and just attempt some real players, starting with the media.

'I'll have a chat on Monday with Alan White my literary agent and get him involved. Maybe we should aim to hit a couple of the High Street banks or one of the utility companies, who seem to be getting bad PR!'

'Or the Government!' laughed Kevin in reply.

That evening they went to sample the local beer at The Sheepcote Arms two miles away on the edge of the moors. Kevin listened fascinated as George expounded on some of his ideas to attract sponsorship.

'He's a one man marketing miracle,' mused Kevin, fully realising that 30 odd years in the Armed Services hardly prepared him for this particular aspect of commercial life.

'I think we should try and get a charity onboard. Look at what Fiennes and Stroud achieved for theirs, when they did that trans-Antarctic trek,' George continued, 'it gives the trip a clean purposeful and 'feel good' image and gets away from the usual doe ball question of Why!'

'Do you know,' said Kevin, 'that is the one question I find hardest to honestly answer. I do know at certain times it may be the personal challenge whilst at others it's not wanting to let somebody down. How about you?'

'It is just something that gives me the greatest pleasure, not when I'm actually involved as there are usually too many things happening around you for time to become philosophical. I would say it's more the shared experience and right now that means another Tetley Special!' cried George.

Later that week George had a break through in media interest when *Newsweek* broached the subject of possible sponsorship with Alan White, subject to a proviso of exclusive media rights. The *Newsweek* market research team had discerned a small but definite rise in UK sales when *Time* used their article on George the year before and they were ready to make an offer of £10,000 for an involvement.

Given the short time available to explore alternatives, George had no qualms in signing up for their offer (half of the envisaged budget) on the understanding that they would also run a full page on his preferred charity, the British Heart Foundation.

Newsweek envisaged two articles about George. A short introduction piece in June, with a longer follow-up in September. With this agreement secured so soon and knowing that Richard would top up as required, he felt extremely relieved and positive about their prospects.

As usual, The Royal Geographical Society were extremely helpful and whilst not producing any money, gave something even more useful, their endorsement. Clutching this, George then approached the Danish Embassy in Knightsbridge for their diplomatic clearance. Anne, the tourism officer he arranged to meet, a young, nubile and attractive blond girl, was most enthusiastic, offering any assistance they might need.

She explained that as the expedition did not involve movement on the Greenland ice cap, they would not require special communication clearances, or produce a financial bond to cover the costs of an air search and rescue. As three of them had visited Greenland before the team had extra credibility. This, combined with the stated Danish wish to encourage tourism and, compared with the bureaucracy of climbing for example in the Indian sub-continent, would almost mean a team leader's holiday.

George felt that he had to find a publicity angle that would allow *Newsweek* the opportunity to develop their account of the first attempt to climb Ketil freestyle. As so often happened, the answer came on his morning run. He would ask *Newsweek* in their first article to advertise a competition for the British Heart Foundation, whereby members of the public had the chance to win a good prize, by estimating how many feet they would climb up Ketil on a designated day, based on donations of a penny a foot.

He was sure either *Newsweek* or the Foundation could drum up some prizes to make it an attractive proposition. He made a mental note to ask the Foundation appeals manager to advise on collection of the donations - possibly by a High Street bank? They would also need slots on prime-time television and radio to get the story out.

The same evening Kevin was responding to urgent messages on his answer phone, by fax and email from Henry to contact him immediately. Against his better judgement, he phoned the Houston office and having spoken to Debbie was connected through.

'Kevin!' cried Henry, 'you don't know how happy I am you called. RW is giving me very heavy pressure for a progress report and time frame.'

'My assessment,' replied Kevin, 'is that we shall be on schedule to reach Nanortalik by air on 24 July, where we will meet up with our sea freight and the two locally hired inflatable rubber boats and outboard engines. That will see us in the Tasermiut Fjord base camp by the 27th at the latest. Then returning to Nanortalik three weeks later and back in London by the 22nd August.'

'RW will be mighty pleased with that news,' murmured Henry and in a more relaxed manner went on, 'RW is also getting a little paranoid about how George will raise the budget.'

Kevin laughed and said, 'He seems to have it all in hand. *Newsweek* are talking of being the main sponsor and I understand Paul is ready to top up the difference. Making any enquiries could possibly attract George's attention – so I would suggest that we keep a watching brief and go with the flow.'

'I know we have talked about it before,' replied Henry, 'can I just remind you how vital it is that we keep everything about our interest discreet and secure.'

'No problems this end,' Kevin reassured him. 'I'll try and keep to a weekly call timetable – say Monday morning your time?'

'I look forward to that pal – take good care,' said Henry as he hung up and faced the window, unaware of the interest the call had generated in his outer office. Debbie carefully replaced the telephone and slipped a small note pad into her bag.

'I know someone who will be pleased with these details,' she mused, already anticipating how much pleasure she would derive from Jake's extra attentions, as she coyly revealed the new snippets.

In North Wales, having obtained Albert Kurt's contact details from the Alpine Club secretariat, Hugh composed a list of questions to ask about the Ketil climb. On calling, he was fortunate to find Albert at home and agreeable to see him later that week at his office in Zurich. Leaving the Anglesey cottage in the early hours, Hugh quickly sped along the empty A5, M54 and M6, to arrive at Birmingham airport in plenty of time to catch the morning flight to Zurich.

By 11.30am he was exchanging pleasantries with Albert in his office and deciding that Yes! they had met some years previously at the Brenva bivouac hut, above Courmayeur on the Italian side of Mt Blanc. Having broken the ice, with a welcoming smile, Albert quickly switched on a slide projector showing his pictures of the climb and indicated the route they had pioneered some years before.

They had climbed using siege tactics – fixing rope permanently to the climb, then descending to spend the night at base camp. Each morning saw them re-ascend to their high point to add more fixed rope. They continued this routine for ten days until they were two thirds of the way up and then they climbed continuously for a 72-hour period to the summit.

'What gear do you think we need for the route?' began Hugh.

Albert replied, 'I would recommend 20 assorted pitons, 3 sets of friends and chocs, 3 times 60 metre of 11mm climbing rope and 2 times 60 metre of 9mm haulage rope. We also took a hand drill and 10 bolts for emergency use. Of course you will need full body harnesses, jumars, ettriers, slings, etc.'

'Did you find any sleeping platforms?' asked Hugh.

Albert laughed and replied, 'Only two places really – one quite low and the other only 100 metres from the top. To free climb it completely you will need the American portaledges to sleep in.'

'Any drinking water on the wall?' queried Hugh.

Albert nodded, 'A small seep here and there – but it really depends on the weather and I guess water availability is the key problem – as no way can you haul up enough for more than what, three days? Even that would be a lot of weight, at say two litres a day for each of you that would be 18 kilos of water alone.

'Thinking about it, I don't remember more than two days in a row when we did not have rain or snow as Ketil seemed to attract any weather in the area. Whilst that would be a problem for lots of people, for you it could make all the difference!'

'Are night temperatures cold?' asked Hugh.

'Not really,' Albert replied. 'You should not need any warmer gear than you would use in the Alps on a similar climb at the same time of year. We did have a two day storm the last time, but the visit before that was more or less clear for a whole month except for the short daily flurry passing through.'

'How is the rock?' queried Hugh. 'Is it flaky or sound?'

'It is really beautiful granite, initially plates until the upper half of the route, when it gives way to the crack system. Mostly finger and hand ones, with some long lay backs and chimneys,' Albert explained, smiling in memory.

They went through the slides once more and Albert agreed to copy and forward certain ones. As it had now reached lunchtime, Hugh asked if he could take him out to a nearby restaurant.

'That is most kind but I must say no as I am meeting a client in 30 minutes,' Albert replied.

'In that case may I say how grateful we are for all your help and advice,' Hugh said then asked, 'Is there anything that we can do for you?'

Albert answered slowly, 'I count the route on Ketil as one of my most finest climbing achievements. It is so gigantic, so committing. Do be successful and yes! Give my best wishes to Eric Larsen at Nanortalik – you'll like him he's a good guy.'

Shaking Hugh's hand in farewell at the outer door, Albert's cheerful 'Gluck Haben' rang in his ears as he made his way onto the airport train.

On the uneventful return journey to Birmingham, Hugh thought over all Albert had said and tried to visualise the monster wall that was Ketil. Putting the climbing problems aside, the two key logistic areas to concentrate on would be firstly to carry and drink enough water and secondly, having a bomb proof portaledge ensemble for rest and sleep.

He anticipated at least 20 days being necessary to complete the route, which would require a lot of water, food and fuel. Realistically the two haul sacks could not be more than 90lbs each to start with.

It was going to be an interesting exercise working out the priorities of weight and he noted to get hold of the new self-ratchet pulleys immediately and try them out at the maximum weight.

'That will concentrate the mind a bit,' he decided, arriving at Birmingham. Before leaving the car park he made a couple of calls - one to Joe Brown's shop in Llanberis, near Snowdon. He placed an urgent order for a couple of Exotica wall hauliers, two haul bags, a two man and a single man portaledge and two Wilderness hand drills, with drill bits and a selection of bolts. The other call was to George, with a resume of his visit to Albert Kurt.

'Well if he reckons it can be done,' George responded, 'we'll just have to prove him right! I am hoping we can have another get together here next weekend – perhaps you may have the new slides available then and we can discuss your visit today and what came out of it.'

'Right you're on! I look forward to that,' replied Hugh.

As he was bypassing Telford on the M54 a natural apprehension began to clear. Driving through Capel Curig into a magnificent sunset, with a dramatic view of Snowdonia and the Glyders massif finally sweeping away his concern for success on Ketil.

'It cannot be harder than El Cap – just a bit more iffy with the weather,' Hugh said to himself, carefully negotiating the narrow main street of Bethesda township before reaching the new trunk road leading to Anglesey and Jane.

That same evening, two hundred miles south at his country cottage, Kevin was quietly congratulating himself on making such good progress with Eric Larsen, the tourist officer at *Nanortalik*. He had begun by faxing an introduction letter seven hours before, just after lunch when he calculated with the six-hour time difference, Eric would be opening up his office. Within two hours Eric made a return contact by email saying he was ready to assist in any way possible and requesting full details of dates, names, aim, objectives and specific requirements.

These centred on three items:

* The local hire of inflatable craft, VHF radios, engines, fuel and immersion suits.
* Assistance with the provision of base cooking gas.
* Clearance to use an Immarsat mobile telephone station.

The first two were quickly dealt with and then Eric went on to declare that permission to use the Immarsat would first have to be obtained from the Danish Embassy in London, but should not be difficult.

Finally, he called Eric direct and thanked him for all his help and assistance. Over an excellent line Eric responded, 'It is a duty and my pleasure to ensure you all have a good visit to my area. I will email you about what food can be obtained here in Nanortalik, rather than spend money sea freighting from Copenhagen. The other items will be ready when you arrive and we can spend as much time as you need for getting ready before you go up the Tasermiut.'

'We will probably need at least a day and a night with you,' replied Kevin, 'before I push off, if there is anything you want us to bring, just fire off a message and it will get freighted out with our gear in June.'

Eric also wore a self-satisfied smile as he finished the phone call. He'd now been in Nanortalik over six years and had witnessed the summer tourist population swell from a couple of dozen to nearly 400, with every indication of making 500 this summer.

The short Greenland spring had already arrived, with both daylight and temperatures rising daily to an average of -1 degree C. For him this was the best time of the year, as the snow topped peaks began to loose their white shrouds and the ice choked sea fjords first cracked and then revealed dark, deep, open water. This was the time when the local Inuit hunters began to make serious preparations for the annual seal hunt. Only 100 years previously, if this had failed, the whole community faced starvation.

Born in Denmark and aged 29, Eric as a rebellious teenager had developed an interest in Greenland exploration. When the occasion arose to crew on his Uncle Jens' small trading ship that regularly sailed between the two countries, Eric quickly took the opportunity and spent the next few years spell bound by the experience.

His first voyage took him to Reykjavik, capital of Iceland, then across the Denmark Straits to Ammassalik, eastern Greenland, before swinging north to Narsaq, a port on the more populated south western seaboard, where the Labrador Sea meets the North Atlantic Ocean. It was here, on a clear sparkling morning that he saw his first real iceberg, bowling along in the southerly current after breaking out of the grip of the winter pack ice in Baffin Bay. It would have calved from a permanent glacier on north west Greenland the year before, its benign appearance giving a totally wrong impression to the horrors it could bring to the busy North Atlantic shipping lanes on a storm lashed night.

Typically, one-fifth to one-seventh of an iceberg protrudes above the water. The submerged core is made of rock-hard, freshwater ice, with an average age of 5,000 years, but some may date back to the last Ice Age. In their glory, they can tower hundreds of feet above the water. Riding the Labrador Current, some of the icebergs make it to the North Atlantic, whilst many are lost to grounding in shallow water or simply disintegrate. Weakened by the sun, they sometimes collapse in a great, splashing mess, leaving a litter of 'growlers'.

During the voyage Uncle Jens loaned him a fascinating book written by K J Krogh titled *Viking Greenland* which he eagerly devoured. This graphically described the exploits of Icelandic settlers – possibly slaves buying their freedom – who in 960AD began to establish colonies along both the west and east Greenland coastlines. This first migration, organised and led by Eric the Red, set sail from Iceland in 25 ships, of which only fourteen survived. Whilst the climate was warmer than today, it was still a perilous journey in open boats.

Information gleaned from archeological surveys indicates that these Norse settlers were first and foremost farmers, growing root crops for themselves and hay to feed their cattle. Contact with the local Inuit was friendly with both peoples leading separate and peaceful existences. Four hundred years later their presence totally ceased. It is thought this was due in part to a climate change of minus a few degrees stopping growth of hay for the cattle, plus a reverse migration of the young adults seeking improved prospects elsewhere.

Whilst unloading at Narsaq, Eric requested Uncle Jens for a couple of hours shore leave to locate the site of Dyrnes, thought to be the largest Norse settlement in the whole of Greenland in the mid-13th century. With a warning of not to be longer than four hours, or they would miss the tide, Eric quickly located the site and spent an hour lying in the lush grass, with its profusion of wild flowers, trying to envisage life here 600 years ago.

Even in winter, it was always a few degrees above freezing, the major reason for the Norseman's choice of the site. The church and farm buildings faced east across a wide sweep of the valley. Whilst the south facing bay provided good shelter for boats, easily pulled up the gently shelving beach for winter repairs and storage. Reluctantly he made his way back to the ship, vowing to return when he had more time to assimilate and absorb the true nature of the settlement.

For the next couple of years Uncle Jens taught him all he knew of the seafarer's life, Greenlandic history and Danish interests. As their cargos varied with each visit and required different ports of call, in that time Eric called at the majority of the small townships, villages and hamlets that cling precariously to the shoreline and narrow belt of rocky wind swept tundra leading up to the enormous inland ice cap.

Eric learnt that with a summit at over 10,000 feet above sea level, the enormous Greenland Ice Cap generates daily control over the Northern Hemisphere weather patterns. Recently, a European environmental venture, the Greenland Ice Core Project, has extracted cores of ice from down to 4,000 feet and back 4,000 years in time, giving important insights into climatic and pollution variant changes and providing a measurable constant.

His increasing interest in the Norse colonial period led Eric to develop an awareness of the Inuit and their culture. He discovered that the Danish Government had made efforts in the recent past to help ease their rapid transition from the traditional Inuit way of life, closely attuned to the environment, to the more artificial complexities of a modern Western society. The traditional kayak has for instance been replaced by fibreglass boats, powered by outboard engines. Progress yes, in that sea travel is now easier and safer, but a hunter requires a cash surplus to buy his boat, engine and fuel.

The gradual erosion of the Inuit culture, largely unaffected by the Norse settlers, started when Hans Egede, a 17th century Danish missionary, set out to look for the Norse colonies. Nothing had been heard from them for several hundred years and no one realised that they had disappeared, probably at around the time Columbus discovered America, the continent that they had visited from Greenland, 500 years earlier. Undeterred, Egede embarked instead on the conversion of the Inuit from Animistic beliefs to Christianity.

Trade and religion went hand in hand and the Danes assumed colonial rights, imposing a trade monopoly and closing Greenland to all but Danish shipping until 1950. Since the granting of Home Rule in 1979 a new sense of national identity emerged and most places now have two names, one Danish, one Greenlandic.

Of a total population of 55,000 more than four-fifths are Inuit, meaning 'people' and much preferred to Eskimo, 'eaters of raw flesh'. The majority of the remaining one-fifth are Danes.

CHAPTER 6

On his 18th birthday Eric volunteered for service with the Frogman Marine Korp (FMK), the Danish equivalent of the UK Special Boat Service or US Seals, based in Isefjord, north Zealand. First he had to complete a year's basic training for the submarine service, before being considered for selection. Fortunately, Ingar Lund his immediate supervising officer, was taking a career break from the specialist unit and recognising his potential and obvious zeal, helped Eric prepare mentally and physically for what was to lie ahead.

FMK recruits all face the same initial selection, which is divided into three phases. Psychological and physical tests, two days of physical examination, and finally, aptitude itself. Throughout the aptitude phase the potential frogman must show qualities of will power, leadership, teamwork and endurance, when staying in and working underwater and ashore.

Normally 200 apply for the initial selection, of whom about 60 will start the basic training, with only six expected to complete the whole of the 32-week package.

During this the students will experience:

4 weeks	Terrestrial navigation, cross country movement on foot and swimming.
1 week	Endurance and will power.
2 weeks	Weapon training and demolition
3 weeks	Navigation and sailing small inflatables and kayaks.
2 weeks	Scuba diving
4 weeks	Patrol tactics
8 weeks	Tactical close circuit oxygen diving
1 week	Tactical exercise, including 120 km march with 55 kg of equipment
5 weeks	Final exercise comprising all skills learnt during training.

After qualification the new members of FMK join already existing patrols. Hereafter each frogman will specialise further in different fields.

Eric discovered the rigours of life aboard Uncle Jens' boat had prepared him well for fitting into a five man closely-knit *Frogmandskropset* team. In addition to combat swimmer/frogman, he specialised further as a unit level explosive expert, easily shouldering the individual demands and responsibility this called for. During a final year of service he was drafted into the national counter terrorist team, undertaking even more specialist training in close quarter combat and covert surveillance.

Whilst enjoying the comradeship and job satisfaction of being in the unit, Eric recognised his destiny was to lie with Greenland, realising how much he missed the empty frozen wilderness, the longer he stayed away. Following his end of tour party, the next step was to ask Uncle Jens for the return of his crew man job. Uncle Jens was highly delighted and declared he could re-join the ship, but only after accepting a promotion to become the second mate. Eric responded immediately and boarded.

Soon after, during a visit to Nuuk town-ship, the ship developed a radio fault that required locating and installing a spare part. This gave them a four-day enforced wait, during which Eric became friendly with an Inuit hunter of his own age named Kaj. Following a long exhausting day visiting various seal hunting spots, Kaj invited him back to his humble homestead for some much needed food and drink.

His wife Aka made them welcome and fussed over preparing a simple meal, whilst Kaj and Eric played outside with Gitte, their four year old daughter. After eating a sumptuous banquet of smoked haddock and just as Eric was about to make his farewell, Aka's younger sister, Edda, arrived.

She had recently returned home from teacher training college in Copenhagen where she'd graduated with a degree – one of the first Inuit females to do so. Aka and Edda were very close and as Aka's house had a spare room, Edda stayed there, rather than at her parent's smaller house. Whilst her mannerisms, bearing and clothes were Danish, once she began talking animatedly with Aka, or playing with Gitte, she exhibited the fun and laughter of an Inuit girl. Eric was completely captivated.

Hanna his regular girlfriend in Denmark was most certainly much prettier, but with a serious approach to life. Edda with her irrepressible sense of fun, had a much more relaxed attitude. Later, back aboard the ship and reflecting on a great day ashore, Eric quietly made a decision to keep in touch with Edda, which he began by writing her a short letter, care of Kaj.

They began an exchange of correspondence that led to further meetings firstly at Kaj and Aka's home when next he visited Nuuk. Partly out of curiosity and partly as an excuse to be in her company, Eric persuaded Edda to teach him Inuktikut, the native Inuit language. She was waiting for an assistant teacher's post to become available at Nanortalik Township, near Cape Farewell and welcomed this opportunity to improve her knowledge of this slightly older, tall, strong and blond Dane in his early twenties.

She immediately ascertained that Eric possessed a sensitivity towards the Inuit people and their culture, not commonly shown by his fellow countrymen. It was another three months before she moved to Nanortalik and a year before they were married in the church at Nuuk.

Meanwhile, Eric had been recruited by the Home Government to introduce and administrate tourism to the area, with Nanortalik as the hub. Along with Agnete the medical assistant and her husband Frode who ran the KNI Co-operative store, the foursome effectively formed the governing nucleus of the small community of 2,450 souls in winter, that rose to 2,850 in the spring and summer months.

Founded in 1797, Nanortalik (meaning 'Place of the Bears') was a safe harbour for any ships in passage around Cape Farewell. In particular, for the many British and Dutch whalers who hunted almost to extinction the giant Bowhead whale in these waters during the nineteenth century. Whales were not only hunted for whale oil for fuel but also for their whalebone or baleen. This had numerous uses in the nineteenth century amongst which was in the fashion industry, as it was used in women's corsets.

The Bowhead received its name from the high arched lower jaw that resembles the shape of an archer's bow. They live at the southern edge of the Arctic ice during winters and move into leads through broken and melting ice during summer. Their broad back has no dorsal fin, which may make it easier to swim beneath ice floes.

Bowhead whales feed on plankton and consume about two tons a day by skimming through the water with their mouths open. Water flows into the mouth and through the baleen, which traps the food inside near the tongue to be swallowed. Bowheads usually travel alone or in small groups, known as pods of up to six animals. They are slow swimmers and will retreat under ice when alarmed. Their only known predator, besides man, is the killer whale.

Whilst the early explorers made little impact on the Inuit way of life, when the whalers wintered over, they employed Inuit men and women to work at their bases and also aboard the whaling ships themselves. Naturally this eroded traditional ways of life. With the decline of whaling and a discernible fall of fish stocks, the local Inuit's very survival rested with hunting, in particular seals – for their food, warmth and clothing, as nothing of the seal was ever wasted.

The fashion industries demand for white fox fur led many Inuit to become solitary trappers, so that with the emergence of the Green Peace lobby - and a loss of revenue from the diminished markets for seal skins, Inuit dependence on Government welfare increased, along with increased child abuse, alcoholism and solvent abuse amongst the young.

As a race, the Inuit seem to have a lower tolerance of alcohol than other races and recent surveys indicate their average consumption of alcohol is double that of Denmark and four times that of Sweden. The Inuit, in common with other northern peoples often suffer from winter depression, linked to alcoholism and high suicide rates. They know it as *perlerorneq* 'the burden' – long before Seasonal Associated Disorder (SAD) was medically acknowledged elsewhere and attributed to lack of sunlight, therefore Vitamin D, during the long northern winters.

One of the first measures Eric introduced was the establishment of a small gift shop at the Seamen's Hostel, which comprised the only restaurant and tourist accommodation in the township. The Government owned KNI store had been the sole point of sale for all tourist souvenirs, which without any competition were cheap and shoddy.

The gift shop at the hostel stocked only locally made crafts of wood, bone and soap stone, keeping more than a dozen families busy throughout the year, in particular during the long winter months. The standard improved with the increased practise of half forgotten skills, to such an extent that they were now sending a surplus to Nuuk, for sale in the airport shop.

As tourism officer, Eric spent his first year making contact with all of the specialist holiday concerns in Europe, Australasia and North America, extolling the delights of nature to be found in his area and emphasising how welcoming was the traditional Inuit culture.

In addition he linked up the Nanortalik Tourism website far and wide. This would always be a chicken and egg situation, along with Government tax concessions to hotel, aircraft and helicopter operators in a bold bid to improve internal communications and infrastructure.

Eric's next step was to actively encourage the younger men to learn and participate in the traditional skills of hunting and watermanship – before they became forgotten. In this he was given tremendous help by Edda, who as an acknowledged voice of the female Inuit, quietly supported her husband's desire for the community to retain some of their traditional skills, which had evolved to ensure their continued survival in the harsh cold environment.

He cajoled his superiors incessantly for cash to subsidise a hunter's skidoo, outboard motor, boat, fuel, clothing, guns and ammunition – 'assisting self help' – and it worked. Almost every family now had a male who was involved with both hunting and fishing, or guiding the increasing number of wealthy tourist groups that arrived. This also meant that with more restaurant meals to be prepared and rooms in the hostel to be serviced, employment opportunities increased for the younger Inuit girls, giving them more independence.

This generation was the first to be fully processed through the new schooling system of the Home Rule Government and if the more intelligent were to stay in Nanortalik, useful occupations had to be found, in addition to traditional child bearing and home making.

Eric was very conscious of the tremendous potential for exploratory mountaineering that existed within his area and took every opportunity to publicise and stimulate an awareness, particularly within Europe, with whom most Inuit felt more of an affinity than either Japan or North America.

When two years earlier Albert Kurt and his Swiss-German team had spent a month climbing on Ketil it had been a useful chance for Eric to fully understand how best to help a climbing team in its endeavours. These were not men who needed cosseting like tourists, but who relished the wilderness and felt at one with their chosen environment. However, they would always need some help with essentials such as transportation, communications and fuel. What Eric liked most was an expedition ethos of self-containment that said 'Leave nothing but footprints – take nothing but photographs.'

When Albert Kurt's team passed through for their one night transit stop in Nanortalik after their climb, Eric enquired how best they thought he could assist future mountaineering parties. In the last two years he had tried hard to put into practise their suggestions.

These had included maintaining an information data-base about visiting teams, their aims, objectives and results, and holding for hire inflatable boats and Mariner outboard engines, immersion suits, search and rescue beacons, VHF communications and cooking gas bottles.

In turn this meant full time employment for two Inuit handymen to service the equipment and to keep it in good working order. Again this helped to infuse useful employment into the local economy and removed two more families off the vicious cycle of welfare dependency.

Eric quickly discovered that with just a little guaranteed money coming into the home each month for essential items of fuel, basic foodstuffs and the occasional luxury, that the Inuit ethos of self-sufficiency derived from fishing and seal hunting quickly emerged. Whilst he could not find work for all – anything at all was an improvement and already he could detect a rise in self esteem amongst the young, amid their positive talk of a bright future as Greenlanders, rather than as a backward colony of Denmark.

The municipality was run democratically with an elected council that was answerable to the Home Government at Nuuk. The position of Eric, Edda and other government employees was similar to in-house consultants; they could make recommendations but it was up to the council to endorse them for implementation. Frequently Eric would find council discussion bogged down in examination of minutiae.

Talking this over with Edda, she reminded him that the Inuit needed to feel that every aspect of a proposal or plan had been examined, as once underway, it was too late and Greenland had never suffered fools gladly. There were other occasions when he felt his voice, calling for a sense of animal conservation whilst hunting was alone, as he did not share the Inuit faith in nature's reproductive strength to complete the cycle of life.

Eric spent many hours trying to explain that if, for example, all the musk ox were hunted out, then the fragile ecological structure of which they were part, would be irreparable and lost for ever. In turn the elders would sagely point out that it had been outsiders who had destroyed the bowhead whale and not the Inuit people, with each settlement taking only one or two a year.

As discussion reached far into the night, Eric would wearily leave and stroll the half mile to his combined house and office, using the ten minute walk to marvel at the natural geographical harbour created by a sheltered scattering of islands and headlands at the entrance to Tasermiut Fjord, which gave the town its name.

The vastness of the locality, brilliant twinkling stars and the clear sharp night sky was always a delight to behold – never failing to amaze and stimulate him. He would reach their new two storey wood built house and whistling contentedly skip up the outside staircase to the front door where he was always met by a warm and welcoming Edda.

He continued to absorb the history of the Norse settlers from their arrival in 986AD. Their name for Tasermiut Fjord was Ketil Fjord, called after the original settler who had arrived with Erik the Red's colonisation group from Iceland. The community had been well established with over twenty independent family groups, whilst most of the other settlements had been further north, around Gardar.

Their farms were based on the typical long house of Iceland and Norway, consisting of a single long room, which could be divided by wooden partitions. The entrance was on the end side of the house, which had rounded corners, giving an oval ground plan. Building materials used were turf, stone and timber.

Extra farm buildings, which included cowsheds and barns, were placed near the farmhouse and many farms had both drainage and water reservoirs. The passage house was a variant of the long house, in which a corridor running the length of the house linked the rooms.

It was thought that the colder winters of the 13th century caused a new type of farm to be developed, known as the centralised farm. All the rooms were in a single block around the all-important cow shed, which had as few outer walls as possible. Each farm was virtually self-sufficient and each settlement had a subsistence economy, which did not depend on imports or exports.

Pollen analysis of peat cores have shown that in the early stages of the Norse settlement, extensive areas of birch and willow scrub, many forming regular forests were cleared to make way for grasslands. The homesteaders brought with them cattle, pigs, sheep, goats, horses and dogs. Sheep were the most numerous farm animal and were probably capable of remaining outside all winter in mild years. Cattle were even more important than sheep, as dairy products formed an essential part of the settlers' diet.

Stalls for ten or a dozen animals have been excavated at many farms, whilst at Gardar, the Bishop's farm could house as many as a hundred cattle. Some of the farmers probably grew corn and the food provided by the farm animals would have been supplemented by hunting seals and reindeer and fishing.

From the very start the Norse farming economy was marginal, their biggest headache being to grow enough feed to keep the cattle alive for the two hundred or so days they had to be kept indoors in the winter. Assuming that the settlements survived well into the 15th century, it is easy to venture that they must have been squeezed out of existence afterwards by the inexorable laws of economics and climatic change. Certainly not by the Inuit with whom they had both friendly and hostile encounters, but no more than that.

Shortly before the start of the steady erosion of the farming base of their economy by climatic deterioration, the Norse had fallen under the twin ravenous clutches of both the ecclesiastical and royal bureaucracies of Norway. Together they sucked dry the economic life-blood of the colony. On top of a subsistence economy, they now had the equivalent of a market economy, but one in which surpluses, instead of being sold, were given away to church and king, bringing nothing of economic value in return.

It was these outrageous demands on an ailing economy, which finally caused the extinction of the Norse settlers. Eric was able to piece together these facts and by being able to follow-up on the ground what he read, had a clear understanding of an almost forgotten epic of Norse history.

An awareness of Inuit cultural history was made real by Eric's stubborn study of the language, expertly taught by Edda. She would insist on a daily conversation of at least ten minutes in Inuktituk, the Inuit language and deftly encouraged his learning and practise of at least five new words per day.

His fascination with his fellow men meant that wherever he travelled, there would nearly always be somebody who had heard of him and wanted to engage in a conversation. It was not long before Edda diligently taught him the famous Inuit poem by Uvanuk:

> *'The Great Sea has set me in motion*
> *Set me adrift*
> *And I move as a weed in the river.*
> *The arch of sky*
> *And mightiness of storms*
> *Encompasses me,*
> *And I am left Trembling with joy'*

The nomadic Inuit were influenced very little by their contact with the Norsemen, as the mainstay of their existence was the seal and musk ox. These were essential for food, summer tents, clothing, and fuel for giving light and warmth in winter by blubber lamp and, above all for covering the boats and kayaks.

Inuit society was a network of dispersed ever-moving hunter groups held together by kinship; smaller family-sizes in summer, larger for collective musk ox and seal hunting in the autumn and spring. They were self-supporting, sharing and egalitarian. In the winter they would set up a communal shelter half-underground of perhaps seven or eight families living quite amicably together without quarrelling or stealing, in one rectangular house. The walls were built of stone, the roof of wooden rafters covered with bushes, turf and lastly earth. The narrow entrance passage would be 20 to 30 feet long. Inside, the floor was of flagstones and the walls were hung with sealskins.

Along the rear part of this roughly rectangular structure ran a sleeping platform eighteen inches above the floor and divided by sealskin partitions or cubicles each four feet wide. Each cubicle was occupied by married members of a single family, together with their daughters and small children, that is a man, his wife or wives (bigamy was not particularly rare) and up to six children.

The married people slept with their feet towards the rear wall of the house; the unmarried daughters slept at the foot end and the unmarried men, teenage boys and any guests slept on a narrow bench along the front of the house. Each married woman tended the blubber lamp in front of her cubicle and the heat of several lamps permitted normal indoor clothing to consist of very scanty sealskin underpants for the adults and birthday suits for the children.

In these houses the long dark winter night was enlivened by all sorts of entertainments, prominent amongst them being shamanistic seances, drum song contests and the telling of lengthy stories with much gesticulation which, if not obscene, were often descriptive of hunting adventures and successes. The game of 'turning out the lights', otherwise known as wife exchange, was also played by adults, especially when there were guests in the house. Some of the best hunters, particularly shamans, were notable womanisers.

Too much attention should not be given to these carryings-on, for there were many long-term stable relationships – although a legal marriage as such did not exist. The only thing, which might be taken to denote it, was the birth of a child; the nuclear family was the ultimate social reality.

The family group was not knitted together by any public laws and institutions, much less by compulsion or penalties, but by voluntary agreement based on a mixture of self-interest and fear. The habitual division of labour amongst all Inuit was that man alone hunted and the women alone were responsible for turning the results of the hunt into fuel, food and clothing, and for the management of the household.

Shortly after he and Edda had settled into Nanortalik, another of the long-term tourism measures Eric initiated was the construction of a replica 12th century Norse house, based on archeological plans he discovered at the museum in Nuuk. It was placed on a suitable headland, not far from the centre of town, overlooking the harbour and within easy walking distance of the heliport. He made contact with the Danish Polar Institute in Copenhagen and they acted as the main sponsor, helping to generate funding for the three year project.

Now, every spring a Scandinavian volunteer archaeology student group came to live for three months, just as the Norse settlers had, applying the same methods of agriculture and practising the same methods of self sufficiency. They quickly become inured to being a historical showcase, giving life (and smells) to the demonstration that included appropriate domestic animals loaned for the season from the existing hill farms at Tasiusaq village, 20 miles further up Tasermiut Fjord.

Spurred on by this success Eric discussed with Edda the possibility of the local Inuit perhaps building a similar winter dwelling. After some negotiations, Edda persuaded a group of elders to take on the venture and the following year they completed a structure, just off the beach at Usek, a small Inuit community half way to Tasiusaq. Constructed of natural materials, it stimulated further awareness of local culture amongst the inhabitants and was soon joined by three sea worthy kayaks, sets of harpoons, plus other hunting and fishing items on display along with articles of home-made clothing and seal skin boots.

Once the initiative had proven successful, Eric was able to make a strong case for government funds to employ a permanent custodian of what was soon to become a large family sized encampment of four dwellings.

These two cultural exhibits, along with the attractions of the thermal hot springs at Uunartoq and the largest natural woodland in Greenland at

Qinngua Valley, plus the imposing mountain landscape to the north and east, gave Eric hope for encouraging more naturalist tourism to the area – armed only with a camera, fishing rod or ice axe!

There was always the odd expedition to grab the headlines of whatever country had initiated an attempt to climb amongst the numerous virgin peaks that littered the coastline, or to trek across the immense inland ice cap. Some did little to stir the imagination, whilst others grabbed it hard and really made an emotional impact.

One such recent expedition was that by Rune Gjeldnes and Torry Larsen, members of the Norwegian Marinejeger Korp, the same unit that had produced Borge Ausland, the first man ever to travel solo, unsupported, trans-polar across first the Arctic Ocean and then Antarctica. Eric had once been on an exchange attachment with this unit, working closely with Borge on a winter warfare exercise in northern Norway. They had built up a friendship, so when Borge contacted him and asked his help with the project, Eric readily agreed to further the ethos of Norwegian polar exploration in the footsteps of Nansen and Amundsun.

Rune and Torry planned to travel unsupported north from Cape Farewell, the extreme southern most tip of Greenland to Cap Morris Jesup, the very northern point. Eric helped to organise the safety cover in his area when the pair parachuted from an MC-130 Hercules of the 7th Special Operation Squadron, USAF.

They were dropped from an altitude of 10,000 feet (3,300m) above sea level at N60.30 onto the ice cap, twenty kilometres north of *Tasermiut Fjord*. From here, they moved south on foot and by kayak over 100 km and around to the seaward side of Cape Farewell, just off Eggers Island at N59.45 North Latitude.

The journey was not without its problems, surmounting unknown glaciers and cliffs encumbered with kayaks. At one stage their progress was halted by being unceremoniously dumped into the sea, when their kayak overturned and they were in the water at 0 degrees Celsius for 15 minutes without dry suits, before righting the kayak and getting to shore. Following further adventures they made it as close to Cap Farewell as the heavy drifting sea ice would allow.

There, after a ceremonial dip into the sea, they then climbed back up the mountainous headland and returned to the parachute drop zone site; here to marry up with all the stores and equipment needed to make the first, unsupported and continuous 86-day journey to Cap Morris Jesup.

After returning to the air drop site and a reorganisation, the next phase was to gain the high central plateau. The first part involved negotiation of steep mountainous terrain with heavy sleds of 175 kilos, and in addition they experienced some very bad spring weather. The high central plateau (62N to 82N), known as the Inland Ice, is an immense, wind blasted landscape extending monotonously for thousands of miles. It is a frozen wasteland, and the desolate plateau has an average altitude of 6,600 feet (2,000m) above sea level. In some places the ice cap can be over 9,000 feet (3,000m) deep.

Except for maintaining a government enforced daily satellite communication link with their support base, they did not have any further human contact until their completion of the world's first south-north traverse of Greenland, unsupported through 23 degrees of latitude.

They kept weights to a minimum by using a new composite drink, rich in added minerals and vitamins, instead of freeze-dried foods, the only other viable alternative. Another innovation they used was wind sails. When attached to a competent user on favourable terrain and with suitable wind conditions, they give the sledge hauling skier tremendous benefits for the time/distance ratio; saving both fuel and food weights and justifying the extra load, once they had been used for a relatively short time period. The wind sails however were potentially lethal and they had trained hard in the preceding year by doing a 31 day west–east traverse across Greenland, a total of 870 kilometres.

CHAPTER 7

Only two degrees further south, at Latitude 57.17 North, Longitude 6.11 West, on the Isle of Skye, north west Scotland lies the Sligachen Hotel from where, over the Easter holiday weekend Hugh and Rick planned to climb the Cullin Ridge. Arriving late on Good Friday evening, following a nerve racking haul north, they quickly re-made an old friendship with Jimmy Moore, the resident mountain guide, who knew all there was to know about the local area, route information and who was doing what, and when.

'Conditions are as good as you will ever find lads,' advised Jimmy, a 40-year-old, slim wiry man of average height, with the quiet relaxed competence that is a hallmark of mountain guides.

Jimmy smiled before continuing, 'It's been well below zero the last couple of nights and all the classic ice routes are in good nick especially Hose Pipe Gully and The Streak and I know how close you came to knocking them off your last time here Hugh! I've also heard that Ian Douglas and Mickey Weaver are visiting as well – so you may well have company.'

A couple more beers, a laughing farewell and it was time for them to drive to the road head and quickly get into their sleeping, plus bivouac bags, down beside the car for a few hours rest. By seven o' clock in the morning they were walking up the snow slope to their climb, meeting crisply clear tracks – maybe left by Mickey and Ian from the day before?

With Hugh initially in the lead, they quickly completed a second ascent of Hose Pipe with time to spare. Undaunted, rejuvenated and relishing the fine clear cold conditions, their thoughts turned to a second challenge The Streak. To make a speedy approach they quickly lightened their rucsacs' weight and with crampons making a reassuring crunch at every step, they independently climbed up South Gully to a high amphitheatre that contained the climb. This was a continuous narrow ice stream that culminated in an icicle-ridden overhang.

'Let's go for it,' cried Hugh.

Rick could never be accused of dithering when faced with severity, as they both felt an irresistible urge to meet the imminent challenge. In such situations it is unwise to ignore the potential lateness of the day and the fact that they had left quite a bit of survival gear a thousand feet below. Quickly soloing a couple of short grade three sections saved some time and meant the lack of gear was not really noticeable until they gained the line proper and had effectively committed themselves.

Rick led off on a single 9mm rope, with time not being unduly wasted by placing protection, as they did not have a great deal with them to place! Progress was fast and after a gradually steepening ice ramp, followed by a short swearing-packed struggle with a brittle monster icicle, led past a small overhang to an airy stance, from where the rest of the line was clearly visible.

'Desperate! Just the way you like it,' shouted Rick, as a couple of more steep and spectacular pitches on perfect ice led to the obvious crux of the climb. Here, the water seeping through the over-hanging rock spire above had frozen to form two huge icicles, one dropping from a point midway across the roof and another adorning the lip.

From a constricted belay in a shallow ice cave it looked just possible to climb up beneath the roof and cross it by stepping from one monster icicle to the other, before moving round onto the front face and then pulling up to the easier ground above. A series of lurches and much scrambling of crampon-clad boots took Hugh to the outer face of the icicle.

It was easier than it looked and a couple of quick moves on bomb-proof axe placements soon had the thin winter sun glinting in Hugh's eyes, as the friendly upper slopes came in reach. Rick speedily followed and without wasting any precious time, they quickly moved down the easy west flank in the gathering gloom to collect their gear, so foolishly abandoned earlier and made the hotel an hour later. Their minds zinging on an adrenaline high from making the second ascent of a route that may be in condition to climb only once a year.

At the hotel bar they encountered the two veteran mountaineers, Ian Douglas and Mickey Weaver who waving them over to the alcove by the roaring fire, made room for them to sink into welcoming chairs.

'Hi lads – what are you having?' queried Mickey, a smiling, bearded and barrel-chested Mancunian, and former top class mountaineer, who now had investments in outdoor pursuits equipment outlets in the north west.

'Jimmy said you were having a look at Hose Pipe and Streak...

interesting in places eh! How did it go?' grinned Ian, a rangy, shaggy giant of a man, who was one of Briton's greatest living climbers, and at 50 years old was still highly active.

'The crux on Streak certainly concentrated my mind,' laughed Hugh. 'By that time we only had a couple of old Russian titanium ice screws – as in the flap to make a quick ascent, we'd left our sacks at the bottom.'

Both Ian and Mickey laughed before Ian replied, 'Congratulations I don't think it will be repeated that often – the forecast is for a thaw over the next 24 hours – so that's probably it for this year.'

The foursome continued chatting amicably for the next couple of hours about past climbs and mutual friends, with the odd guarded reference to their future aspirations. Experienced mountaineers will usually have a private agenda of hopes for the future, which they are usually quite protective about, wanting to be the first up a specific route – or even a first ascent up a dwindling number of the world's virgin mountains.

Knowing he had been there, Rick casually mentioned to Ian about his involvement with Hugh, George and Kevin's visit to Tasermiut Fjord and an attempt to free climb Ketil.

Ian's interest was instant and he remarked, 'You'll have a ball. Miles of unclimbed granite alongside the fjord and then you get Ketil - a magnificent huge pillar at the end, with the ice cap as a back drop. I visited a couple of years ago for two days to have a quick look. There's enough virgin rock there to keep you going for the rest of your life. And a great guy at Nanortalik, the heliport where you can hire an inflatable and engines. Eric Larsen is his name and he is married to Edda a local Inuit girl, who is an assistant teacher. You'll like them!'

The hotel owner eventually persuaded them to leave about mid-night into a mild, windy night, which was the forerunner of a stormy and wet weekend that curtailed any more mountaineering. They waited until Sunday and then pronouncing it a wash out headed south – quite pleased that they had at least snatched what they did from the fickle Scottish winter climbing season.

Both were also delighted with how each had performed, complementing the other's strengths and weaknesses, as whilst Hugh was without doubt the one with an eye for a new line, Rick had better technical experience and expertise with hardware. He was less trusting of new devices than most, always trying where possible to double-up on protection, especially on abseils.

They had shared the euphoria that overcoming a savage mountain route gave to the fortunate. Both were mature enough to realise that it was 'when nature has her back turned' that they could become 'conquistadors of the useless!' They'd lost friends killed in climbing accidents, which only heightened their perception and love of the wild corners of the world, especially those under threat from the aspirations and greed of their fellow human beings.

As Hugh dropped Rick off at his home in a rain soaked Lake District, he turned down the offer of food and drink and making farewells and promised to contact George and tell him what Ian had said about Ketil and Eric Larsen.

~ ~ ~ ~ ~ ~ ~ ~ ~ ~ ~ ~ ~ ~ ~

In Houston, Debbie had slowly come to terms with Jake's latest request. They had met for the holiday at her condominium, for what she hoped would be three full days of pleasurable time together. Upon arrival, Jake embraced her passionately, making her feel very special, before reclining in an easy chair to drink a cold beer.

His throw away lines came right out of the blue and were quite simple - either Debbie found out what was behind Project Alpha, including names, places and dates, or his boss would force him to move to the Azerbaijan office very soon.

Of course Jake did not want to be parted and couldn't bear the thought of not seeing her at least every two weeks, but she knew the oil industry as well as anyone, and his boss was not a man to mince his words, or make an idle threat! Debbie had prepared herself for this moment, ever since she found herself full of wanton thoughts at their regular meets.

'Why does everything I love and hold dear turn into a nightmare?' she asked, leisurely reclining and sipping a cold vodka and tonic.

'My thoughts entirely sweetheart,' responded Jake, 'but he's such a bastard and I think he really means it! The last place I want to be is with some third world towel heads in stinking Azerbaijan.'

'I have already given you all that has passed my way,' Debbie whispered. 'What on earth is so important that you are asking me to risk my whole career with a company that's been so good to me?'

'Honey, my sweet baby,' cajoled Jake, 'if I knew the answer to that I wouldn't be wasting our loving time even talking about it. Why don't we hold it for now? Leave it for the morning - what do you say? Good, let's take a long slow shower together and forget about it until then eh?'

Much later, Debbie stared at the ceiling as Jake contentedly sighed in his sleep beside her, naked, tanned and muscular. She kept passing over in her mind all that she had heard and seen written about Project Alpha, trying desperately to piece together a mental jigsaw of times, people, and events.

Suddenly she started with a little cry which caused Jake to stir but not wake up. The phone numbers of that call which pleased Henry her boss so much - from whom? What was the name he'd used? Yes she had it now Kevin, and she had meant to pass it on but somehow she'd forgotten in the excitement of seeing Jake again.

I wonder what it's worth money wise, she pondered. Maybe that was an angle to try, as Jake's continued presence in her life was now a big question mark, just like all the other men since Pete, her first lover and one of the last men to be killed in Vietnam, at only 21.

Compared with him, Jake was just a nice, convenient, warm body, when occasionally she needed reminding of how a woman should feel. Yes! That was the right decision and having made it, she easily slipped off into a deep slumber.

Not ten miles away, Henry Williams, the person who had been central to their conversation was arriving home, tired and late from yet another visit to UK, Norway and Holland. He was well pleased with Project Alpha and had told Kevin just that, when they met for dinner the night before at Au Bon Accueil another gem of a restaurant in London. Whilst the surroundings were relaxed, Monsieur le Patron could not have been more civil and attentive, catering to their every need without fawning or false courtesy.

Savouring his fresh Dover sole, Kevin informed Henry of their preparations so far, especially regarding arrangements George was making with *Newsweek*. Desperately trying to concentrate on what Kevin was saying, Henry was finding it difficult to focus away from his dish of succulent calve's liver and smoked bacon, he had started to eat.

In between mouthfuls he exclaimed, 'I'll tell you something Kevin old buddy - you certainly know some excellent eating spots in this town. Looking at Project Alpha what is your next milestone to complete?'

'I guess it must be taking all of our gear to Copenhagen by 12 June ready for it to sail to Nanortalik on the 20th' replied Kevin, then continued, 'I will take it there myself, direct to the shippers, via a night ferry.'

'And after that, what are the flight details?' queried Henry.

'They are booked for the 21 July from Copenhagen, after arriving on an earlier flight from Heathrow,' explained Kevin, 'direct into Narsarsuaq, for an overnight stop, then catch the morning heli shuttle into Nanortalik to arrive abut mid-day.'

'I'll make sure then that Barney delivers the seismic gear on the 1st of June,' answered Henry.

'Perhaps it would be best if I met him at Swindon station and took delivery there,' Kevin replied, wiping his plate with a piece of bread.

'Good idea. Before we split remind me to give you his numbers and then you can make the arrangements,' said Henry as he wiped up the sauce and speaking before a final mouthful said, 'Give me 24 hours to contact him and let him know you'll be in touch.'

Henry garaged the car and quietly let himself into the large modern house in a secluded leafy suburb of Houston that he shared with Catherine, wife number two of eight years and Helen their bouncy daughter, fast approaching six - that marvellous age of femininity.

His first marriage to Barbara had been both eventful and traumatic; producing David now aged 20 and busy studying Law in Philadelphia. Barbara had remarried soon after the divorce and was content at last with Harry Cohen, a Jewish businessman who successfully dealt in antiques, mainly for the New York nouveau rich jet set.

Perching contentedly at the breakfast bar, Henry poured himself a thirst-quenching schooner of beer and thought over the developments produced by the last couple of days. Whilst never quite satisfied with everything, he never would be, it was certainly gratifying to see how the key events appeared to be coming together nicely and called for him to give another update to RW, possibly later that day if Debbie could fix him with a slot.

It was 2am and, making a mental note to call the office as soon as he woke, he finished the beer and crept into the guest suite for a shower, before falling into a deep sleep in the spare bed. He knew that Catherine would ensure that he was not woken until he had slept off the jet lag by late morning.

'Morning honey,' breathed Catherine gently in his ear, as she slipped naked into the bed and snuggled up alongside him. 'Helen has gone to school and I've put the answer-phone on.'

'Seems to me you have thought of everything,' whispered Henry, refusing to open his eyes and tenderly reached to stroke her slim rounded hips and smooth thighs.

Later, as they recovered and let heart beats become normal, Henry spoke of his trip in outline and caught up on the family happenings. After a shave and a shower he phoned Debbie and asked her to book him in with RW as soon as possible. Sounding her normal friendly self, Debbie promised to do what she could before ringing off. Pledging that he would get home as quickly as possible, Henry turned into the late morning traffic and headed downtown.

True to her word, Debbie had arranged a ten minute slot with RW immediately after lunch and glided away to fetch him coffee, whilst he quickly glanced through the contents of his in-tray.

As she placed the cup down on the desk she turned to him and speaking quietly said, 'This Project Alpha is certainly an important item, judging by the response it's receiving upstairs.'

'Debbie, when we pull this one off, it will be bonuses all round and possibly a promotion... I just hope those crazy Limeys can pull it off. Oh yes! Would you ask the technical support boys for a map of southern Greenland please – a one to a million will be fine and also a gazetteer of Denmark.'

Henry had thought on the trip home about increasing Debbie's involvement and knowledge. He considered that with the project reaching a critical level, there would be times soon when she may have to act quickly on his behalf and as his PA, he did not enjoy keeping her in the dark. After he had briefed RW would be a good moment he decided, quickly listing the main up-date points on a small white card.

Upon her return to the outer office, Debbie took a deep breath to help steady her nerves, as a sharp pang of conscience pricked her mind. Being with Henry and thinking of disloyalty was all proving just a little too much. Whilst alone with Jake it had been relatively easy to negotiate a good financial arrangement for each new piece of accurate information about Project Alpha she produced.

In reality, the mental turmoil frightened her. Then, focussing on the excellent financial benefits to be safely credited to a numbered Cayman

Isles offshore bank account, she phoned the technical branch and requested immediate delivery of the map and gazetteer.

Henry returned from briefing RW cheerful and smiling. Pinning the
Greenland map to his flip chart, he motioned Debbie to a seat and quickly gave her an overview of Project Alpha – after first pointing out its
commercial value to any competitor and reminding her of company policy for dealing with breaches of security.

He then continued, 'If we know what to bid for in any future auction
for the exploration rights, we could save ourselves millions of dollars and
not be held to ransom by the Danes. It's like the Alaska Polar Shelf field
or the North Sea before anyone started sniffing about.'

'Will the information produced by Kevin Roach's trials be apparent to
him?' asked Debbie fighting to constrain her curiosity.

'No. He will merely safeguard the recordings until they are handed
over to our courier at this place Narsarsuaq. Come to think of it, I may
even go myself!' replied Henry

Later that evening Debbie placed a call to Jake's number and using an
agreed simple shrouded method of speech, made arrangements for an
immediate meet during her lunch break the next day at a nearby hotel.

CHAPTER 8

George winced as Jane Fulbright the *Newsweek* interviewer enquired what Phoebe and the family thought of his disappearances away on expeditions. Giving his usual bland stock item to disguise his ire at her amateur and inept attempts to seek a headline, he battled on through the interview. Only the familiar surroundings of the Royal Geographical Society in Knightsbridge, where George suggested they meet - with its memorabilia of famous explorers on display - saved him from being rude.

Even her offer of a free lunch on expenses and, if he read her body language right, the possibility of a closer liaison, did little to reduce his tension at the futility of it all. He reminded himself that beggars cannot be choosers, as he ran through the usual list of reasons why mountaineers constantly seek to ascend isolated and unclimbed peaks, or climbed them by a different route than anyone else.

Thank goodness dear Camilla had arranged to meet him later, the thought of which brightened him up and brought a smile to his lips. Jane must have anticipated she'd made a break through, as she plunged on remorselessly with her questions. George found himself explaining that a mountaineer has two conflicting motives.

Firstly - their acceptance of risk; the spirit of adventure that includes the climber's desire to explore the unknown (with the added attraction of gambling in a high risk game) and of playing his own appraisal against the natural elements of wind, storm, cold, rock, snow and ice. Secondly - the basic factors for their own self-preservation.

He made the point strongly that he hoped the climb would act to focus attention for the British Heart Foundation Charity and invited *Newsweek* readers to sponsor their progress on the climb as part of their fund raising effort. One of the ways they could do this was to send £5 to the foundation's head office, asking for a signed postcard to be sent back to them upon the team's arrival in Nanortalik. This would be a photograph of Ketil itself.

He also spoke about how they intended to take Rupert, a cuddly toy bear donated by the Heart Foundation with them to the summit of Ketil

- so that upon their return Rupert could be auctioned off by a famous personality, such as the charismatic actor, Brian Blessed.

Following a photo call in the Society's garden, where festooned in climbing gear and he posed pointing at the roof, as if scouting out a burglary route, the session ended and George could make good his escape to an afternoon dalliance with Camilla. At her most sensual and voluptuous self, she demanded and gave in return true ardour, with a massive measure of humour and gaiety. So much so that by the time of his participation that evening in a symposium at the Alpine Club on mountaineering in Greenland, he'd shrugged off his cantankerous mood and was in fine humour.

The evening was made even more enjoyable by the presence of Iain Mackenzie, an insolent, humourous and likeable rogue of nearly 60, who had climbed hard in his day. Iain was in great demand as an after dinner speaker at climbing club annual functions, where his wry, anarchic wit - aimed mainly at himself - had the collective gaggle entertained. Tonight he had begun by asking about the possibilities still open for making first ascents in the Sweizerland area of eastern Greenland.

Then without a pause for breath, he took up a commentary on the after dinner speeches he'd made over the previous twelve months. His vivid word pictures describing classic idiosyncrasies of club dinners, from the alcoholic daze associated with a university thrash, to the more formal restrained gentlemanly atmosphere of the Alpine Club. This led him quickly onto comments about memorials to dead climbers. He finished on a story about the intended last request of a famous friend (happily still climbing) - whose ambition was to die at the age of eighty seven, shot by a jealous husband and to have his ashes ceremonially flushed down the club's toilet!

George spoke for ten minutes on his future plans for climbing Ketil and received a quietly enthusiastic reception form the assembled throng. This included several geriatric gentlemen who appeared to be nodding off, before making reference to a dynamic event of yesteryear, when without satellite communications, Gortex shell clothing and plastic boots - they had survived on pemmican, Kendal mint cake and oatmeal porridge, whilst pushing back the exploration boundaries of the known mountain world.

He declined to comment on a hypothetical homily injected by Iain, on the ethics of commercial expeditions; other than to state his belief they should voluntarily constrain their activities to the lesser ranges and stay well within the capabilities and aptitude of their clients.

This received a few gentle hand-claps, plus a boisterous, 'Hear, Hear!' from a member of the first successful Everest 1953 team led by John Hunt. As he was leaving, copies of a short article caught his eye, written by a member's daughter for her university Sports Science degree and he put one into his document case for reading later on the train home. It was entitled 'Mountaineering: is it worth the risk?' and went on to say:

'In order to establish whether mountaineering is seen as a dangerous sport the term 'dangerous' must be defined; the dictionary states that it is 'a liability or exposure to harm, risk or peril.' The definition of what is harmful is already known, so what is risk? The Oxford dictionary defines risky as 'hazardous, full of risk'.

'Ever since the beginning of time man has wanted to overcome the boundaries of their physical and mental capacity. In the absence of conditions for physical survival, modern man seeks to create a challenge, which is unknown and to overcome that challenge (ancient man didn't seek challenges such as climbing mountains, they were too busy surviving).

'Mountains are an example of one such challenge. However climbers not only climb the mountain, but also conquer their own fear of failure. Mother Nature in the form of mountains are not conquered but are recognised as being greater and more powerful than the person is, and therefore respected because of this.

'The people who choose to climb mountains are in their various ways accepting with delight this challenge, in order to prove themselves against the peak, as well as being fascinated by their mystery and beauty.

'The desire to prove or find one's self is of course well known, and is seen as the main motive for climbing. What compels climbers to fight against weather, the cold and of course physical discomfort, and possibly death in order to stand for a moment, on a cone of snow or a pile of rocks which form a summit? Is it the notion of death, which invites climbers up to the tallest peaks of the world?

'The motivation for mountaineers is to engage in activities in the mountains whereby they are acting spontaneously and not under compulsion. The attraction for some mountaineers is discovering where the risks lie in developing skills and gaining the experience to measure up to them. Discovering where the risks lie is only gained through experience of climbing.

'Death is a real risk whilst climbing. It is faced everyday whilst on the mountain and climbers in order to reach the summit must accept this fact and not underestimate its power. Climbing mountains unfortunately takes lives and Mt Everest is certainly not an exception.

'The statistics show that one in eight climbers will die in an attempt on Everest. To climbers the statistics of death are noted and they are prepared for the inevitable but it does not absorb all of their thoughts, because if it did, then the challenge would never be completed.

'Novice climbers with little climbing experience are usually the ones preoccupied with their own death. This is through fear if nothing else, and these climbers are usually more at risk of never returning from the mountain.

'Mountaineering and danger/risk are interchangeable. Without danger mountaineering would not be what it is, as it would not be a challenge against the elements and your self. Danger is to climbers as time is to athletes, without the element of time to conquer there would be no challenge. If athletes were expected to run the 100m sprint in a minute then the task would be easy, everyone could experience it, and it would not be defined as challenging.

'The same applies to mountaineering. If everyone could climb Mt Everest with great ease and nobody died in the attempt then it would not be classed as challenging or dangerous, it would be just like walking up the stairs. So the element of danger is important to climbers, as they live and breathe for that danger, they enjoy the thrill of experiencing the magnificent views at the summit and the thrill of meeting head on the forces of nature.

'The dangers are accepted and welcomed as part of the process of climbing a mountain. The degree of danger is measured in terms of how serious the outcome of that situation is, and the frequency of dangerous situations already taken place. Everyone in the world once they are born is on their own path to death, so in theory everyone is dying.

'Mountaineering could be said to create a more authentic life for yourself, take control of your life and live it to the full, experience everything you possibly can in the time you have. The pursuit of mountaineering should imply a certain feeling for the mountain scene, as well as sensitivity in regard to other people who wish to enjoy the mountains.

'Mountaineering in all its aspects should be pursued as a matter of personal choice for its own sake, whether from a sense of adventure or from a desire to acquire knowledge or fresh experience. A basic element in mountaineering is the presence of serious risk in varying degrees. Without this element it would lose something as vital as is competition in organised games.

'Those who are introduced to mountaineering must be safeguarded against accidents arising from the exposure to risks that are beyond their experience. At the same time, they should not be taught attitudes or practices which, by overplaying safety, may stultify enjoyment and restrict their ability to progress in climbing with all its attendant challenges and opportunities. By becoming prevalent, such attitudes and practices deprive mountaineering of its unique characteristics and charm.

'Mountaineering is a pastime that most people like to enjoy with a few friends, or occasionally, alone. Some are more gregarious. But whether they go alone or in smaller groups, all would wish to preserve a sense of remoteness and an element of wilderness in the mountains.

'Death is revealed to us as a 'loss'. We only understand death if it is given to us in the form of an analogue, or a description for example describing a pain as 'stabbing.' So understanding our own death will be of great difficulty, as you never see yourself as an object in the world, because you see yourself from your viewpoint - you are you - and you see other people around you, not yourself.

'The subject of where people go after death is more frightening than death itself. It is being scared of the unknown and until reaching that point in your life cycle you will never know. So mountaineers see their death not from their own viewpoint but how it will affect other people including friends and family.

'The perception of risk however varies from person to person. Mountaineers have different perceived risks than, for instance, train drivers; there are different hazards for each to identify.

'Mountaineers also tend to have different personality traits from other sportsmen or women. They are usually confident people, with higher self-esteem and self worth than other people. With this in mind, would this affect the way they think about their own death?

'Would their death be just like a climbing expedition, the lucky people will have the opportunity to climb and reach the top, and the unlucky climbers will not be chosen and die? Could dying be put down to luck

73

in mountaineering? Perhaps it does not matter how much experience you have but when it is time to die, it is time.

'Mountaineers are in a sense bridging the gap between life and death, every time they take a risk and climb a mountain they are getting closer to death, whereas non-climbers rarely put themselves in such situations.

'Mountaineers are willing to in a sense put their life on the line to experience a sport in its real sense. Mountains do not have boundaries, nets or goals like organised sports do. Climbers do not attempt to beat others personal bests, they are there for personal success.

'In conclusion climbers are playing with life and death in a sense but they are truly aware of it. They must be, otherwise they wouldn't climb again and again. Climbers understand that they can only control these hazards or dangers to a certain degree and the rest is down to Mother Nature.

'They thrive on the fact that there is a perceived danger involved. Their motivation comes from finding these risks and overcoming them, this gives them immense gratification. Climbers are not obsessed with death, they are aware of it, and put it into context. It is non-climbers who are more concerned with dying in the sport, possibly due to a lack of statistical knowledge concerning death and mountaineering'

'And I couldn't have said it better,' remarked George as his train headed north.

The next morning George had a long chat by telephone with Kevin and confirmed the suitability of the logistical arrangements he wanted to make. They discussed every aspect of the move, trying to envisage where and why it may go wrong and how to avert its possible happening. With just eight weeks to go, the plan was fast consuming their lives and the steadily mounting excitement started to place their thoughts of all else, including personal family needs, at a lower level of priority.

Fortunately, the wives had been through this aspect of the man they married many times before and whilst not enjoying having to play second fiddle, knew that to remonstrate would only add further strain. The girls preferred to be supportive, knowing full well that they would return scourged of the wanderlust, seeking ways to repay their appreciation and gain solace - until the next time!

'I would like us all to get together for a weekend's climbing and chat before we ship the gear. I was hoping for next weekend at Malham Cove

- how does that fit with you?' asked George.

'That would be good for me,' replied Kevin, 'how about the others?'

'I've been in touch with Hugh and he can make it and I've left a message with Helen for Rick to get in touch,' said George. 'He'll come I'm sure and I'll book us all into The Raven for B&B on expedition funds as we are working-up.'

'Make that doubles and we can bring the girls to have a get-together and a good chat for when we are away,' suggested Kevin.

'You're right! Let's pray for some sunshine and go for a rendezvous at The Raven on Friday evening,' chuckled George. 'I'll get in touch with the others and ask them to bring their gear, so we can give it a going over on the main overhang.'

'So long as all you expect me to do is take photographs and make the brews, I look forward to it. Bye will be in touch,' answered Kevin.

The weather on the following weekend was reasonable and following a happy reunion at The Raven on Friday evening, they sat down to a supper of traditional Yorkshire pudding, gravy, vegetables and local sausages, followed by rhubarb crumble and ice cream.

'How did the *Newsweek* interview go,' queried Hugh.

'Better than I thought possible and I got in all the cries for the charity,' replied George. 'Unfortunately as you know, what they want is a heroic disaster story to head-line - especially if there is an angle to do with either environmental issues, political correctness or minority rights.'

'So we swap Kevin for a Mongolian transvestite employed by Green Peace,' Rick laughingly suggested.

'How does that leave you for funds?' Jane enquired.

'*Newsweek* have sent their cheque and I have a strong promise of one for the balance from a personal friend,' George answered and avoiding eye contact with Phoebe went on, 'He's never reneged yet and I don't anticipate he'll start now, so I guess we are already in the black.'

'That makes a nice change - usually it's still panic stations at this stage,' laughed Gillian, 'Let's just hope he stays sweet.'

'Fortunately I know someone close to him to handle my case and I've not been let down yet,' declared George with a smile.

'The *Newsweek* coverage will certainly help if you are. Not many people I know can attract that kind of publicity,' stated Rick.

'Does that mean we are famous darling?' Phoebe said in a stage whisper. 'Will I now get to meet Heads of State as your supportive wife, or is a dirty weekend at The Raven my limit of exploitation?' she coyly asked to delighted cries of laughter from the others.

Next morning the weather started fine enough and after breakfast they left the girls to their own resources and walked to the cove, dominated by a huge amphitheatre over 300 feet high, the wings of which gradually tail away into the hillside. The climb they had decided to attempt is known as Central Wall Direct graded with an A2 difficulty and one of the most popular artificial aid climbs in the country.

Upon arrival they found that a pair of climbers had already started and were making good progress, so that by the time they had prepared their own gear, the front pair were over half way up and beginning to ascend the over hanging top pitch.

'Have you any objections if I lead off?' asked George. 'It's ten years since I was last on this one, but I do remember that it went OK for me.'

'Not a problem with me mate,' replied Hugh, I want to have a crack with these new haulage devices. So maybe if Rick climbs second and then goes through, I can come up to where you are and haul up the sacks, whilst Rick cracks on.'

'It will certainly be bloody good to try out my new bolting kit - as if for real - not that I expect to use it,' laughed George.

'Except in an emergency that is,' Rick remarked. 'After all we are trying to make a clean ascent of Ketil.'

Rick was referring to a method of a climber providing protection by hand drilling a hole in the rock, into which is inserted a metal expansion bolt with a hook, from where a climber could attach himself or his rope and thereby arrested a fall, should one happen.

Walter Bonatti one of the world's most famous climbers once remarked, 'With the use of expansion bolts, the sense of the unforeseen almost entirely disappears and so too the challenge of the climb itself and the meaning of the word 'impossible'. The spirit of the climb itself is killed. It becomes merely harsh and brutal, with no reason why it should be done at all.'

This subject of 'bolting' split the UK climbing community in two. There are those who condone a liberal use and those who believe the rock route should be left virgin after an ascent. As their aim was a 'clean' ascent of Ketil, removing all of the ropes and paraphernalia as they went along, they belonged to the latter group and did not envisage their use except in a dire emergency.

Another area of concern that always generates debate is the use of radio communications, as on big climbs they are notoriously problematical and unreliable. One recent development has been to join two head sets through a thin cable that runs through the climbing rope itself. Called 'a talking rope' these are an excellent innovation if used correctly on certain types of climb, but with the threesome taking turns at lead climbing and then moving in support, it would prove more of a hindrance than a help.

Most of the protection they required on today's route up Central Wall Direct was already in place, so the trio could concentrate on individual techniques and revive their knowledge of each other's personal idiosyncrasies and improve communications. Kevin watched intently from ground level as they made steady progress up the route, noting how each would find certain stages harder than others would.

Rick was the steadfast technician, checking each bolt and piton placement thoroughly before committing his weight or safety. Hugh yodelled his delight with the performance of the new devices that made haulage of the 100lbs dead weight in the haul bag smooth and trouble free. George made up for what he lacked in finesse and style, with a strong and dynamic approach to the job in hand - always trying to be best placed in the middle, where he could best see and influence the other two.

The day passed without incident, except for a prolonged mid-afternoon shower and it was a jovial and happy team that later made it back to The Raven, to meet up with the girls over a huge pot of tea and cakes beside the welcome fire.

'We had a nice walk over to Settle for lunch and then decided to catch the bus back. How was your day?' asked Phoebe.

'Except for dropping my hammer and nearly killing Hugh, pretty successful I would say,' George replied. 'I'd like to have a go with the haulage clamps tomorrow and convince myself they are as foolproof as Hugh says.'

'So long as you don't dump the haul bag on me!' Hugh laughed a retort.

The next day saw them trying out the vital sleeping platforms that

Hugh had obtained from America. Called the A5 Expedition Portaledge they were the brainchild of the famous American big wall climber John Middendorf. After he'd graduated from Stanford University with a degree in mechanical engineering in 1983, John began a full time climbing career, climbing every day of the year whilst making a living working for the YOSAR (Yosemite Search and Rescue) and rigging climbs for films and commercials.

After years of climbing, his skills and opportunities advanced to the point where he became one of the finest climbers of his era. His creative approach to climbing and developing innovative equipment brought him international credibility and acclaim, as did his flair for writing mountaineering books and making films. In 1987 John started up A5 his own equipment manufacturing concern, with the intention of revolutionising the existing standards of design in a full range of mountaineering equipment.

Before John's introduction of A5 portaledges, climbers resorted to a wide variety of systems for spending the night on big walls. In Yosemite, the recognised centre of knowledge, climbers would often bring wood platforms or steel rigid-framed cots. In more remote places, where weight was an issue, climbers sometimes relied on hammocks, which besides being very cramped did not offer adequate protection from the elements.

Advances in big wall climbing standards were severely limited by the lack of an adequate and versatile bivouac system. A good big wall bivouac system needs to be lightweight, compact, easy to set up and waterproof. Using his unique combination of engineering and climbing skills, John evolved the A5 Expedition Portaledge system for one, two or three person occupation. He devised a system where a lightweight alloy tube matrix within an extremely strong floor cloth forms a solid floor, from which a pyramid of tent walls containing suspension strops lead upwards to a safe single point anchor system.

In 1992 his 18-day climb of the Great Trango Tower in Pakistan set a new standard for lightweight extreme big wall climbing. Success was largely due to John's A5 Expedition Portaledge, withstanding several severe Himalayan storms whilst suspended on a sheer cliff at 20,000 feet.

John continues to design and test materials and equipment that are at the leading edge of technology and use of which are crucial to push out the boundaries of big wall mountaineering.

Fortunately both Hugh and Rick had used the portaledge before and so were able to quickly introduce George to its construction and use. The first time they did it all at ground level and then spent three hours preparing a position only twenty-foot up the wall, before they occupied it.

Whilst this was going on, the girls arrived and joining Kevin had an impromptu picnic lunch, as they watched the antics of the other three setting up the portaledge. The remainder of the weekend passed in the same relaxed manner, with everyone in the group getting on well, with no noticeable areas of friction.

CHAPTER 9

Across the Atlantic, Jake was briefing his boss Dana Sutherland, on findings to date about Project Alpha.

He concluded, 'I'll call you once I've tied down the main players and have some ideas on how to conduct the next phase. In case you need to reach me quickly and my mobile is kaput, I'm booked into the Chelsea Hotel on Sloane Street near Harrods, Knightsbridge.'

'Good hunting and remember - not a word of this gets out - EVER!' she replied menacingly.

Jake chuckled to himself as he drove to catch a night flight to London Heathrow. 'If only the bitch realised that I know about her numbered Swiss bank account,' he smilingly consoled himself, 'plus the string of young studs she supplies with Crack to give her a good weekly servicing at that fancy Penthouse.'

'Letting that lot out would just about torpedo her chances of becoming US Business Woman of the Year,' he said to himself. 'How naîve some people were if they thought that 'ole Jake did not cover his ass.'

Dana Sutherland, the subject of his ruminations was engrossed with her own damage limitation scheme, should Jake's operation turn sour. During her steady rise to becoming president of Arrow Oil, she had acquired some very useful and discreet contacts, which would do just about anything - if the price was right.

A total career animal, she had graduated thirty years previously with a law degree and had quickly become immersed in the maverick world of oil. Starting in their legal negotiating department, she joined just as the Alaskan Polar Shelf was opened up. This demanded someone who could combine a clear vision of the environmental issues at stake, with the ability to convince hard-nosed Alaskan Congressmen that everyone was a winner.

Her colleagues had plenty of experience, but mainly gained in a rough-neck world of oil exploration in the Middle East. Employing all of her analytical intelligence, warm charm and a deadly survival instinct, she quickly rose to head the department by winning some extremely lucrative contracts, against fierce competition.

Then the North Sea Field opened and with it Dana's ability, as vice-president research and exploration, to extract from the Brits and Norwegians 'First Choice' status. Her capacity to use every trick in the book, plus some she invented, including a rumoured illicit liaison with Wayne Burgess, the head of a competitor, gave rise to a positive profile amongst the macho culture of the oil industry. Fully exploiting her knack of providing clear unique concepts, when all those around her were lost for ideas, she was unanimously voted in as president, when Larry Hoffenheim resigned due to ill health two years previously.

Since that time she'd strongly consolidated her position and still took a keen interest in her old department of research and exploration. Jake's well paid role in the department, as a part-time field operative was not irreplaceable and she had already ensured that his salary and expenses were provided for via a holding company with no direct links to Arrow Oil. She also knew of his conviction for fraud twenty years previously, when under his real name of Johnny Norman he had served a three-year prison sentence.

It was a custom in research and exploration that field operatives managed their own source needs without reference to head office, unless cash over $10,000 was required. To date, she had not seen any reference to any source regarding Project Alpha, which was not surprising, given Jake's track record as an operative who much preferred to work alone.

'A real mustang that one,' reflected Dana, glancing at the time and reminding herself that tonight was party night in her suite upstairs. Last week it had been Richard of the wry smile. And tonight?

'A change is as good as a rest - I'll give Wayne the once over,' she slowly purred and expectantly reached for her private mobile phone. Even at 54 her libido was strong and demanding and she worked out at a bespoke health club three times a week. Inheriting an excellent bone structure, she had always watched her weight, almost to a point of anorexia. Still with bumps and curves unimpaired by childbirth, an adroit dress sense and regular visits to Colin, her brilliant hairdresser, gave her a glow of sexuality and calm confidence that far exceeded her five foot five inches.

Her first five years had been so intriguing that any thoughts of getting married and settling down to raise a family were soon brushed aside. Aged 35, she was making serious money, owning outright a pretty town house, top of the range car and enjoyed regular holidays to exotic locations. In addition, with a large pool of willing males available to meet her physical needs and a hectic lifestyle that provided all the stimulation she needed, marriage was discounted. Only over the last few years had she resorted to more blatant means of savouring the attentions of young, good-looking males for the night.

Rather than money, she would pass on a handful of cocaine sachets, which she felt did not have the same blatant sense of commercial barter. Never a user herself, she'd found a steady supplier in Tony Bond, whom to date had applied an utmost discretion. What she did not know was that Tony had once shared a cell in New York with Jake Norris. There they'd survived after forming a firm friendship and still kept in touch. For old time's sake, he'd once let Jake know he was supplying Dana his boss, on a weekly basis, but he didn't think she herself was a user.

Arriving at Heathrow the next morning on a damp grey day, Jake quickly spotted a chauffeur holding up his name card and gratefully settled into the rear leather seat as they treaded their way along the M4, then the West Way into Knightsbridge and to his Chelsea Hotel. Treated as an old friend rather than just another businessman, he quickly settled into his corner suite over-looking the gardens across the busy street.

A short call from a nearby public phone box gave him contact with Freddie Hill, an ex-British Telecom engineer who Jake had used in the past. An hour later found the two quietly nursing glasses of Boddingtons Gold in a small pub off Battersea Park Road. Jake slipped Freddie a note with the unlisted number he wanted checking and they made arrangements for a meet the next day at 11.30am at a pub in Parsons Green.

'All I can say is that he owes my client some money,' stated Jake, 'besides giving him a lot of grief over the last year.'

'Don't worry we'll soon have a name and address for you,' replied Freddie, 'I've never let you down yet. Oh yes! Can I have a hundred on account and then you can bung me the rest once I've given you the griff on matey.'

'OK but remember this is just between us two and not all of greater London Town,' Jake responded, quickly palming two new fifty pound notes swiftly into Freddie's waiting hand.

'Now have I ever let you down Mr Brown,' said Freddie. 'Don't worry it'll be safe with me.'

Outside, Jake hailed a cab and asked to be taken to Liverpool Street

Railway Station. Instead of buying a train ticket, he visited the concourse coffee shop and loitering over a cappuccino, whilst ostentatiously reading a magazine, he checked for any faces taking an interest in him amongst the thin gathering of afternoon passengers. Once satisfied he was not the subject of anyone's undue attention, he slipped outside then, via back streets lined with small specialist businesses, spent twenty minutes walking to the Alpine Club. Mary, the club's formidable librarian answered the intercom request for entry off the narrow street, beckoned him upstairs and gently fussed over his intrusion into her hallowed domain.

'Tasermiut Fjord, southern Greenland eh!' she enquired, pushing forward a file marked 'Greenland.' 'Start with this lot whilst I dig out anything else we may have.'

An hour later saw Jake making his way back to Liverpool Street his inner coat pocket holding four photostat copies of mountaineering articles of the Tasermiut Fjord area. A final stop of the day was a call into Stanford's near Leicester Square. There he purchased maps of southern Greenland and a *Lonely Planet Guide*. When he was once again ensconced in his suite at the hotel, Jake asked the concierge for a self-hire car to be made available the following day and ordered a light meal of Scottish salmon, green salad and fruit, along with a cold bottle of welcome Chablis.

Following the hugely enjoyable meal, washed down with half the bottle of wine and determined that the detrimental effects of 'jet lag' was delayed until his body clock had adjusted to the local time zone he telephoned an escort agency in Belgravia, which he'd reviewed on the internet. After a friendly chat with Jean the receptionist, to discuss his preferences, an hour later 'Sara' arrived. A striking mid twenties brunette, with long legs, an easy relaxed manner and a figure to die for.

Pouring a glass of wine and slipping off her shoes, she curled up in a chair opposite and purred, 'My answer to everything normal - without pain and with protection - is OK! And how long do you want me for?'

The next morning, after a refreshing and deep night's sleep Jake ate a hearty English breakfast, before assimilating as much about Greenland and in particular the area of Tasermiut Fjord as possible. Meeting a smiling Freddie as planned, they exchanged envelopes over a glass, before making a friendly departure and farewell. Waiting until he'd returned to the hotel before opening his envelope, Jake gave a small 'whoopee' to see the name revealed. 'Kevin Hearne, eh! Well at four to one, the odds are not that long.' He pondered, going back to the *Newsweek* article and the small profile headshot of Kevin and his short biography in the article on George Merryweather and his latest expedition.

'So now at least we know who one of the players is and where he lives,' Jake chortled, 'and thank you Debbie for catching it. As my old sergeant used to say, time spent in reccon is seldom wasted! So guess I'll have a quick flip along to Royal Berkshire this afternoon and have me a quick look around.'

Before leaving, he made fresh travel arrangements for departure the next day to Copenhagen, in time to link up with the flight to Narsarsuaq the Greenland air hub, near Nuuk the small capital. Once there he hoped to find some reasonable excuse, possibly associated with tourism, giving him the chance to visit Nanortalik and then to see what happened.

Once he'd cleared the M4-M25 junction, the afternoon visit to Royal Berkshire passed smoothly, particularly when he had purchased an Ordnance Survey 1:10,000 scale map of the Malmesbury area. This gave the name of Kevin's cottage and the rest of what he wanted was straight-forward enough. On a second and final drive past, he caught sight of what he surmised was the family car, disgorging a middle age couple and their shopping. The male was of a similar age to Kevin and had the dress and bearing of an ex-military person. More importantly to Jake was proof of a family dog in residence, as it came running around from the rear to greet them.

It was late in the evening before he returned to central London, where he ordered from room service a medium rare sirloin steak with salad, washed down with Beaujolais. Stifling a yawn and murmuring out loud, 'Sorry Sara honey, I guess it will have to wait for a return visit, I'm plumb tuckered out,' before he called reception to book a morning call and chauffeur car to Heathrow.

The 737 made a long slow descent into Narsarsuaq giving the assort-ed passengers plenty of time to familiarise themselves with the majestic sweep of barren inland ice below. The fierce mountain range hugged the coast spectacularly and was dissected with long sea green fjords, their colours giving a welcome visual relief from the glaring white desolation that is 95% of Greenland.

Following baggage retrieval and friendly arrival formalities, Jake con-firmed his onward helicopter flight the next day to Nanortalik and took a cab to a small family hotel in town, booked by the airline. After a short stroll to give himself a gentle leg stretch following the flight, he enjoyed a supper of fish, before mentally going over his chosen cover story. Affecting his role as a self employed travel writer, he hoped the three day visit would allow him a good opportunity to absorb a feel for the area, in particular Tasermiut Fjord.

'It really depends on how I get on with Eric,' he reflected, pouring over the maps once again.

Whilst he had a variety of options available, his over-riding concern was to keep a low profile, making sure that no-one sensed his real mission. The bumpy 90 minute helicopter ride next day to Nanortalik proved noisy, cold and uneventful. Circling to make a final run-in from the bay Jake could make out a welcoming reception group at the heliport. Its outline picked out in bright yellow, this was no more than a large level concrete circle on a flat area near the shore line, well clear of the buildings and consisting of a wind sock, two fuel tanks and a small wooden hut that sprouted a radio antenna.

As they crowded round the hut waiting for their bags to be off-loaded, loud cries and shrieks of delight filled the air as families and old friends were re-united. Introducing himself, Eric helped to gather Jake's bags and mouthing pleasantries with a smile, he smoothly shepherded Jake, in a calm and untroubled manner through the crush of excited humanity to his waiting jeep.

'I'll soon have you into the Seamen's Hostel,' Eric said. 'Arrival of the helicopter here is a highlight of the day, as a lot of these folk have been away visiting kin, or at college - and there's not much else to distract from a welcome.'

A short drive of a mile on the graded road, leaving behind clouds of dust, quickly got them to the hostel, which was a weather beaten, single storey, white painted wooden structure, of indeterminable age with a red roof. Inside, a stone fireplace dominated the main lounge, with the eating area on one side and a dozen lounging chairs around the huge TV next to the fire.

'Hi there! Welcome to Nanortalik,' beamed a fresh-faced Inuit woman of about twenty with a relaxed smile. 'My name is Nauja and we have reserved you a room that overlooks the bay. Would you first fill in our registration form please and then make yourself at home.'

'I'll come round before dinner and we can have a chat about tomorrow,' said Eric, shaking hands with Jake and waving farewell to Nauja.

Having unpacked and enjoyed a fresh coffee beside the fire, Jake took a stroll around the immediate vicinity for an hour, enjoying the fresh salty air and brisk breeze. Rocky, snow topped hills dominated the horseshoe shaped cluster of islands that sheltered the calm deep waters of the bay, forming a natural harbour. Tied up at the small quay was a tired looking coastal steamer and two fishing boats, with the rest of the community clustered round, marked by a short church spire in its centre.

As the gathering night crept in, Jake moved back inside the hostel and was busy admiring the local Inuit artefacts on show, inter-spaced with old photographs of whaling ships and bearded sailors, when his thoughts were interrupted.

'They slaughtered every Bow Head here and successfully wiped them out,' came Eric's sombre voice from behind him. 'That, their diseases and alcohol nearly did for the Inuit. It was the nearest they ever came to genocide and let's hope that it'll never happen again.'

'My sentiments exactly!' replied Jake. 'Will you join me for a beer whilst we sort out an itinerary?' Later, after asking Nauya for another can of beer each, Eric summarised the next day's arrangement.

'I'll collect you at 8.30 and we can look at the maps in my office, whilst I describe the attractions to you. Then perhaps after lunch with my family we can have a look at what Nanortalik has to offer and get you fitted out and everything ready for our visit to Tasiussaq and up the Tasermiut.'

'Sounds good to me,' replied Jake, 'I'll look forward to that.'

They parted company soon after amicably enough, Eric to rejoin Edda and Jake to make contact with base at Arrow Oil, to let them know his probable return date. By 7.30 Jake had sent an email from his laptop via the satellite phone and guided by wonderful kitchen smells, soon found him in the eating area for supper.

The only other hostel resident that night was a Gustav, a representative of KNI the Local Government co-operative that maintained stores in the isolated communities and seated at the same table they enjoyed a wholesome meal of local lamb casserole with Danish beer. Chatting with Gustav, a Dane who had lived and worked in Greenland for ten years, gave Jake an ideal opportunity to rehearse his pseudo story of being a self-employed travel writer, building up a fictitious family home, wife and children.

The presence of Nauya, first serving the meal and then joining them for coffee in the lounge area, helped him to elaborate on a plausible tale, using his sister Julie's family as a guide to the children's names, gender, age and interests. After some gentle questioning, Nauya also talked a little about Eric and Edda's background and their status in the community. This helped to confirm Jake's initial appreciation of Eric as a mild mannered, well-motivated and cheerful individual, who loved Greenland and held a deep respect for the Inuit people, their culture and traditions.

It also transpired that Nauya was an avid user of the internet and email, the use of which had transformed the lives of most young Inuit, making it possible for them to 'chat' cheaply, both with their friends in Greenland's widely dispersed communities and also to join overseas 'cyber forums' most especially in Denmark.

Asking Jake what satellite phone he was using she confirmed its coverage of the area as the most reliable available. Just after 9.30 Nauya's friend called by to pick her up and after a final exchange of friendly banter, she departed, leaving them to watch the CNN News.

Back in his room, Jake's thoughts as he lay on the comfortable bed under the thick warm quilt, were of satisfaction that he had made the trip and of how he was looking forward to the next couple of days - building up a knowledge of the people and the area. Thinking out loud as he dropped off into a deep slumber, 'I could sure get to like this and to think I'm being paid for being here.'

Eric collected him the next morning as promised and together they walked round the block to his combined house and office. The tourism office had a separate entrance and was essentially a self-contained unit, with a large open plan main office and two smaller ones at the back, ready for any expansion and storage space. Eric shepherded him in and introduced Jake to a slim rangy Inuit young man aged about twenty one.

'I'd like you to meet my assistant Yann who was born in these parts and has just completed a degree in tourism management at Copenhagen University.'

'Pleased to meet you Yann,' said Jake shaking hands, 'this is certainly a great place you have here.'

'Yes it is,' replied Yann politely, 'and I am so glad you like it.'

Eric suggested that Jake should take a seat facing the office wall map and poured them all some coffee that was freshly percolating, before beginning an informal introduction briefing.

He started with, 'I suggest that I orientate you first, explain the general geography and weather patterns of the area, before moving onto the human history, the animal habitat and finishing with a present day demographic, political and logistic overview. Please feel free to ask any questions as they come to mind and I promise we will get back on track once you're happy with an answer. That will probably take us an hour or more and then I thought we could discuss in more detail what we do tomorrow and any specific points you may have. Then we can have some lunch and after that I thought we would get you fitted out for tomorrow and finally have a look around town. How does that sound to you?'

'That all sounds pretty good to me,' replied Jake. 'As I explained earlier, I've been commissioned to write an article that will feature in popular consumer magazines in North America. The client operates expedition tours by chartering Russian research vessels such as *Multanovskiy* and *Molchanov* - plus the icebreaker *Kapitan Khlebnikov*. As you know the icebreaker has been active every summer going to the North Pole and through the North West Passage and they are now trying to stimulate an interest in using the two smaller ships around Greenland.'

'I am sure we can help show there is lots to see and do in our area,' said Eric. 'I'll start by pointing out a few of our main landmarks.'

Eric talked enthusiastically for the next couple of hours, answering Jake's questions to the best of his knowledge and bringing Yann into the discussion when he needed assistance with local detail. He explained that Yann was Nauja's elder brother and that their father, as a founder member of the town council, was very influential in local affairs. Jake explained in more detail what he knew of the Russian ship's *modus operandi*, how the 42 passengers she carried were accommodated and fed, how many 'expedition staff' were usually available and their particular roles and skills. A ship's doctor was always present, just a little important given most of the passengers were over 50 years old.

'I can only tell you what I saw them do when I visited the Antarctic Peninsular on *Molcharnov* last season,' said Jake. 'They gave great interest lectures on-board, in particular explaining basic environmental issues, managed all the crew liaison with the passengers, manned the Zodiac inflatable trips to shore, where they then escorted them and ensured everyone had a great time, in total safety. A very professional operation.'

Eric outlined a plan and timetable for their activities, starting early the next day when they would depart with the dawn at 7.00am by his Avon Rigid Inflatable Boat (RIB). Travelling up the Tasermiut Fjord, to make a first call at Usek and visit the Inuit replica village, before moving on to Tasiusaq, halfway up the fjord before reaching the inland icecap, near Ketil.

'At Tasiusaq,' Eric said, 'we can make a decision on should we go further, dependent upon how the weather is looking and if the engines and radio are working OK. Any sea ice should have melted up there by now and with any luck we will get to Ketil by noon, getting us back here by last light. Just in case, I have prepared an emergency rucsac each, with sleeping and bivouac bag, food, medical first aid kit, fuel and stove. We can upturn the RIB to sleep under, if it comes to that. I now want to fit you up with a dry suit to keep the cold out. I'll also take a rifle, just in case, as we don't want to be a polar bear's spring snack!'

Continuing in same vein until it was time for lunch, they left the tourist office by one door of the building, only to re-enter it by a separate one, direct into Eric's house. Edda was there to make them welcome. Lunch was a relaxed affair of excellent Arctic char and vegetables, with fruit-cake to follow. Jake expressed his admiration for both the wholesome food and the homely, comfortable décor and furnishings that made such a statement about them both. It was of classic Danish lines, sensitively broken by Inuit artefacts and carvings, with pride of place taken by a polar bear skin.

Sensing his interest, Edda explained that traditional Inuit art had several functions - religious, magical, decorative and toys, or just for something to do. The artist studies the raw piece of stone until he 'sees' a shape within it of an animal or person. He roughly chisels it out before refining it with files and then sandpaper. The idea that there is firstly an image of an animal containing the essence of the animal within the stone and secondly this needs to be released by the artist, has its origins in the Inuit beliefs that human acts of creativity freed the universe from a dormant state.

Yann now took over and led Jake to the tourist office store close by, where he fitted him with a suitably sized dry suit and checked out the VHF radio they would use next day tuned on to Channel 16. Back in the office Eric was ready to take him on a tour of Nanortalik, starting with the reproduction Norse long house near the heliport, the KNI store, church, jetty, school and hospital, before dropping off back at the Seamen's Hostel.

The remainder of the short afternoon passed quickly, as Jake absorbed everything Eric said and took plenty of photographs, whilst asking hopefully intelligent questions about the township and its inhabitants.

'I trust that gives you a good overview?' enquired Eric parking his jeep outside the Seamen's Hostel. 'We can discuss any further queries you have tomorrow. I'll just come in to tell Nauja about my joining you for an early breakfast and then I must leave you as I have a town council meeting to attend in an hour.'

'Well, Eric it certainly has been an interesting day and I thank you for that,' said Jake as he followed him into the hostel, 'I'll certainly be up and ready for breakfast with you in the morning.'

Returning to his room, Jake mulled over the sights and sounds he had been exposed to since his arrival. More importantly his impression of Eric, sensing that behind a pleasant urbane exterior, lurked a formidable and highly competent person, dedicated to the future of Greenland and fair play for the Inuit people.

'I'm pretty sure that could well be an advantage in some way,' he reflected, climbing out of his clothes and into a hot shower. Before supper, he set up his laptop and as a diary entry, typed in some bullet points to remind him of the day's events. These, together with the brochures and maps Yann had given him, would provide all the key elements needed to maintain his fictional cover story, at the same time as providing any information he might require in the future. In the dining area, he was the only guest at supper, Gustav having returned to Nuuk on the day's helicopter shuttle.

As he took his seat, Nauja smilingly described what was on the menu, suggesting the musk ox steak, cheerfully adding, 'To help keep your strength,' as she casually brushed past him with a water jug. He was not sure if this was a slight innuendo and replied in kind.

'I'll probably need every bit of help! I could really do damage to a beer right now. Would you like to join me?'

Nodding an affirmative Nauya slipped back into the kitchen to give the order to the chef and, collecting a couple of beer cans and glasses, returned.

'Did you get to visit Yann whilst he was at university in Copenhagen?'

Jake asked, as Nauja poured two glasses of beer and joined him.

'You bet,' she giggled. 'He never knew he had so many friends.'

'From my recollection of Copenhagen,' Jake said, 'it is expensive, clean and the beer was excellent, with the sexiest girls on the planet and as much shit to smoke as anyone could ever want!'

'A real mixture of all that,' Nauja laughingly said. 'The Copenhagen night life was certainly pretty demanding. The real highlights were the 'freebie' trips with Yann, to theme parks where we were feted like VIPs, with all booze and food free.'

'For a young innocent Inuit girl it must have been awesome,' Jake remarked, 'did you find it overpowering and all too much?'

'Well I certainly would not call myself innocent,' Nauja chuckled, 'we Inuit girls probably know more about the facts of life earlier than most. Our long, dark winter's nights were certainly not wasted watching television. I don't think the Danes had anything to teach me in that area, other than homosexuality, which is virtually unknown here.'

'Yes that would be a real waste! How about us sharing a spliff - are you into that?' asked Jake suggestively.

'I would say that is the best news I've had all day,' Nauya answered with a smile, 'let's get the meal eaten and then I'll definitely join you later.'

CHAPTER 10

The next morning, despite feeling a little queasy, Jake's breakfast meeting with Eric went as planned and Jake mentioned his concern about their meeting any polar bears. After thinking for a short while, Eric told him all about their habitat and life style, using a recent event to illustrate the main features.

'A month ago,' he said, 'not far inland from Nanortalik, near Usek, Arne, the shepherd from Tasiussaq and Nauja's boyfriend met up with Aka, who is Edda's elder brother. They intended to spend a week up Tasermiut Fjord, where it was still frozen near Ketil. For the last five years they had made the same visit to hunt polar bear. As spring arrived and temperatures rose, seals the polar bear's favourite snack, were very active catching Arctic char, that in turn bred extensively on plankton in the areas where the sea ice was breaking up after the long winter freeze.'

Pausing, Eric checked he had caught Jake's full attention - he was sitting cradling his morning mug of coffee, listening intently.

'Aka, as an Inuit hunter was able to take two bears annually as his birthright, whilst Arne had obtained permission to take one. They planned to take a RIB as far up the fjord as possible, berth her on dry land somewhere prominent, before heading off using skis over the sea ice, taking turns to pull all their gear in a one man sledge. For longer journeys husky dogs could be used, but in the confines of the fjord their presence, smell and barks would frighten off both bears and seal.'

'The pelt of a polar bear is a highly treasured item for an Inuit family, as it provides excellent insulation as a warm mattress cover. It is the animal most feared by them and they have many stories woven into their culture from their days of hunting by spears bows and arrows. Polar bears, other than family groups of females and young, are solitary most of the year,' Eric continued.

'During the breeding season in late March, April and May, males actively seek out females by following their tracks on the sea ice. Bears are polygamous, and the male remains with a receptive female for only a relatively short time and then seeks another female. Pregnant females seek out denning areas in late October and November and denning occurs both on land and sea ice. Young are born in the den in December and a litter of two is common. They will emerge from the den in late March or early April when the cubs weigh about 15 pounds. Young remain with the mother until they are about 28 months old.

'Females can breed again at about the same time they separate from their young, so normally they can produce litters every third year and have a life expectancy of about 20 to 25 years. Their main food is seals, which they capture by waiting for them at breathing holes and at the edge of leads or cracks in the ice. The polar bear's keen sense of smell, sharp claws, patience, strength, speed and the camouflaging white coat aid in procuring food.'

Taking a break to refill his coffee cup and eat some muffins, Eric enjoyed recounting about his favourite animal - the king of the frozen north, with no superior predator, other than man himself.

'After leaving the RIB on the north shore of the fjord, they skied for a full day and set up camp nearly opposite Ketil. They made four forays out from here for a full day each in different directions before cutting fresh bear tracks heading towards the inland icecap. They followed, moving slowly and as quietly as possible, hunting rifles out of their protective carrying bags, slung over one shoulder, loaded and ready for use.

'A few hours later and just before they would have to return in the failing light, they came across an area where the bears had obviously made a seal kill, with lots of blood and discarded flesh brightly marking the spot near a breathing hole. As Arne bent to investigate the hole in detail, from out of the corner of his left eye he glimpsed a white mass, moving at speed straight for him. He instantly stood to turn and unslung his rifle in less than a second, but not fast enough to bring the weapon to a firing position. As if in a slow motion movie the bear bore down on him and just before his instant death, a shot rang out, fired by Aka, that brought the animal down literally at his feet. Aka had made a reactive shot from twenty meters distance, aimed at the bear's skull, which hitting its target, had stopped it in its tracks and close enough for Arne to smell its rancid breath, tinged by seal blubber. It transpired they had inadvertently crossed between the mother and her two cubs, which fortunately were nearly 28 months old. They scampered off with an excellent probability of survival.'

Suitably impressed Jake expressed his thanks for Eric's rivetting account and timely realisation that man's survival here was merely a very small part of the mosaic of a neutral or even antagonistic environment.

Outside the weather was stable with little wind, as they loaded their gear and departed in the 5.4 metre long RIB just as the first rays of daylight hit the surrounding snow covered hilltops. Once out in the main channel, Eric demonstrated his prowess with the inflatable by opening up the throttle on the two powerful 40 HP outboard motors and they quickly adopted a cruise position, skimming over the calm water. Within an hour they had reached Usek. They headed into a tiny cove, where a small boat was beached and Jake could make out an earth covered rocky mound a few hundred yards inland, with thin tendrils of smoke rising into the still air from one end.

'Ah! Here comes Udda. He's Yann and Nauja's father and the chief here,' exclaimed Eric, as the short but powerfully built man caught their bowline and hauled the front of the RIB onto the pebbly beach. Offloading a full animal skin bag, Eric grabbed the man in a bear hug and together they danced a short jig, delighted to see each other. Jabbering away to Udda in Inuit, Eric first made the RIB secure and then introduced Jake. Udda gave a short formal greeting in English and led them off towards the mound.

'We'll only stay a short time as Udda is opening up the replica winter house for the season,' continued Eric, 'it'll give you some idea of what visitors will experience and I want to push on to Tasiussaq whilst the weather is still good.'

Following Udda into the entrance, Jake ducked through the small opening and was immediately assailed by the pungent smell of burning seal blubber, as his eyes adjusted to the near darkness and the sting of smoke. Udda waited patiently until Jake's vision allowed him to follow down the narrow passage to a raised area where two small blubber stoves were burning. Despite the near darkness, the area gave out a sense of warmth and quiet well being. The walls were made up of flat and oval shaped rocks snugly layered into a double dry wall and fitted into place above a shallow depression, scooped out of the gravel earth. This gave an internal height of eight feet or so, before the convex roof which was made of curved whalebones with whole whale skins and held in place by large sods and earth. Udda's sleeping bag and mat were in a corner of the platform, where he ushered Jake and Eric to sit down, as he busily prepared them some coffee.

'It's amazing how quiet and warm it is,' exclaimed Jake squinting in the gloom, 'how long would it have taken to them to build a shelter like this each winter?'

'Quite a while from scratch, but once they'd built it the family group would return year after year, replacing the roof each time, which would only take them a few days,' replied Eric.

'You'll notice how everything has its place and they had a ritual for what was worn where, keeping here inside on the sleep platform only the minimum of equipment, clothing and footwear. After we've had some coffee, I'll ask Udda to give us a quick tour and then we must depart, if we want to make Tasiussaq and Ketil.'

Thirty minutes later the snarl of the outboard motors cut the silence as once again Eric picked up to cruising speed. Whilst Eric sat at the transom, gripping the wheel with his left and working the throttle bar with his right hand, Jake got himself comfortable jammed mid-ships amongst their gear, sitting on his rucsac and pushing back into the firm air filled bulwarks on the left hand side of the RIB. The barren rocky mountains on the north side plunged steeply into the fjord without respite, whilst on his right the slopes were much more gentle and covered with green scrub below the snowline, which he estimated to be lying at about the 2,000 foot level. He was also conscious of just how intrusive they were in this wilderness playground, as since leaving Usek astern, there was not one single sign of man's presence.

'At this rate we should make Tasiussaq in about forty minutes,' shouted Eric above the roar of the engines, 'you'll first see some sheep shelters up on the hillside to the right, where the peninsular comes down to meet the main fjord. The village is at the bottom, sheltered from the fjord.'

As anticipated they made excellent progress and, passing several isolated sheep sheds opposite Tasiussaq, they nosed into a natural harbour at the mouth of a tranquil bay. The hamlet appeared asleep and only as they approached the last hundred metres to the huddle of dinghies above the high water line, did a person appear out of a small shack and hurried over to meet them. With a well practised pull on the thrown bowline, just as the swell and their impetus carried them forward, the bearded giant grabbed the bulwark haul line and tugged them onto the pebbled beach. Having secured them to a tether line, he helped catch the offered parcel and boomed out a welcome to Eric. Shouting a greeting in reply, Eric grabbed his hand excitedly and introduced Jake.

'Jake meet Arne, an old comrade of mine from the Danish Navy. We spent a couple of years together in the submarine service and then bumped into to each other here. Small world eh! Arne is a full time shepherd with over 2,000 sheep to look after and also acts as the Tasiussaq policeman when needed.'

Arne led them to his ramshackle hut, the inside of which was amazingly comfortable, clean and neat with a scrubbed wooden floor. In addition to a small table with bench seats on two sides, substantial shelves, filled mainly with books, lined all available wall space, with a corner sink leading to a small water closet. Pride of place was given to a white polar bear skin, next to a pot-bellied iron stove at the opposite end from the entrance, that provided both heating and cooking. A door gave access to a small bunkroom with a surprisingly small bed next to a desk with a satellite phone coupled to a laptop and a VHF radio set up, all linked into a diesel generator outside.

'All the comforts of home,' remarked Eric, 'Arne joins in our nightly 'cyber chat' sessions and is Nauja's boyfriend, but still flirts outrageously with all the girls and probably knows more local gossip than anyone else in the area.'

'I'll call Yann and let him know you're here,' Arne said reaching for the handset and talking in Inuit to Nanortalik before turning to them and reporting, 'he says everything is in control and to enjoy the trip.'

'We should be back here in three hours, depending of course on the weather,' offered Eric, as declining another offer of coffee, they made their way back to the Avon RIB.

'I'll try to make sure I am here and will listen out for you on my mobile Channel 16,' Arne cried, effortlessly pushing them back into the water and waving them off.

As they chugged away, Jake tried to memorise the layout of the hamlet as they turned into the main fjord and picked up speed. The weather remained calm, with an increase in trash ice registering the fact that on the horizon they could see the cliffs of inland ice meeting the sky. After thirty minutes Eric throttled down and asked Jake if he would like a turn in control whilst he answered an urgent call of nature and dug out a steel flask of hot chocolate from his rucsac.

After changing over and relieving himself over the side, Eric poured them both a drink, then peered forward with his binoculars and exclaimed, 'It looks like the brash continues to increase. We'll push on for another hour or so and then take another view on the situation. At least we should be able to spot Ketil if nothing else!'

'Whatever you say,' Jake nervously replied, 'you're the boss and it's sure been really fascinating already.'

As Eric had predicted, an hour later found them confronted with a barrier of swirling trash ice, through which they bumped and swerved an erratic, slow, zigzag course. Jake had changed over once again and was kneeling in the forepeak, where armed with a boat hook he was busily engaged pushing ice blocks away from the bow.

Eric eased to a gentle halt beside a block the size of a small car and focused his binoculars towards the inland icecap before turning to Jake to inform him, 'We'll get a good view of Ketil from here - have a look.'

Jake took the proffered binoculars and focused where Eric had indicated. Filling the lenses was an enormous perpendicular rock face, which appeared to be leaning out slightly over the fjord. Behind he could make out the inland icecap and at the bottom of the face was a thin slither of shoreline, before the green/blue water ice of the fjord.

'Are you telling me that people climb up that!' Jake whispered in awe, 'it only confirms what I've always suspected - they are definitely born with a screw loose!'

'Only the world's big boys come to play on Ketil,' noted Eric, 'the massive commitment they need mirrors the size and Ketil does not suffer fools gladly. It is such a short season and the two reasons combined mean that only a limited number of teams have made an attempt. There is a strong one coming from Britain soon and we shall be involved with providing some logistics.'

'Well I am certainly impressed,' said Jake, 'could I just get some long range shots from here - with you in the front of the boat. Also, if you do not mind, I'll get the Brits' contact details off you when we get home tonight.'

Ten minutes later found them steadily heading down-fjord through the trash ice towards Tasiussaq, which they reached without incident. Staying off shore Eric made a call to Arne and chatted away about the journey and confirmed his intention of heading straight back to Nanortalik. Arne promised to radio that information ahead to Yann, with his updated estimated arrival timings. The next couple of hours cruising passed incident free, with Eric giving a running commentary on all the bird life he could see. Plus at one point they sighted only two hundred yards away a school of 'harp' seals numbering about ten, that sped along effortlessly giving the impression of the water 'boiling'.

They continued on past Usek, keeping a look out for Udda, who was nowhere to be seen in the gathering gloom, as dark rain laden clouds scuttled up the fjord to meet them. By the time they beached by Eric's office, there had been a steady drizzle for an hour and they were more than pleased they had worn the wet suits for the journey. It was also dark enough to need head torches whilst unloading the RIB, helped by Yann.

'The helicopter shuttle does not happen until early tomorrow afternoon,' remarked Eric, 'so we'll have plenty of time in the morning to go over any more details you want. Have a good night's sleep and I'll see you then.'

'Many thanks for a mightily interesting day,' Jake replied, 'and yes I'll look forward to catching you late morning with any further questions. Bye!'

En-route to his room at the Seamen's Hostel, Jake caught sight of Nauja and gave out a load shout to gain her attention. Turning round she waved and smiled, mouthing she would see him later, before swinging her way into the kitchen. Once in his room, Jake eased out of his clothes and whilst the bath filled, sat wrapped in a towel and reflected on the experiences that day.

He had been really impressed with Eric, whose passion and knowledge for all things environmental came shining through. Tasermiut Fjord had been singularly impressive and he would not forget quickly the sense of magnificence it left on his inner feelings - something that had not happened for a long, long time. The meetings with Udda and Arne had also registered as special events and he grinned, realising that he'd been smitten by the ambience radiated in the fjord.

'Well dear Dana Sutherland and Arrow Oil,' he muttered, stepping into the welcoming bath, 'you've certainly given me something new to think about. And as for those crazy Limeys, I'll just have to try and make some kind of contact with Kevin Hearne before they get here.'

Later, as he enjoyed a fillet of freshly caught Greenland cod, baked with herbs and served by Nauja with vegetables, potato and a thick tartare sauce, he reflected to her about what he had sensed and absorbed during the visit, in particular his experiences that day with Eric in the RIB.

'You really have a very special place here,' he said, 'and I'll have no trouble writing up a nice article to encourage tourism - both for people coming here for a short visit and those seeking a more serious adventure - not to mention the friendly staff,' he laughed.

'That would be fantastic,' replied Nauja fussing over him. Pouring another can of beer she inquired suggestively, 'Have you any strength left to share another joint later, as the one last night has really wet my appetite?'

Deliberately leaning over Jake's shoulder to give him the chance to inhale her freshly applied body spray, Nauja sensuously looked deep into his eyes and, gently stroking his hand, quietly said in a low murmur, 'It's not an early start tomorrow morning so you can sleep-in as long as you like. Tonight you can tell me more all about your impressions of Usek and Ketil.'

Casually patting and stroking her buttock, Jake stared straight back saying, 'That will be my pleasure. Why don't I grab a six pack and meet up with you in my room after your finished? I'll roll us a couple of nice fat spliffs whilst I am waiting.'

Just across from them in the village Eric was deep in conversation with Yann, who had called round to join him and Edda for dinner. Eric summarised his meeting with Udda and Arne and the remainder of his day with Jake, before observing, 'We probably had the best mix possible of good weather most of the day, so he could get some great shots of the fjord and mountains, then the sea ice near Ketil, before we headed back here, with some light rain for the last hour. Hopefully that will give him a reasonable overview and he seemed satisfied with the experience. If the article is well received, who knows it could produce 50 or maybe 100 tourists next season. He certainly was impressed with Ketil when I told him about the British attempt this season.'

'I understand from Nauja,' said Yann, 'that Jake seems a genuine type of guy and has been quite impressed by what he has seen. Let's hope he writes well enough to get the environmental and native protection messages across with humour and the passion that they are worth protecting.'

'Which reminds me,' said Eric, 'I've had an email from a UK outfit called 'Chisholm Expeditions' the brainchild of a Ruari Chisholm, the first man ever to climb the seven summits and walk to both poles. He has initiated a clean up of the Ukraine Base on the Antarctic Peninsular. His aim is to raise global awareness of Antarctica environmental issues and by helping the Ukrainians, demonstrate how we can achieve it by co-operation, rather than conflict.

'To help raise the money he persuaded corporate sponsors to buy and adapt an ocean going yacht named *Antarctica*. Sponsor representatives help crew with a professional team to visit the project and experience Antarctica. After which, when all fired up, they take on a commitment to spread the word in their respective spheres of influence. They want to visit here this season and motor up the fjord to meet the British team on Ketil.'

'Hey you two, eat up!' hectored Edda with a laugh, 'before the food goes cold, then you can continue talking about *Antarctica* later.'

What Yann had avoided to mention was Nauya's interesting snippet about what she'd seen on Jake's laptop. Whilst cleaning his room, a natural nosiness had been aroused by the open machine and flipping it on she'd read a couple of his emails. An earlier one had been interesting, giving brief outline details of Jake's preparation for being a writer prior to his arrival in Greenland. Another, to someone called Debbie, besides being laced with graphic sexual innuendo, also mentioned the pressure he was under to provide his boss in Texas with even more details of a Project Alpha? Not being a fool, Nauya decided the less she said about it the better, but as she'd always shared everything with Yann and wanted someone else to know about her findings, telling him seemed a logical thing to do. They'd both decided to keep quiet about it with Eric, so as not to worry him or Edda, but they would tell Arne and Ata.

Once they had eaten and cleared away Yann, intrigued by Eric's graphic descriptions of Chisholm Expeditions, asked if he could be excused and quickly going next door and using the office computer, he looked it up on the internet. His search revealed a very informative web site. Yann spent a couple of hours absorbing Ruari Chisholm's vision, so that when the next morning Jake called into the office to say his thanks and find out the British team's contact details, Yann was also able to brief him in detail about the *Antarctica* project and their stated wishes.

'Combined with the British attempt on Ketil,' he remarked, 'it should provide a great focus for attracting the right kind of world attention to the region. Your article could act as the vital trigger!'

'That's very kind of you to say so,' replied a smiling Jake. 'I'll see what I can do. Right now I am thinking that I should pay a return visit when both the Brit climbers and *Antarctica* are here. Maybe even getting a lift up Tasermiut Fjord aboard her, which would make for some stunning photography. If you could let me have their contact details, I'll get in touch with both and see what I can arrange.'

'I thought you may want something like that, so I've noted them for you,' laughed Yann, passing Jake a list of their contact details.

'Thanks,' said Jake, 'I'll keep you posted on how I get on with them both. If I may, I'd like to use you and Eric as an initial reference when I make contact.'

CHAPTER 11

Kevin Hearne, the man pivotal to Jake's thoughts was fully engaged making frantic final preparations in the controlled, but seemingly chaotic style of any expedition - anywhere. He had centralised all of the gear to be shipped at his cottage and hired a 20 foot-freight container to store it securely. He would take it all in a large hired van to Copenhagen to meet and load onto a freighter, to be taken first to Iceland and then to Nanortalik. Food was their biggest bulk item, even allowing for the lots of items that he had asked Eric to have ready from KNI sources. Because food was always the most contentious item on any expedition, Kevin had spent a great deal of time and effort to ensure they had more than enough, plus lots of variety.

Having spent many days with the Royal Marines isolated in some challenging places, Kevin knew the importance of having the right balance. Morale was equally important as the physiological aspect of adequate nutrition and what constituted 'wall scran' when climbing was an item that had concentrated all their minds. George, a self confessed Mars bar addict was quite happy to live on nothing else, whilst Rick had developed a home made muesli concept of calculating a bagged mix of nuts, raisins, fudge, oatmeal with chocolate flakes per person, per day. Hugh meanwhile would happily subsist on 'big soups' for the rest of his life.

As an adequate fluid intake was the most important dietary aspect of the proposed twenty days climbing Ketil, Kevin wanted to ensure that every opportunity was taken to try and make their drinks as welcome as possible. With the team's acceptance, he restricted the fluid component for the wall to orange powder, hot chocolate, soups, with only a little tea and coffee and some experimental energy drinks with plenty of sugar.

With caffeine being such a strong diuretic and dehydration a major concern he'd discounted much coffee and tea, except at the base camp. Here he planned to have an assortment of attractive and balanced menus, that should satisfy most of their cravings. To ensure getting this right, he'd spoken at length with Nigel, an old pal from his Service climbing days, who was an acknowledged UK guru on expedition nutrition. Based close to Wells Cathedral, Nigel's latest business and entrepreneurial venture was called High & Wild, an adventure travel company that ran specialist trips worldwide.

Stealing a whole day to see him and discuss the issues, Kevin decided to cycle over. He persuaded himself that it was the best way to combine both business and pleasure and knowing Nigel, he'd not be fazed by seeing him arrive hot, sweaty and thirsty. Selecting a route that would keep him off the main A class roads, but at the same time keep him away from hills and in the general direction, Kevin eased round to the east of Bath and then headed straight for Wells. It took him three hours and upon arrival, after a refreshing drink, he had been amused to be given a familiarisation tour of the ancient city aboard Nigel's latest marketing toy - an imported Indian tuk-tuk motorised trishaw. He negotiated this through the narrow, congested and winding streets with humourous ease, raising quite a few smiles of interest and waves from bemused members of the public.

'I'd certainly work hard on really making the few days in base before the trio start the climb, a mega boost for their vitamin intake, without overloading the digestive system,' Nigel suggested, 'ensuring that they are very well hydrated in the final 24 hours - with no alcohol or heavy activity in that period. The final two meals are vital, with lots of vegetables and protein in the first and lots of carbohydrates in the second. Are you sure you do not need me to come and cook for you?'

'Thanks for the offer,' replied Kevin, laughing a retort, as he departed for a return cycle ride, 'but we cannot take you away from High & Wild for that long!'

Kevin had listed all the rations and climbing gear and placed them in lockable plastic storage kegs, which he'd numbered for quick reference and retrieval. The bulky tentage, spare sleeping bags, mats and base camp stores he stowed in large canvas lockable kit bags. Wherever possible, he split up a group of items into two or three lots and stored them in separate containers, so that if one was lost in transit, there were replacements still available in the others. He well remembered one trip when all their tea, milk powder and sugar for a whole month was placed in one keg, which had indeed been irretrievably lost, with a massive blow to morale for a British team!

The stores' container was also hooked up into the garage electrical supply to allow the use inside of a small space heater and some lights. With a sturdy Chubb lock on the container door, a trigger alarm inside and the area well illuminated by a pair of movement sensitive flood lights, Kevin felt confident that no one could tamper with the vital climbing and camping equipment, clothing and food supplies. He'd decided to include the seismic instruments in the sea freight, well insulated and padded in a Pelican box with good locks and marked 'Emergency Resuscitation.' Separate was an auger pole with a radio antennae mast kit and, secreted in three large sealed tins of chocolate drink mix, he'd hidden a kilo of low velocity mining explosive. The dozen electrical detonators he placed in the base medical kit, shorted out, insulted and well wrapped in bandages.

The Immarsat briefcase satellite phone and a rugged Husky laptop would accompany him on the flight out in just over a month's time. To ensure the phone and other batteries were kept fully charged at the base camp, he packed in the boxes a couple of solar panels, a transformer unit, power adapters and battery connections. Eric had agreed to provide a large fully charged truck battery and as an extra precaution Kevin had also packed a tiny wind generator, designed for use on yachts.

Using an encryption device that resembled a personal organiser, he expected emailing out the coded test results securely direct to Houston, shortly after the test. So if he was in any way compromised, at least some of the product would have got through. The results would also be downloaded onto separate floppy discs, for safe storage until their delivery. Not for the first time, Kevin reflected on how getting a trip together called for a wide range of skills and disciplines, recalling what Mike Banks, a famous Royal Marine climber of the 1950s and 60s had recorded after making the first ascent of the Himalayan giant Rakaposhi:

'Every expedition has, in its nature, a foreground, a middle distance and a background. The foreground is the planning and preparation, the hopes, the frustrations, those utterly insuperable obstacles - which are always overcome just at the moment of desperation and abandonment. The brawny adventurer finds himself secretary and drudge, his idealism and athleticism floundering in a flood of paper. These preliminaries to action, although they make dull reading are part of the very fabric of expeditioning. They put the organisers, good rough hill men, to a harsh test when they find themselves on trial as businessmen, diplomats, photographers, linguists, communication specialists, paramedics, travel agents and caterers. They must find time to guess - it is with regret that customers are informed that errors cannot be rectified after they have left the country - and to dream!'

'You can now add pseudo geologist to that list!' smiled Kevin, working away on a packing content list for Danish customs. He was going to have a mildly manic couple of weeks as, in addition to getting the van load to Copenhagen for shipping, he had also been asked by Aces High, the Bristol management training company if he would be interested in helping to facilitate on a couple of courses lined up over the next period. They were team-building interventions at an outdoor centre venue in central Wales with an unpronounceable name, located in a semi-remote area of hill farms, forestry, open moor land, with a couple of large reservoirs and rocky outcrops available if required. All this and yet the area was still only an hour's drive away from motorway and railway links.

Kevin enjoyed working with the outfit, as it was challenging and the remuneration always helped with the boarding school fees. To help minimise costs he'd booked on a night ferry from Dover the following evening and had allowed himself three clear days to drive from Calais to Copenhagen and back. First via Belgium, the Netherlands and then across northern Germany to Puttgarden, for another ferry over to Redbyhavn in Denmark and onto Copenhagen. All things being equal, this should get him back in plenty of time to fulfil his task in Wales with Aces High.

George was also rushing around, engaged on seemingly endless publicity related junkets, the most recent being a trip to New York to give a presentation at the Explorers Club. This would help sell any subsequent material in the huge North American outdoor book market, currently undergoing a renaissance fuelled by media desire to show American folk heroes' in rugged outdoor scenarios. For the Ketil climb his biggest fear was not of failing, but for one of the team having to drop out at the last minute and he'd used the trip to also make a quick call on Bucky Burrows, an old climbing buddy.

A native of Montana, Bucky had robustly promised that should the unfortunate happen, he was more than happy to step quickly into the breach. George knew the others would welcome him into the slot, as Bucky was a leading veteran exponent of epic 'Big Wall' climbing techniques, notably on Baffin Island where he had more than six new hard routes to his credit. George had called for a final team meeting the following week once Kevin had returned from Copenhagen, when he hoped they could iron out any last minute problems. He intended to introduce the subject then and explain Bucky's nomination and agreement to act as their reserve.

He'd also be able to brief them about the interest being shown by Ruari Chisholm and a proposed visit to base camp by his yacht *Antarctica*. Roger Chantell, Ruari's operation's manager had recently contacted him and they'd agreed it would be useful for both their goals to collaborate in this small way, meaning even more publicity for the Ketil team for no outlay, other than Kevin giving them a small amount of entertaining.

Shortly after he'd made contact with George, Roger received an email from Jake Norris, which after describing who he was, explained about his recent visit to Nanortalik and what he hoped to achieve with a write-up. He went on to ask if he could possibly hitch a lift on *Antarctica* to photograph the yacht and Ketil. Roger discussed the issue with Lucinda, Ruari's public relation's manager and she contacted Jake to find out who had commissioned him and what story line was contemplated. Following a short flurry of messages and telephone calls, Lucinda decided that Jake's article could be useful and recommended assisting him, on the understanding they agreed to check his draft for errors before publication.

With a wry smile on his face, it was a cheerful Jake who jauntily strode into Dana Sutherland's penthouse office at Arrow Oil to give his report.

'So what have you got for me?' she queried motioning him to sit opposite her small uncluttered desk.

'My initial visit was successful,' he confidently replied, 'and I've arranged for a follow-up meet with Kevin Hearne, the Ketil team base camp manager once they have started their climb, in my capacity as a travel writer. I hope to arrive there aboard *Antarctica* a yacht belonging to Chisholm Expeditions who plan making a call at the base camp.'

'Any compromises?' quizzed Dana.

'None I'm aware of,' Jake replied. 'I also seemed to have passed muster with Lucinda, the media person for Chisholm Expeditions who was quite inquisitive.'

'I do hope you're right, or I'll have your balls made into a pair castanets!' she smiled menacingly, concluding the interview.

CHAPTER 12

K evin sighed with relief as he drove the now empty van west bound off the M25 and onto the M4 en-route home from Dover. The three-day round-trip to Copenhagen had been well over 1200 miles, and included four ferry journeys, an overnight stop near Hamburg, with hurriedly snatched periods for meals, sleep and no change of clothes.

The next sixty or so miles home could not pass quickly enough. He'd spoken with Gillian soon after docking, so he knew that in another hour or so she'd be welcoming him home once again, for what must be the thousandth time. Then a long shower and a hot meal whilst catching up on all the family happenings and a deep sleep for eight hours or more would ease the kinks from his back and numbness from his brain. It was a glorious day, with a robust June sun contrasting brilliantly with the green countryside as he sped along, counting the junctions.

Copenhagen had passed without incident, especially after meeting with the shipping agent at their dockside storage area. Verbally checking for any hazardous items, he showed more interest in ensuring that the paperwork was correct, than with the actual contents. Kevin had watched anxiously as the stevedores loaded the gear concisely into a ten-foot cage, with the numbered keg containing the explosives and the black medical box containing the detonators being placed central to the load. He took a deep breath when the nearly full cage was securely padlocked and placed in a bonded area, ready for lowering into the bowels of the freight ship *MV Broberg* in a few days time.

During the long drive on the European motorways, he'd pondered the ethics and risks of involvement with Henry, his biggest concern being the shipment of the explosive and detonators. Firstly, in case they were discovered and secondly, the potential hazard they could present by falling into the wrong hands. He was happy they did not represent a danger whilst they were separated in transit, being less of a potential hazard aboard ship than the diesel fuel, or, for that matter any alcohol.

Also it would be unusual that expedition plastic kegs were identified as being worth stealing in a prosperous place such as Copenhagen, or rifled in transit aboard a Danish ship. He estimated the chances of anything untoward happening to the load once in Nanortalik, as minimal.

Another major anxiety was for any activity that would effect the professional status of the fellow team members, should the full truth of his involvement with Henry ever leak out. So far as possible, he'd double-checked the most vulnerable points to date and could spot no apparent weaknesses that would backfire on them. By keeping the lads completely in the dark, he knew that if his true mission were to be discovered, they should not be compromised by his actions.

On the major plus side, the fiscal incentive would mean he could relax a little for meeting the boys' annual school fees, as thirty years' service with the Royal Marines had not prepared him mentally for such expenditure. Whilst the job as a self-employed management trainer was lucrative and enjoyable when 'on the case' there had been and would continue to be slack periods, as the first sniff of a recession was enough for most companies to close down their training budgets.

Like some of his former colleagues, he could always go onto the 'security circuit' but felt that being somebody's watchdog, gate keeper or potential bullet stopper, was not something he could eagerly rush into. Others had cleverly used their hard won skills and knowledge to very good effect, finding well paid employment as consultants for the specialist security equipment companies that have flourished as a result of the Services expertise gained containing the IRA threat for thirty years. Plus there were other deployments such as Dhofar, Falklands, Bosnia, Kuwait, Sierra Leone and Iraq. It was from one of these individuals, who had long owed him a favour, that he'd obtained the explosive, whilst the electrical detonators had mysteriously appeared from a tin secreted in his shed that he had long forgotten about.

Seeing the signs for Junction 17, he dismissed all other thoughts from his mind other than Gillian and home. Within ten minutes he would be explaining where he'd been, what and where he'd eaten and how much sleep he needed to catch up on. He would leave any expedition business until the morning, concentrating instead on keeping awake long enough to eat whatever Gillian had prepared and converse intelligently until tiredness overtook and he crashed out. Fortunately, he'd remembered to buy some of her favourite perfume on the Channel ferry, so his Brownie point score would be positive.

Stopping the van in the area vacated by the hired container, he grabbed his travel bag and sauntered easily into the house, catching Gillian on the phone to a friend. Smiling and waving 'Hello' he flipped the kettle on and busied himself making a fresh pot of tea, as she ended her conversation and gave him a big hug and a welcome kiss. Wrinkling her nose and pushing him away she laughingly asked, 'And guess who's not coming any closer until they've had a shower?'

Whilst he did as bid, Gillian prepared a simple but tasty meal of cheese and broccoli quiche with a tossed green salad and chunks of fresh wholemeal bread, washed down with an Australian Chardonnay. Between mouthfuls, they quickly brought each other up to date on the children's welfare, family news and neighbourhood gossip, before discussing their priorities for the next couple of days. A couple of hours later Kevin's eyes were shutting and he needed no persuasion to crawl into bed to a deep, untroubled sleep.

The next morning after returning the hired van, he concentrated on letting everyone know that the freight was on its way aboard *MV Broberg* sending a copy of the load manifest to Eric for checking off upon its arrival at Nanortalik in three weeks or so.

Then in the afternoon he chased up his involvement with Aces High for their forthcoming team building events in Wales and lastly spoke with George about the final team meeting. Gillian had a couple of planned engagements locally for lunch with friends then a visit in the afternoon, with them both getting together for supper and an early night, especially for Kevin to capitalise on his Brownie points!

Two days later found him at an outdoor centre near Machynlleth in central Wales preparing for the arrival that night of a ten strong mixed gender management team travelling from London. They were due to arrive by supper time, after which it would be a quick series of safety briefs and preparation for a short walk on paths around the local countryside, hopefully finishing and getting to bed by 1am.

The aim of the Aces High intervention was to provide the client with an atmosphere where they could develop a meaningful discussion on a handful of concerns. Peter, the client's boss, was a fervent advocate of using the atmosphere of the shared experience, generated by outdoor activities, to formulate new concepts and thought.

Not everyone was such an ardent supporter - indeed the majority initially were usually totally against being plucked from their comfortable surroundings and asked to do what, on the face of it were silly tasks. Kevin had yet to work with a group who had not departed having both enjoyed themselves enormously and achieved far in excess of what they thought possible.

By creating a level playing field where none of the team has any particular expertise or knowledge and by controlling the tempo, the true nature of good team leadership and teamwork can be demonstrated, with participation by the individual and without the normal distractions associated with the work place. To remove a macho image allied with outdoor activities, as the most weather beaten of the trainers Kevin always started off any course by asking the participants to divide into two groups - men in one, women in the other.

He then wrote: 'A woman without her man is nothing' on the white board and asked each group to punctuate it correctly. The men mostly wrote: 'A woman without her man, is nothing!' And the women wrote, sometimes with a little gentle persuasion: 'A woman: without her, man is nothing!' This invariably broke the ice and defused any leaning towards a 'boys only' culture, before it started.

Besides Kevin, there were two other trainers, Tony and Paul. The junior partner in Aces High, Tony was designated chief trainer and they had successfully worked together before on a wide variety of courses and venues. Whilst Kevin's expertise centred on being completely unflappable, he also brought with him a confidence born of meeting adversity head on, both as an operational soldier and an amateur mountaineer.

Tony at 38 was the youngest and had started his professional career as a graduate line manager in a high tech corporation. He'd found his particular forté was helping people and had naturally developed into an excellent trainer, with an interest in the theory, as well as delivery. Currently studying at the Open University for a post graduate degree in personal development, he had invested in Aces High with the purchase of some shares. Paul had been a policeman in a previous life, when at 42, following an involvement on duty in a horrific road traffic accident, he'd taken early retirement on health grounds.

The threesome were family men and enjoyed the mental stimulus that each new course brought. This one was no exception and the next three days flew by, as they facilitated interesting challenges and experiences for the client group to safely surmount, turning the generated feeling of team achievement and empathy into their addressing of work related issues. These short periods of outdoor activities mentally loosened up and stimulated the group; helping to centre their thoughts more effectively on the work related issues. The relaxed, atmosphere of the centre certainly helping those possibly slightly inhibited by the more formal surroundings of the work place.

Kevin normally gave an interest lecture at the end of the second day, using his experiences as a mountaineer to illustrate an aspect of non-commercial team leadership and teamwork. With a tray of slides he transported the audience to the dizzy heights of the world's highest and coldest mountains and this particular time finished by describing his involvement with the forthcoming attempt on Ketil and even managed to extract some donations for the Heart Foundation.

It went down so well that when they retired for the last hour to support the local economy in the pub, the group happily buttonholed him. They were very interested in his straightforward concept that the mystical subject of effective team leadership could perhaps best be summed up by focus on the leader's vital 'Big Five' of Vision, Plan, Motivate, Empower and Communicate.

Having studied the subject a little, Kevin was also a convert for KISS, as in 'Keep It Simple Stupid.' He enthused that this should be combined with another Services' homily known as the 'Seven Ps' which stated: Prior Preparation and Planning, Prevents Piss Poor Performance!

Whilst Kevin was spreading the gospel of human resource training in Wales, 'across the pond' Jake was building up his cover as a travel writer. By plagiarising excerpts of recognised experts and putting his signature block at the bottom, he'd made up a small professional and impressive looking portfolio, complete with photographs. For the casual viewer it would certainly pass muster.

His disguise included worn and battered hand luggage, complete with old torn destination stickers from exotic places, a used 35mm Leica, a Sony digital camera and a fabric document case that had seen better days, well-worn travel clothes plus a shabby multi-pocketed waistcoat. He certainly looked the part. His state of the art Immarsat phone and a top quality laptop were the only items that were kept looking new, straight out of their wrapping, as a successful travel writer would insist on only the best for these items.

He'd kept in email contact with Nauja and Yann, slowly building on the image already fabricated with them and receiving more and more personal replies, especially from Nauja, who treated him as a confidant of long standing. He was pleased not to have followed an initial instinct of making a direct play for having sex with her heavenly body. This way he could assimilate a friendship that could have a huge beneficial return.

He more than made up for any frustrations with Debbie upon return. In exchange for a wild and passionate night of sex, plus a useful sum in $100 bills, she kept him abreast of developments between Kevin and Henry and news that the expedition freight was loaded and en-route to Nanortalik aboard *MV Broberg*.

Deciding that life was treating him very fairly; he absorbed all information possible on both Chisholm Expeditions and their yacht *Antarctica*. Not being a sailor presented a small concern and finding a reputable sailing school near San Diego that offered a beginner course on ocean going yachts of the same size and design, he booked onto a five day program with them. Whilst the chances of *Antarctica* using sails in Tasermiut Fjord were minimal, at least he'd be less of a passenger and more of a crew member, able to ask suitable questions and make all the right noises.

~ ~ ~ ~ ~ ~ ~ ~ ~ ~ ~ ~ ~ ~ ~ ~ ~

At his Peak District cottage, George was thinking about what he'd forgotten to do, whilst preparing for the final team-meet at the coming weekend, before their planned departure in less than two weeks. With the news from Kevin that the sea freight was well on its way and confirmation from the bank that *Newsweek* had credited their account, he was feeling pretty relaxed as he reviewed their outstanding few items. These were mainly to do with the final media departure meeting arrangements and last minute loose ends with the British Heart Foundation. That would involve a visit to town next week and an opportunity to say an extra special 'thank you' to Camilla. He'd also begun to focus more clearly on the climb itself, working out scenarios of what may happen, why and when.

These seemed to naturally centre upon five possible eventualities:
* A minor sickness or injury that may require evacuation before becoming serious.
* Illness or traumatic injury requiring an immediate evacuation.
* An equipment loss or failure that stopped further progress.
* Prolonged vicious weather conditions that sapped their energy and drained resolve.
* Insufficient water and food available, forcing a withdrawal.

He intended going through each one with the team, trying to identify areas where they could attempt to cut down on the percentage chances of anything happening. They'd all had a really thorough medical and dental examination by a climbing doctor friend George trusted. He also knew that Kevin had already thought in depth about what he could personally achieve to lessen the chances and what action he would take on each scenario. Experience told him that whatever occurred it would be the least expected and have further unforeseen complications.

They would retain with them one of the two RIBs hired from Eric, for getting themselves to Nanortalik for this very reason. Fortunately, one of the skills Kevin had picked up with the Royal Marines was the use and maintenance of RIBs and their engines. So that would give them the option if all else failed, i.e. no communications and in non-flying poor weather conditions, of getting the casualty by team self help to Nanortalik. Both George and Kevin were First Aid trained to a reasonable level and felt competent enough to stabilise trauma injuries, administer drips, morphine and immobilise a patient for transit to a medical facility.

The local helicopter Search and Rescue (SAR) service would be a best probable means of moving a seriously injured casualty. They would request this by alerting Eric's office on either the VHF Maritime Channel 16 that he would hire to them, or by satellite telephone to his office or home. Either Eric or Yann always maintained a presence in Nanortalik to safeguard this facility, so George was content they had an evacuation plan. Kevin had organised team insurance cover with a specialist company for this very eventuality and whilst it was not cheap, it gave them a necessary peace of mind.

As well as Kevin keeping an eye on the climbers by binoculars, George would maintain a radio link, with Kevin on a listening watch during daylight hours and only agreeing to catch some sleep when George had closed down for the night. Even then he would keep the radio switched on at full volume close to his ear, which he knew from its previous use like this would get a response from him after a minute or so. Kevin would hold a comprehensive array of medical gear, drugs and medicines that also included an emergency bottle of medical oxygen.

Eric hoped to be able to pass on a 24-hour weather forecast each morning and any imminent severe warnings he received from Nuuk, that should in theory enable them on Ketil to select a site and prepare for a stormy bivouac. Finally he planned that for the first few days at base camp they concentrated on checking and double-checking all of their climbing gear, clothing, food, fuel, cooking and bivouac equipment. He was going to propose that they started off with twelve pints of water each and replenished that whenever the opportunity arose, either from rain, snow or ice on the face. Even so, that amount equalled 36lbs in weight and double the two pounds a day per person allocated for food and fuel.

If the workload and weather were both reasonable, they could probably eke out the twelve pints each to last three or four days. If it was a high workload and cold they would need more hot fluids to maintain a core body temperature, reducing the time the twelve pints would last each man to no more than three days. This area gave George more cause for concern than did any other, including the actual climbing itself.

'At least then we know what we are doing and it's up to us,' he grunted to himself. 'Right now the best place to be is on the climb doing it, rather than all this waiting and talking about the dammed job'

Reaching for the telephone he rang Kevin, 'How does Saturday lunch look to you for a team meeting here?'

'Spot on,' replied Kevin, 'I'll go through the movement plan and produce us all an aide memoir of personal gear to take, documentation, timings, flight details, etc, as well as a full list of all the kit and food that's been shipped. That should help to concentrate everyone's minds, whilst we still have a little time to put anything right.'

George answered, 'Good on you Kevin. I'll cover finance, public relations, communications, medical and how I see the climb tactics unfolding and what I consider are the five show stoppers.'

As departure day loomed closer, Kevin also took the opportunity to revise the notes he'd written all those months ago in the Scottish training camp near Aberdeen about getting seismic readings in Tasermiut Fjord. One excerpt he'd learnt off by heart was:

Seismic methods depend upon velocities of acoustical energy in earth materials. Accordingly, they involve the generation of a short pulse of seismic energy and the permanent recording of the arrival of the seismic pulse at distant locations, with the time intervals after the pulse instant determined to millisecond accuracy. Some types of explosive or the impact of a mass furnishes the energy, which is detected by sensitive seismometers operating into electronic amplifiers and a suitable recorder. Wave (or optical) theory of travel time, refection, absorption, diffraction

and reflection, are available to seismic interpretation and quite different
principles are involved than with 'potential' methods, which include
gravity, magnetic and electrical techniques.

As he could not afford to carry any documents or material that would indicate what his covert purpose entailed, it was essential that everything applicable was committed to memory. He'd also browsed the internet for information of petroleum exploitation in the area, finding a useful source on the Government of Greenland web site for their Bureau of Minerals and Petroleum. Here he discovered all the historical exploration areas, the background to current licensing policy for speculative seismic surveys and who were the main players to date.

Saturday's team meeting went well and they all left George's cottage feeling their mental, physical and practical preparations were complete and were now raring to go. They would keep themselves physically fit for the next ten days before the flight, by gently ticking over and making sure they did not incur any injuries. Each had their own way of trying to make the departure from loved ones as painless as possible. Even though all the girls had been through it many times before, it never came any easier for them. Fortunately, the use of satellite phones and emails softened the blow of suddenly being left alone at home, whilst climbers were off to some remote area doing their own chauvinistic thing. Knowing there was a speedy communication link to use in an emergency reduced the pressure on them all a little.

Kevin and Gillian always kept the last 24 hours absolutely clear of any appointments, allowing them plenty of time to make their final preparations with minimum distractions. They tried to enjoy supper at a decent restaurant on the final night, returning home tipsy, making love passionately before collapsing contentedly into a deep sleep.

Hugh and Jane pretended that nothing untoward was about to happen, right up to the final farewells being made at home. Jane never travelled to the departure airport, finding the emotions involved far too traumatic and demanding.

Helen and Rick had a theory that the more fuss equalled more stress for both. So they carried on with what for them passed as a normal life, both quietly giving space to the other, treating the whole event like a weekly shopping trip.

For George and Phoebe it was going to be very hard indeed, as Phoebe had recently visited her doctor for a check-up, only to be told that a small lump she'd discovered on her right breast would require further investigation. Initially she'd considered not telling George, but in the build-up of the last few days, she blurted it out in a flood of tears. His shocked reaction soon gave way to cool logic and he proposed cancelling his involvement with Ketil. Phoebe would have none of that and insisted that he carried on, without telling anyone else. She'd also try to keep it a secret until they shared the biopsy results upon his return.

'Phew, thank goodness that's all over', said George as the BA flight climbed to cruising altitude outbound for Copenhagen. 'If I never see another camera, reporter or microphone again, it'll still be too soon.'

Seated next to him Kevin grinned widely in approval, remembering the scene below at Heathrow they had so recently departed from. Meeting the media always gave him the shivers and today had not been any different, with opinionated interviewers imposing their tricky questions, hoping for a throw away quote they could mould into a good quotation or headline.

Fortunately for the three of them, George was the one the media wanted and he'd borne the brunt of the scrum, with Kevin, Hugh and Rick as a supporting act. As expected, it had been hard work trying to get the Heart Foundation link mentioned, with the more cynical of the throng making snide sounding comments questioning their integrity. They'd a job to do and the sooner it was done the better for all concerned, so they bit the bullet and co-operated fully.

'Hopefully that will be the last until we get home,' Kevin said. 'I don't expect any when we change flights in Copenhagen.'

'Aye, with any luck you're right,' George replied and, eyeing the breakfast tray chuckled, 'better tuck in, as we do not know what the next one might be!'

Their change at Copenhagen onto a Greenlandair flight passed smoothly without any media interest and they settled down for a further six hours before the late afternoon descent into Narsarsuaq and a night stop.

CHAPTER 13

Glancing through the complementary in-flight magazine and its map of Greenland in relation to North America, from out of the blue, thoughts of Oag Mackenzie filled Kevin's mind. Five years previously Oag had asked him to be expedition manager for his attempt to travel solo and unsupported to the North Pole starting from the ice runway at Ward Hunt Island - the accepted launch point for such bids from Canada.

He'd known Oag a few years and respected his integrity and determination to do something completely 'off the wall'. A very proud Highlander from near Wick and a great bear of a man, Oag was one of a handful of servicemen to have successfully completed all of their 'Big Three' selections - Commando, Parachute and Special Air Service Regiments.

After discussing the concept with Gillian who was supportive, he got together with Oag and they went into more detail about the concept before he gave an answer. Oag envisaged a flight forward by Twin Otter from an airhead at Resolute Bay to a launch site on Ward Hunt Island early in the short season. He reasoned that by starting early, in temperatures of minus 45C and below, he would encounter less 'open water' the scourge of man haul attempts to the North Pole.

As the season progresses, the ice cap breaks-up into independent ice islands that move with the Polar drift, an ever-present ocean current, which flows from the North Pole in the direction of Ward Hunt Island. So effectively, any attempt would be like walking up a moving elevator - stop and you go backwards!

Whilst not a proposition that Kevin could personally aspire to, he had to admire Oag for his guts and daring in even considering an attempt. Working on the premise that it takes one to know one, he agreed to accept the task. Initially this entailed setting up a familiarisation training programme during one season, then making the attempt the next. Thought was given to mounting from Russia and 'going with the flow' from Siberia, unfortunately this had to be discounted as too expensive.

To gain experience and credibility Oag would have to train somewhere suitable and after various options were looked at, an approach was made to Alert the Canadian Forces Base in the extreme north of Canada, where the northern tip of Ellesmere Island nearly meets North West Greenland. From here Oag made forays onto the live sea ice, starting off with single one day trips, then steadily increasing duration to a final trip of twenty days.

This gave ample opportunity to test out various concepts of clothing, food and equipment as he was going over the very same Polar ice terrain he would meet in an attempt from Ward Hunt Island. Where independent ice islands met one another, they pushed together with enormous power and formed large pressure ridges, some sixty feet high! These could run at right angles to a chosen line of march and would have to be surmounted by the intrepid explorer. Even more agonising was the man-haul sledge or 'pulk', which for a solo, unsupported attempt would have a start weight of 400 pounds plus. So the task was enormous.

How to survive in extremely low temperatures, moving a huge work-load over treacherous terrain, with forward progress reversed whilst you slept? To do this solo with no re-supply, must be one of the world's greatest exploration challenges. Oag rose magnificently to the event the following year, following a prolonged period of fund raising, equipment and food preparation.

Being a vegetarian, he had to select a daily diet that would be palatable and would satisfy the criteria of low weight with sufficient calories. This was achieved with a combination of freeze-dried vegetables and fish, potato powder, oatmeal, orange and chocolate drink, fudge bars and ghee fat. The vital heat to melt ice for water and warm his food was provided by using naptha fuel rationed to 300ml per day using an MSR stove.

Clothing gave Oag lots of grief, as the workload was such that no matter how slowly undertaken, it caused him to sweat. This had to vent to the outside surface quickly to freeze and be brushed off. It was found a combination of Duofold expedition weight underwear, a Ventile shirt, worn under a multi-layer system of Phoenix fleece jacket and salopettes with a final Ventile over suit, proved to be highly efficient.

Marginally less full of grief, was the problem of what sleeping bag to use? Duck down feathers provide the best insulation, but when wet or damp, they matt into clumps and are impossible to dry under these circumstances. Body moisture, naturally produced as we sleep, will usually evaporate through a sleeping bag without any complication. However in extremes of cold this does not happen and it becomes trapped in the 'loft' material. If this is down, the bag soon becomes useless, providing no warmth for the occupant. Man-made fibres tend not to matt as quickly and can be dried out by wind and stove produced heat. Whilst not as warm as down, they are usually preferred. Another option is to first getting into a thin vapour barrier inner bag, thereby trapping all the moisture close to the body. The negative side of this is that the wearer's underwear becomes damp and needs changing next morning immediately on getting out of the bag, unless intending to start the day's man-haul very cold indeed.

So quite a dilemma and with no complete answer, it becomes one of personal choice. Oag decided to go with two Norwegian Ajungilak 'Quallofil' bags and a 'Buffalo' inner bag without using a vapour barrier bag. He hoped that the first would last 25 to 30 days. Another aspect is exhaled breath, which will cling to the outside layer of the bag, melting at the first sign of warmth.

They landed at the first attempt onto the ice runway at Ward Hunt Island on 8 March, where the collection of huts had once been a military weather station, now long abandoned. Knowing that two world famous Polar explorers - Misha Malakhov and Richard Weber - might be at Ward Hunt, it came as no surprise to Oag or Kevin when they hurriedly appeared at the sound of the Twin Otter.

They had already been on the Polar ice for nearly a month, returning the day before from taking forward a large load of supplies and caching them to support their endeavour to become the first men ever to go to the pole and return, unsupported. After an exchange of pleasantries, Oag very slowly moved off dragging his two heavy pulks.

These had been designed and manufactured by Roger Daynes of Snowsled in Tetbury, specifically to allow Oag the option of moving the pulks either singularly or in tandem. Lashed side by side, they also allowed for use as an emergency float, should open water have to be negotiated.

Setting off with 445lbs weight of food, fuel and equipment meant that Oag immediately had to shuttle half loads forward, then return and repeat the process. Therefore to travel one nautical mile he would be forced to walk a full three, two of them with loads, over the chaotic pressure ridge boulders of ice, all lying at crazy angles and perched precariously upon each other. Some would rear up sixty feet, so hours each day would be spent finding a way to surmount the obstacles.

Then it was down the reverse side, with the sledges finding their own way, hurtling at an increasing speed before coming to a sudden shuddering stop at a crazy angle, nose into a hole. The amount of unsympathetic use the pulks received, with only minimal damage, speaks volumes for the skills of Roger Daynes. Oag recorded in his diary for day two the temperature was minus 54 degrees Centigrade! Deep in thought Kevin smiled a little. Just to say it was minus 54 degrees Centigrade does not even begin to describe how that magnitude of cold effects human life, regardless of the intense work load in moving around sledges, totalling more than 400lbs.

The cold completely dominates all thoughts and actions. Before the simplest, mundane task such as getting started in the morning, is the need to have a well trialled systematic method with every action carried out in a sequence, to ensure that the body heat gained in the sleeping bag (whilst it is still dry) does not get wasted. It means being conscious that as the head moves out of the bag's protective warmth it will be assaulted with tendrils of hoarfrost created from exhaled breath and clinging like spider-web to the tent walls and layered on the outer sleeping bag.

It means that no bare flesh comes into contact with the metal MSR stove and fuel bottle - easier said than done when it refuses to light and fiddly connections have to be adjusted. It also means that every single item is carefully stowed, so that in an emergency no valuable seconds are lost hunting for a replacement balaclava or glove. Trying to stay warm and dry is the hardest task of all, with a human naturally producing moisture 24 hours a day, without which the body's metabolism would cease to function effectively.

A purring MSR stove is your centre of survival, but whilst melting ice and heating water it will produce moisture that coats anything and everything, meaning it can't be used when the sleeping bag is unpacked and vulnerable. So, no tea in bed!

Having spent three hours getting body and soul ready for the day's toil, stomach and flasks filled, fudge bar readied, daily communication and navigation checks done, with all gear stowed in the pulks, the solo Polar traveller begins the day's haul. In the unremitting pressure ridges, every step will need a calculated placement of the feet amongst the ice rubble to ensure that the ankle does not twist.

Every forward move will be dictated by the heavy pulks refusal to budge, except to obey the laws of gravity. This simple edict will always dictate the day's objective. Deep, soft snow, now regularly encountered, gives a whole new meaning to the word 'drudgery' as the heavy pulks bog down. Kevin shuddered at the thought. At this George turned from reading his book and asked if he was OK.

Kevin laughed and explained what he'd been reminiscing about.

'Give me a steep high mountain anytime,' George replied, 'I cannot think of anything more excruciating than pulling two bath tubs, each weighing 16 stone, continuously over the equivalent of an earthquake zone, completely covered with two feet of snow in nut freezing temperatures.'

'Each to there own I guess,' said Kevin, going on to explain how Oag had persevered for over forty days.

'During the latter half of which Ray McKenna, who'd joined me from UK to form a safety pick-up team and I, moved forward to Lake Hazen with a Twin Otter piloted by Henry Peck with Big Al as crew man.

'There, beside the frozen lake with an ice runway, Baysil, a native of Calcutta and the only tourist hotel operator in Resolute Bay, specialised in taking guests by Twin Otter to the North Pole. He'd set up an overnight staging post that accommodated ten guests in a dormitory.

'The concept was simple. For a Twin Otter flight to land at the North Pole, it needed a fuel cache at 88 Degrees North. This would allow it to land at the Pole and also stage through Lake Hazen for an overnight stop en-route back south to Resolute Bay. It meant that the passengers had a night in a remote part of the High Arctic, making the experience even more memorable.

'The key factor was maintaining a fuel dump at Lake Hazen, from where another Twin Otter could take onboard fuel barrels to cache at 88 Degrees for the North Pole aircraft and also act as a back up. With ski landing gear the Twin Otter is the ideal aircraft for both tasks, even more so in the hands of highly competent pilots such as Henry Peck.

'By co-locating with Henry at Lake Hazen, Ray and I were in the best position to help should Oag have any problems. The satellite beacon communication messages from Oag went first to UK, who forwarded them to Resolute Bay. Here, the final member of the team, Jock Hutton monitored the messages and reacted accordingly.

'Having activated the Lake Hazen base, Henry made an attempt to place fuel down for the second aircraft. Thick cloud prevented a successful landing and after trying several times, Henry returned to Lake Hazen, following seven hours flying on instruments. I met them after landing on the lake and straight away took Henry and Big Al by skidoo up to the hut, a hundred yards and fifty foot above the lake.

'Normally the main battery would be removed from the aircraft but Henry wanted to meet up with his girlfriend BK, have a coffee and cookie and planned latter to return and do it.

'As you know at the main entrance to every hut in the Arctic is a vestibule between the outer and inner doors where the occupants leave their outer boots and clothing. Lake Hazen was no different and having discarded our outer gear, we went inside to sit at the main table in the dining area, sip a drink and eat some of BK's excellent cookies.

'The passenger aircraft was en-route from Resolute and due to arrive in a couple of hours, so BK was preparing supper. Switching the main stove on, she discovered the gas supply was almost non-existent, with obviously the empty cooking gas bottle needing a changeover. Pierre, the general handyman supplied by Baysil promptly disappeared to the back of the kitchen and about a minute later let out a frantic cry for help as a loud 'whoosh' rent the air.

"Propane.' yelled Henry and without further urging or orders, we stampeded for the nearest door. Luckily there were three exit doors to choose from and a pair went for the nearest to them. Bursting through we all tumbled out into the snow gasping for breath, when seconds later with an almighty roar the whole hut blew apart, a huge explosion taking the roof completely off, as a fire ball passed through. Numb with shock, we all made verbal contact and ascertained that everyone was accounted for. With the exception of Pierre, who had sustained a slightly burnt foot, everyone else was OK.

'Henry then yelled out, 'Aircraft,' and the six of us galloped off wildly down the hill through snowdrifts to the lake. The temperature was minus 30 degrees Centigrade, pitch black and no one had a chance to don any outer ware. We were all lightly dressed in track-suit bottoms and tops, wearing sneakers on our feet. No hats, gloves, scarves, overtrousers, parkas or mukluk boots.

"Emergency gear,' Henry ordered, as with BK, he scrambled into the cockpit. Big Al, Ray and I shepherded Pierre into the fuselage and breaking out the emergency gear wrapped him in a sleeping bag. Henry meanwhile was coolly doing his pre-flight checks.

"Fuel her up,' Henry shouted, at the same time starting the engine. Ray got into a jacket, passing two for Henry and BK and a jacket and over trousers to Big Al and I. He pulled on the over trousers and passing me the jacket started to wrestle a full barrel of aviation fuel, whilst I got hold of the manual pump and hose. Within five minutes we'd transferred two barrels and Henry thumbing up as enough, started to manoeuvre and test her flaps for take off.

'Once the door was shut, cabin lights and heaters full on, we could all catch each other's eye and give a supporting smile. Seat belts buckled, we watched anxiously as a super cool Henry ran us out onto the ice landing strip, his main beam easily picking out the red markers that Ray and I had so laboriously placed only a few days before.

'Cheap and effective, these were red plastic bin liner bags filled with snow and tied off. Henry lined up and gently opening the throttle until full revs were achieved then headed off down the strip, making a text book take off. Once airborne, everyone yelled out and laughed with relief, as Henry brought her into a perfect turn, to pass over and circle the site of the hut, now just a red molten smudge, completely destroyed.

'Turning west Henry headed for Eureka, a manned weather station an hour away. He also radioed out the news of the disaster and our lucky salvation. Normally Big Al would have removed the aircraft battery and taken it into the warm hut, with only the lure of BK's coffee and cookies altering that routine. We were very, very lucky indeed, as without a charged battery the engine could not be started and there was no way anyone could have lugged the heavy battery out of the inferno, and survived.

'The staff at Eureka could not have been more welcoming, loaning clothing and footwear, checking over a shocked Pierre, feeding us and setting up beds for the night. It was almost a party atmosphere, as with each passing hour a full realisation of our deliverance sunk in.

'Retiring both exhausted and exhilarated, it was a massive shock when three hours later the fire alarms went off in the sleeping accommodation. Only to discover, as once again we tumbled out into the frozen blackness, that it was false alarm caused by a fault in the electricity circuit!

'Later that morning in our borrowed clothing and footwear we left for Resolute Bay, feeling like shipwreck survivors. Ray's and my first priority would be to beg, buy and borrow sufficient gear for us to be able to effect a rescue of Oag, should he need us. This took a couple of days, after which Henry suggested we might like to join him again at Tanquary Fjord, a tented summer camp site, not far from Lake Hazen (now known throughout the north as 'Blazin' Hazen'), from where he would mount the same ariel fuel re-supplies for North Pole tourist aircraft.

'There, we would also remove every scrap of material from Lake Hazen, shovelling first into empty barrels for loading onto Henry's air-craft then flying to a recognised rubbish dump at Eureka. Meanwhile on the Polar Ice, Oag was experiencing more than his fair share of setbacks, as the mind blowing torturous drudgery ate deep into his reserves of strength and stamina. He was at last fighting his way out of the main pressure ridge area and beginning to make sizeable daily distances, as the temperatures rose to a balmy minus twenty degrees Centigrade.

'To add even more speed he'd ditched one sledge and was relying on a watertight immersion over-suit for any open water obstacle crossings, which Oag had trialled the year before. On day 41 he came upon an open lead about 100 yards wide, cutting across at right angles to his line of march. He zipped into his immersion suit and slipped into the water, prepared to slowly swim across the lead, towing his sledge. Within seconds he knew something was dramatically wrong, as his legs started to feel wet.

'Fighting a way out, he immediately erected the box tent and got inside, before shedding his now soaking trousers and clambering franti-cally into dry ones. (It later transpired that the suit manufacturer had for-gotten to dope the seams). Quickly packing up and moving along one bank for a couple of hours, he came to a spot where the lead had nar-rowed to about fifteen yards, forming a choke point filled with four sep-arate ice floes. His options were extremely limited - he could camp and wait for the lead to close, continue hauling along the southern edge to try and find a better crossing, or attempt a crossing using the ice floes as a bridge.

'Deciding on the latter, he was half way over when floe number three which the pulk was on started to twist over, threatening to dump the pulk into the sea. In desperation, Oag had no option but to make a savage lunge for the far ice, five or six yards away. Using all of his considerable body power he swiftly made the move, but in doing so he heard and felt something rip across his back.

'Making onto the solid ice, a vicious spasm of excruciating pain forced him onto his knees in agony. Retching bile, he gingerly tried to straighten up, but in doing so another savage pain gripped him again, leaving him gasping. Somehow Oag forced himself to slowly erect the tent, push in sleeping mats, bags and kitchen box, before collecting a bag of ice chips to melt into water. He then pushed inside with his shotgun and grunting with effort removed outer layer and boots before wriggling into a semi-frozen bag, trembling and weak with the effort. 'I've done something nasty,' he thought and focusing on immediate survival needs, fired up the stove and started melting the ice chips.

'Fighting nausea and trembling from pain and cold, Oag got down a handful of Fudge squares and a pint mug of hot chocolate. Hitting the system, he began to relax a little, think more clearly and was out of any immediate danger:

'One, his back muscles were obviously severely damaged.

'Two, he would have to rest and use up precious fuel and food, whilst loosing distance gained north, due to ice pack drift.

'Three, the immersion suit gave no protection and finally

'Four, he couldn't take his morphine to combat the pain, for fear of being drugged and unable to defend himself if a polar bear turned up.

'He decided he'd have to take a dose of DF 118 his strongest analgesic, get some nutrition, fluids and rest, before seeing what the next day would bring and then make a final decision.

'The next twelve hours were quite the worst he'd ever spent, fighting assaults from pain and the possibility that the attempt was now over. The next scheduled beacon call was at 7.30am, so he would send out his need for a recovery at that time, helping to emphasise that it was not life or death. The pre-arranged code for this was number 11, which stated that an air evacuation was needed for medical reasons, but was not life or death.

'The message came through to Tanquary Fjord within 30 minutes of Oag setting off the emergency beacon. They had already breakfasted, as Henry was planning to do a North Pole fuel run mid-morning.

"I'll be flying over his location, so we'll make contact and either land to pick him up then, or on the return journey. How does that sound?'

"Mighty fine,' I replied, 'I'll come with you please. Ray can stay here to man the link to us and also to Jock at Resolute.'

'Thirty minutes later we were airborne and within one hour's flying approached the area at 84 degrees of the beacon transmission from Oag. Opening up the ground to air radio and following only two transmissions Oag was on the air, explaining what his injuries were.

'Soon after we spotted his red box tent and saw him slowly get out, bent over to one side. Henry and I had already agreed that if Oag was not in any immediate medical danger that Henry would prefer to land his fuel at 88 degrees North and pick-up Oag on return. As Henry circled 500 foot above him whilst this was explained, Oag said he was more than happy to wait and that he would keep the voice link open.

'Henry then headed off north, entering within ten minutes solid cloud, which continued without let-up for the next two hours, as he probed to locate a hole between 87 and 88 degrees north where he could put down. Finally aborting, he headed off south to pick up Oag and return to Tanquary Fjord. As we got closer with no let-up of the thick cloud, Henry discussed with me what we would do if the weather prevented him effecting a pick-up of Oag. Agreeing that we would try and if it had to be aborted, to then let Oag know we would return again later.

'With less than five miles to go, suddenly there was a break in the cloud base and demonstrating exactly why he was one of the best, Henry put the plane down, with immediate application of reverse thrusts. Stopping fifty yards from where Oag with a definite bent to one side was slowly collapsing his tent. I leapt out and made my way over to Oag as fast as possible in ankle deep snow. We embraced in a bear hug, with Oag saying, 'Sorry to have let you down mate I am really sorry!'

'At which I muttered something conciliatory and bungled him into the back of the aircraft, just so pleased to see him alive after a traumatic three or four hours.

'With once again a display of his superb flying skills, Henry quickly had us airborne, heading for Tanquary Fjord. Ray met us and shepherded us to the cook tent. Here he produced a bottle of Scotch and lining up five full glasses, he proposed a toast to Oag's safe pick-up. With the due deliberation of a true Highlander, Oag slowly raised his glass in salute to Henry and breaking into Gaelic delivered his Clan Mackenzie reply, before sinking the glass in one gulp.

"What in hell's fire is that,' he yelled, 'it tastes nothing like whisky!'

'At which Ray, keeping well out of arm's reach quickly confessed that he'd substituted cold tea for the contents, which he laughingly displayed and passed around.

'It was just the right timing and for Oag it successfully broke the ice to allow them all a rational review of what had happened to him after six solitary, lonely and dangerous weeks.'

CHAPTER 14

Opening his eyes and putting his mind into 'fast forward', Kevin breathed a sigh of relief as they lowered through the clouds for a final run into Narsarsuaq. The barren area of the airport was less than welcoming, with a cold blast of wind straight off the ice cap bidding them hello as they walked over to the arrivals section.

Formalities over and retrieving their bags they quickly boarded a small coach for the short ride to the Greenlandair Hotel in the small township. Having first confirmed the helicopter flight for the next day, they settled in and after an early evening walk to ease cramped leg muscles, devoured a welcome meal before spending an hour in the bar, nursing a night cap.

Kevin had contacted Eric in Nanortalik and confirmed their booking on the next day's scheduled helicopter. Eric said he would meet them upon arrival and make the necessary accommodation arrangements for their stay at the Seaman's Hostel. Eric went on to say, 'I certainly look forward to meeting you and the team and will be honoured if you all have your first meal in Nanortalik tomorrow night at my house.'

'That is most welcome,' replied Kevin. 'We'll look forward to that with pleasure.'

Next morning they departed on time aboard the scheduled helicopter in good, clear weather. The cold, noisy flight gave them an opportunity to gaze out of the window at the contrast between the endless inland ice cap and dark green sea fjords that cut into the white desert, fringed by cathedral like mountains, streaked with ice and snow.

Occasionally, small settlements could be glimpsed clinging precariously to the edge of a fjord, the red roofed buildings clashing with the predominately green, grey or white surrounding backgrounds. Flying over small coastal shipping that kept the scattered settlements alive, it was interesting to speculate on where they were coming from and going to, as like intrusive work ants of the sea they plied their trade.

Eric was there to meet them at the Heli Port and efficiently shepherded them to the Seaman's Hostel, chatting away en-route on the groups that had gone through that summer and who else he had been made aware of. After booking them in, he asked to be excused whilst they unpacked and freshened up, saying he would be back in an hour to take them round to his house for dinner.

Once in his room Kevin set up his laptop and satellite phone and quickly sent a couple of messages, one to Gillian and the other to Henry. The latter read: 'From: Kevin, Project Alpha. Now complete at Narsarsuaq and begin check that all gear has arrived safely tomorrow morning. Weather and local atmosphere is good and we shall probably depart for Ketil in two day's time.'

Besides Eric and Edda and the four team members, the other guests for dinner were Yann, Aka and Kaj. So it was a nice size group that sat down to clam chowder soup, followed by lamb casserole, with vegetables and potatoes. Kevin had bought some good Californian Merlot in Narsarsuaq to help wash it all down, with Eric insisting they try his brandy with their coffee.

The group was a good mix, enjoying the food, wine and company without any arguing or histrionics and an easy flowing conversation ensured everyone relaxed and acted in a normal fashion, as if they'd known each other for some time. Kevin noticed that George was a tad quieter than normal this evening, but put it down to their journey. Around midnight Eric suggested that he take them all home in his pick-up saying, 'I'll be round to pick you all up at 8.30,' as later they piled out of the van at the Seaman's Hostel.

'That will give us plenty of time to show you where I've stored the gear and for you to get it ready for departure the next day. I thought in the afternoon that we could get the wet suits fitted, plus sort out the cooking gas, food and radios ready for departure.'

George replied, 'That sounds good to me - should give us plenty of time to check we have everything and to talk through the communication set-up. May we also suggest that you, Edda, Aka, Kaj and Yann join us tomorrow for dinner at the hostel?'

'That sounds like an excellent idea,' Eric replied, 'I know Nauja will look after us all very well indeed.'

They were very busy the next day, with Kevin giving a secret sigh of relief when Eric showed him straightaway the store with all their kegs, boxes and bags laid out in numerical order.

'I checked them in against the *MV Broberg* cargo manifest you sent me,' Eric said, 'and they tally OK by quantity as well as item numbers.

Please look through them to see they are complete.'

Kevin did as requested and confirmed he was happy that all their items had arrived and none of the locks appeared to have been tampered with. Whilst George and Eric disappeared indoors to discuss the budget items and how the invoice would be paid, Kevin, Hugh and Rick went along with Yann to the KGI store to locate the provisions they'd ordered. They then took them to the storage shed for packing into the spare kegs, ready for out-loading into the RIBs. Following cries of laughter and banter with the two Inuit girls, who ran the store, they soon had a neat pile of goodies outside to load onto Eric's pick-up.

Moving on, Kevin then caused a slight wave of consternation at the post office when he asked to buy 500 postcard stamps, please! Following a few awkward moments whilst the manager was sought, he quickly appeared and opened up the safe for access to his reserve, which was more than enough. Kevin explained what they were doing with the Heart Foundation charity fund raising postcard and the manager agreed it would not be a problem for them to stamp, frank and send the postcards in quantities of about 100 a day. Would this be acceptable?

After a quick lunch at the hostel, they sized and donned the wet suits and checked out the two RIBs they'd use. Aka would coxswain one and Eric the other, leaving the smaller 4.8m boat with them for any emergency cover they may require.

Kevin then went to see the medical team at the town hospital. Here a resident staff nurse manned a first aid and nursing home with an emergency annex that would be activated should a sick patient require it, until air evacuation to Nuuk was feasible. They maintained good communications with the main hospital at Nuuk and the staff nurse explained that a doctor visited weekly to run an out patient surgery and perform minor operations. Any more seriously ill patient was evacuated. An emergency call from Ketil would entail the helicopter from Narsarsuaq bringing the casualty first to Nanortalik and then, depending on the medical severity, a decision would be made for onward movement as required.

Whilst Kevin was busy with this, Hugh and Rick went through with Yann the weather forecast facility and patterns in the Ketil area. They were impressed with the service on offer and as Yann explained more detail, their confidence in the system increased. By early evening they all congregated in the lounge area, sipping beers and waiting for their guests to join them for dinner. George took the opportunity to express his thanks to them all for the hard work they'd done that day and especially for the arrangements Kevin had made with Eric over the previous weeks and months.

He went on, 'I feel we are as prepared for Ketil as we possibly can be. With hard work, a modicum of luck and fair weather we'll make another British first!'

'Hear, hear, we'll drink to that,' echoed the others, raising their cans in a toast to the sentiment.

With that the guests arrived and they settled down to some serious spoiling by Nauya, as they consumed a luscious meal and enjoyed service and attention that would have been the envy of many world famous restaurants. As it was to be an early start the next day, they all bade their farewells and enjoyed an early night.

Next day the morning dawned fresh and cold, with a hint of frost in the air as they breakfasted at 6.00am and vacated their rooms. By 8.00am they were all ready, their stores packed in the two RIBs and with just wet suits to don before departure. The forecast for the day was favourable and Eric promised a reasonably calm transit. They duly clambered into wet suits and made themselves as comfortable as possible amongst all the kegs, rucsacs, storage bags, fuel drums, gas bottles and assorted RIB paraphernalia.

Just before starting up the engines Eric called out, 'We'll call on Arne for coffee at Tasiussaq, as he is your closest neighbour and can provide back-up comms to me if your's fail.'

With that they slipped away from the quay and line astern, with Eric in the lead, they turned into the Tasermiut Fjord and headed inland. Yann and Edda stood waving farewell as the early sun lit up the red roofs of the township. Riding in the lead RIB with Eric were George and Hugh, whilst Kevin and Rick kept Aka company and followed behind. Their stores filled all available space on both RIBs and they'd draped thin cargo nets over the load and lashed everything down, to prevent any untoward movement as they picked up to cruising speed.

With the engine noise it was pointless trying to hold any conversation, each becoming lost in their own thoughts, as regal sights of sharp mountain tops, steep ice slopes leading to green rocky buttresses, tumbling finally into flat calm sea water appeared to meet their gaze at each twist and turn of the fjord.

Half an hour out of Nanortalik they were greeted by one of nature's most amazing spectacles, when they came across a pod of five whales heading down the fjord. With yells of unbridled excitement, cameras were focussed and pictures taken as less then a hundred yards away, first one and then another whale's head and shoulders appeared, blowing off and charging forward majestically to sink gracefully back into the water. The whales waved their tails before their force had them sliding down again into a mystical habitat beneath the surface.

Shortly after this Tasiussaq appeared in view and they swung into the small anchorage and headed for the beach. Arne was there to meet them and after Eric had made the introductions, he led them to his hut where the coffeepot was bubbling away. With everyone squeezed around the small table, Arne filled up the cups and said, 'I'll speak with Kevin every day and monitor Channel 16 all the time. So if you guys need anything, I am here.'

'Like wise,' replied Kevin, 'I'll look forward to hearing from you.'

Coffee over, it was now time to make the last leg for Ketil and, as if to herald the final part of the journey, dark, rain filled clouds began to gather as they swung into the main channel and opened the throttles. An hour later they caught their first view of Ketil as she sat dominating the south side of the fjord in all her brooding majesty. It is always somehow different to arrive at your final destination by sea. This fusion of nature gives the experience a totally unique aspect, sometimes lacking by arrival say on an aircraft. The enormity of the task ahead filled Kevin's mind leaving no space for frivolous thought or emotion.

'Look's a big evil bastard,' he muttered, watching the slate grey clouds stream over the summit. 'Here we go again. We'd better get the tents up quick before this storm hits,' Kevin shouted unnecessarily to the others, busily unloading their stores from the two Avon RIBs one of which would stay with them for emergency back up, if required.

Minutes later, Eric and Aka shouted their farewells as they departed down the fjord, the RIB's engines bursting into life, speeding them away south west, directly into the squally weather. Five hours of daylight remained for them to reach Nanortalik, seventy miles away. Where, except for Arne the solitary shepherd 30 miles down fjord at Tasiussaq, they would be the team's nearest neighbours for the next three weeks.

Setting up two tents with George and Kevin in one and Hugh and Rick sharing the other, they made themselves comfortable, whilst using the available daylight to sort out the various boxes, kegs and containers into two piles. One pile was to remain on the shoreline and the second was for movement up to a base camp below Ketil the following morning.

'It'll be murder here with the mozzies once this rain stops,' said George. 'We'll be much better off up nearer the face, above the scrub line, by that little stream flowing from the small snow field to the bottom right of the face.'

'Looking at the gear outside,' remarked Kevin nodding in agreement, 'I reckon two or maybe three lifts each should get the bulk up there. It'll give me something to do to bring up any of the spares after you've started the climb.'

'I don't know about you Kev,' yawned George, as he climbed into his Anguluk expedition special sleeping bag, 'but I'm ready for a good long kip, which hotel beds somehow don't let me have. Can you please reach my pee bottle?'

The wind and rain beating against the fabric of the double skinned Himalayan Hotel base tent and the warm sleeping bags soon lulled them both into a deep sleep. At some time in the night the wet front passed through, the wind dropped and the new dawn arrived with clear sunny skies and just a hint of frost in the air.

Whilst George prepared a leisurely series of morning brews and bowls of porridge, Kevin set up the Immarsat and sent off a quick test email to Elizabeth and Eric to confirm that they had good communications. Elizabeth would be acting as a relay to Phoebe, Jane and Helen, giving them all a chance to chat over the phone and keep in contact.

As they all clambered out into the bright sunshine, drinking in the clear fresh air and getting their bearings, George suggested, 'I thought we might like to take a stroll to locate a base camp below the face. Perhaps leaving in half an hour?'

None needed any encouragement to get started and by mid-morning they had wandered up to a relatively sheltered area a thousand feet above the fjord, below Ketil. Here, a stream seeping out of a small snowfield meandered quietly through a flat area dominated by a large boulders the size of a house. Evidence could be spotted of previous teams using the same area, in the form of stone rings on flat sites, placed to anchor tent valises.

Selecting a fresh piece of ground and with backs resting against a boulder they donned jackets and squatted comfortably, pulling out flasks and quietly staring hard at the sight of Ketil thrusting upwards above them. Hugh, taking out a small folder with route diagrams and sketches, orientated them to the face and tried to identify the various main features noted by previous expeditions.

'Bloody big isn't it,' announced Kevin to no one in particular, as gazing up he tried to work out the scale. With the base of the face only a mile away, it was difficult to gauge any mid-point marker and for fifteen minutes various 'streaks, corners, ledges, chimneys and cuts' were discussed, as each tried to describe to the others various features on the face.

They all agreed that here was a superb challenge which would demand all their strength, stamina and necessary willpower to surmount its defences. In military terminology they had reached the 'critical point' where you either depart deflated but in one piece to fight another day, or grasp the moment and look to the future. Well aware of what was going through all their minds and determined to keep the momentum going, George quietly, but positively suggested, 'If we put up the two extra tents here and then get back to the beach, we should still have enough time left latter to ferry up another load.'

The rest of the day passed quickly as they erected and secured the tents, then descended to the fjord for another load. By mid-afternoon a prolonged outburst of rain and sleet swept through, giving the whole mountain scene of towering rock spires, sloping to the deep green water with the inland icecap backdrop, a wild beauty almost beyond words. The next loads they ferried up consisted mainly of ropes and climbing gear, so that upon return they could see a marked reduction of the volume to be moved.

'Lads, I reckon another two lifts each tomorrow,' said Kevin, 'will get everything up there, so that the final lift for the following day will just be personal kit and sleeping bags. Anything else I can bring up whilst you concentrate on the climb.'

'I'll get the brew on whilst you're doing the Immarsat,' offered George, as Kevin followed him into the tent.

'Yes! I can certainly do damage to one. I'm parched,' exclaimed Kevin changing his wet socks before manoeuvring the Immarsat antennae. Then switching it on and plugging in the Husky, he continued, 'I'll check to see if we have any messages first and then pass round the Husky for anyone who wants to write up an email. Then I'll send them all later as a batch.'

'Gottcha Kev,' replied George and, passing him a mug of hot tea laughed, 'Get on the outside of that.'

Thanking him and taking a sip before placing it down safely, Kevin made the connection and tapped in his password and address to access their emails. Five came through, one each for himself, Hugh and Rick, with two for George. Closing down the Immarsat, he passed the Husky over for George to read his messages in private and could not help noticing the slight tension in George's eyes as he clicked on to read.

'Nice one from *Newsweek* and another from my contact with Richard D'Ilsey - both wishing us all the best,' and without expressing any emotion George went on to say, 'I'll reply later.'

'Hugh and Rick there are messages for you,' Kevin called out and within moments Hugh's grinning face pushed through the door, as they squirmed inside with boots off, making themselves as unobtrusive as possible inside the crowded space.

Reaching for the laptop Hugh remarked, 'I can never believe how this works so well,' reading the message from Jane before passing the Husky to Rick saying, 'It certainly cuts down on the feeling of being totally out of contact and that's got to be a real bonus for the girls.'

'Yes you're right there,' replied Kevin. 'My first trip to the Himalayas was for nearly four months and during that time I got one airmail letter - trouble was I never read it.'

'How come?' asked George sitting up in the corner, making more room for Hugh and Rick to get comfortable.

'We were making an attempt on Indrasan in the Kulu Himal and progress was good,' recalled Kevin. 'As it was my first big trip, I was on a steep learning curve as a support climber, learning all about siege tactics and altitude. I got one shot in the front for a couple of days when Jimmy Joynt and I occupied Camp 3a, at about 18,000 feet.

'It was a single tunnel tent placed very gingerly on a platform cut across a very small saddle, with very little room outside. Jimmy and I returned at the end of day to find that the lads below had arrived whilst we were out, carrying up much needed climbing gear and rope. Also, inside the tent was an airmail letter from Elizabeth, my wife of six months.

'As always the first priority was a brew and I got the stove going outside whilst getting my double leather boots off to dry.'

Pausing slightly to get the half remembered sequence of events in order he continued, 'It was a restricted perch and I'd carefully placed outside the mugs, brew kit, and boots, with my letter on a coil of rope, being held down with a stone. My plan was to get a brew ready and relaxing with it, read the letter. A short while later the stove started to splutter and flare and whilst making a quick lunge to sort it out, I managed to dislodge the stone holding the letter, just as a small flurry of wind swept the site and took the letter airborne.

'I remember watching fascinated as it spiralled away north into the distance, never to be seen again. Jimmy, witnessing all this turned away and made a discrete departure for ten minutes to check some gear hanging off a storage line below the tent. To say I was a tad disappointed was an understatement,' laughed Kevin in memory.

'After all that, was the climb successful?' asked Rick.

'You bet,' replied Kevin. 'We made a first British ascent and all got home safely in one piece. From then on I learnt to get my priorities right but I have always wondered if some poor unsuspecting soul ever go to read the 'bluey' and what they thought of my love life!'

'Talking of which,' George laughingly interjected, 'I think if tomorrow we concentrate on making the upper camp our base and then we can turn our attentions to climbing the beast. Has anyone got any pressing queries?'

Seeing a negative response, he continued, 'Hugh, could you and Rick get yours typed first and then pass the Husky for Kevin and I to do ours, before Kevin sends the lot as a single call.'

On the next Immarsat call, Kevin downloaded a couple more messages, one of them for George from Phoebe, which brought a smile to his face and a definite change to a more light-hearted mood. Later, as they devoured bowls full of pasta, with a meat and vegetable sauce, George told him of Phoebe's scare, finding a lump on her breast.

'That explains your recent moods,' said Kevin. 'You had me wondering if anything was the matter.'

'Yes,' replied George with a smile, 'now we can get on with what we are here for and knock the bastard off.'

Two days later the team was well established at the new base camp, just below the start of the climb itself. They'd quickly settled into an expedition routine of a total focus on the task ahead and were spending every waking moment checking, rechecking and adjusting their climbing gear and equipment for the wall.

A trial load confirmed that it would be better to have two haulage bags, which even with a minute attention to detail to ensure minimal weight, was still weighing in at 100lbs each. The load with the portaledge was obviously the bulkiest and to offset the weight-bulk ratio, this also contained their three days' water. George was looking after communications, cooking stove and butane/propane fuel, whilst Hugh was Mr Portaledge and haulage, leaving Rick to concentrate on the climbing gear itself.

'What I suggest lads,' said George that evening, 'is that we make a gentle start tomorrow and concentrate on fixing up a couple of hundred feet - aiming to make the first bivouac by early afternoon. Set up the portaledge in slow time for Hugh and I to occupy for the night whilst Rick comes back here. That way if there is anything we discover we need, either during the day or overnight, Rick can bring it back up with him without any hassle, at the same time retrieving the rope and gear. Any points for that?'

Kevin first waited for their replies, then said, 'Why don't I cook us an all-in casserole and special pudding. I've been saving the recipe for tonight. Whilst I am busy with that I suggest that you get on the outside of this,' he smilingly remarked, and reaching into his rucsac produced two bottles of wine, reading out from the label, 'Cabernet Grenache from south eastern Australia. Soft, full flavoured with juicy red fruits and a touch of vanilla oak.'

'Shame about the oak,' laughed Hugh, brandishing his multi-tool, which just happened to include a corkscrew! Reaching for a bottle, he cleared off the wrapping before vigorously extracting the cork to loud cheers from the other three and tipped its contents into each of their mugs.

'Here's to good climbing, bomb proof bivis, fair weather and a safe return,' said George, raising his mug. 'Cheers,' they all raised theirs and replied in kind. The relaxed atmosphere prevailed over the next couple of hours, as eating their final meal together they joked mercilessly.

CHAPTER 15

The morning dawned reasonably fine, with just a light wind and some patches of drizzle. This was soon to clear, as Kevin fired up the morning brew whilst the others made a final pack and check before departure to the start point. Breakfast was a bowl of muesli and another brew, then on with rucsacs and away they went with George and Hugh in the lead, followed by Rick and Kevin, a hundred paces behind.

They estimated that the proposed new route would be a vertical height gain of 4000 feet, split into about 30 pitches. What they had managed to glean from observation in various shades of light with the help of high-resolution binoculars, was that the line started off straightforward, before the first overhang section. It then seemed to take a rising traverse right for well over a thousand feet before another series of overhangs and what looked like a very complicated area of chimneys and corners. These led to the final long, smooth, sweeping crack system that would take them to the summit. George was certain he'd spotted at least one probable site of a water seep. Obviously being able to replenish with water was the major concern and experience told them that it should rain at least once every couple of days and that it would then take the face a full 24 hours to dry out again.

Their gear list read like the contents of a climbing shop in Yosemite, with as many items as possible fitted with clip-in or tie-off loops for ease of security on the climb. What they had in total included:

General	Team climbing gear
Double and single portaledges	3 sets of Friend cam devices
20 days' food	3 sets of wired stoppers
20 litres water	80 karrabiners
2 gas stoves & cook pots	selection of hooks
20 butane/propane cooking	selection of copperheads
gas canister	45 assorted pitons
Haul bags & stuff sacks	bolt kit
3 x 11mm climbing ropes	selection of tie-offs & runners
each of 200 feet	First aid kit
2 x 9mm haulage lines	rope repair kit
each of 200 feet	
2 Exotica wall hauliers	

Personal Gear (per climber)

Full Body Harness	Headlamp
Protective clothing & head over.	Jumar Ascendur Clamps
Swiss army knife & spoon	Descendur Abseil device
Sleeping bag, mat & bivouac bag	Etriers
Toothbrush, paste &	Hammer and holster
face protection cream	
Spare gloves & socks	Climbing Helmet

The overall plan of action called for first climbing and fixing the three 200-foot climbing ropes. Then, when time and conditions allowed, they would move up, install and occupy the portaledges at the new high point. Six hundred feet of rock climbing doesn't sound a great deal. However, pioneering a new route, totally self-contained and continuously over a twenty day period, would call for an extreme degree of mental and physical stamina and a total resolve.

George considered that as a trio they were as strong, both mentally and physically, as any group he'd ever been involved with, each individual's strengths and weaknesses overlapping and complimenting each other. He also considered Kevin to be the best type of support person, who in his time had 'done the business' but now was more than happy to bring a considerable amount of experience and expertise to the party.

By now all three were psyched-out to get started and there were none of the usual pre-climb witticisms and chat normal on such an occasion. For the umpteenth time, each checked their harness, hammer and gear rack, pockets, zips, helmet and finally jumar clamps and safety slings.

With Rick leading off, followed by George then Hugh, they ascended the fixed rope using the jumar clamps. As he went up, Hugh retrieved each belay point in turn, so that the rope hung free below him. On reaching the first belay stance and untying the protection, he was highly conscious this was a definitive mile-stone, as the rope no longer touched flat earth, only steep vertical rock.

It would be at least fifteen more days before they'd walk on a normal slope or surface. Their world was now totally encapsulated in grey perpendicular granite walls, where they'd search for weaknesses of cracks to surmount over-hangs, through buttresses, master chimneys and straddle flakes. It would be savage, uncompromising and very dangerous, with

Mother Nature always ready to remind them just who would have the final word.

On arrival, George and Rick had checked out the portaledges, happily finding them exactly as they'd left them the day before. They quickly unpacked the sleeping mats and bags, clipping on the stuff bags for occupancy later. George had carefully unpacked the stove, gas canister, cook pot and a day's ration of food plus water ready for use later, whilst Rick sorted out the climbing rope in preparation for leading the next pitch.

George would wait until Hugh arrived with the retrieved rope before he joined in support and to lead through. They'd hoped to climb and fix at least two rope lengths while also confirming a suitable climbing routine, before calling it a day. After Hugh had reached them with the third rope, he'd continue with it up the new fix to the high point, ready for use either then, or in the morning.

'It looks like the left hand option could go,' said George, as Rick started his climb.

Stepping gingerly onto the first toeholds Rick placed first his right hand then quickly his left into the crack, jamming them both in deep before he twisted his wrists to offer a safe, even if transitory, anchorage whilst he stepped up his feet. One toe cap went into the crack itself, where the vibram sole gripped solidly into the granite and held firm, whilst the other found a fissure to the left sufficiently wide to give Rick the balance he needed. Releasing one hand he unhooked a Friend and placed it well into the back of the crack. It opened with a resounding crunch, as the cams bit into the walls and held. Clipping the Friend onto the rope and a short cow tail, he breathed a sigh of relief as he took out the other hand jam, to be held by his harness for a short rest.

'How was that?' cried George.

'Good!' Rick called down. 'The crack is sound and just loves the Friends!'

'How does it look from there?' George asked.

'We have a ten foot overhang roof of about A2 split by this crack,' Rick called back before continuing, 'I am pretty sure it will go once I get into it. I'll make certain the next belay is bomb proof, just in case.'

'OK mate – watching and waiting,' George responded.

Rick looked around for protection points and soon spotted a thin crack where he carefully placed a piton and hammered it firmly in, until the metal sang the sweet note of being well and truly secure. Just to make absolutely sure, he also located a home for a No3 wire stopper to counter any pull on the piton.

'That will stop a falling bus,' he mused, well pleased with the handiwork. As he studied the next few moves in detail, he rearranged his equipment rack for speedy retrieval of items in a logical order. Once committed, they had to be placed quickly and effectively, before his upper body strength gave way. He would first locate a Friend into the crack securely, clip in the rope and then step into his etriers clipped into the Friend to aid his balance. Finally he would clip in his harness that would function as a seat whilst he rested and readied himself for a repeat move.

It was all about technique, balance, focus and speed, so that he was not left trying to hold his body-weight by fingertips for more than a couple of seconds. He completed the next move in record time that left him panting for breath as he gently swung underneath the overhanging roof.

It would need just one more placement to get him to the edge, from where he would follow the disappearing crack up and over. Shaking his arms in an attempt to increase the blood circulation, he breathed deeply and concentrated fiercely on getting his next four moves done in a speedy, positive sequence. Reach, place, test and clip-in. Waiting until his heart beat subsided to a reasonable rate, he sharply sucked in breath as he fluidly reached out a Friend in his right hand and simultaneously thrust it into the crack before releasing the cam grip for the sides to lock into the crack.

Taking a bight of climbing rope he quickly clipped it into the short sling dangling down below the Friend, before transferring over one etrier. He now gently transferred his weight over to the new Friend. He watched the cams intently as he allowed increased weight to be transferred and satisfied it would hold, he now unclipped the harness line into the new karrabiner. It all held.

Taking a deep breath, he checked all the placements and back-ups, before shouting down to George's staring anxious face, 'It's a good one! I can reach round to the wall above.'

'Well done pal!' cried George in genuine relief. 'How does she look now?'

Rick had a good look around before shouting back, 'Fairly straight forward, with just a wee bit of exposure to concentrate the mind.'

Unclipping the harness tie, he used the etriers to gain additional height to reach over the overhang lip and explore the crack running through. It felt sound enough and by reaching out of sight, he quickly slotted into position another Friend before resting on his etriers.

Working over a roof lip is one of the most insecure areas for a climber to operate, as he moves from swinging in free air to making contact with the rock again. Maintaining the same steady rhythm, Rick continued to methodically reach, place, test and clip-in for another two more placements into a scoop above the overhangs. Here, the downward drag on the rope meant he could not climb up any more and he signalled for George to join him.

Waiting for George, he absorbed all of the details for the next 200 feet above. It appeared relatively straightforward, with a kink to the left, just about where the next rope length would run out. What amazed him was how time had flown, as it was already mid-day and he'd started climbing at 8am. Four hours to do two hundred feet? The climbing fraternity in Llanberis would certainly have something derogative to say about that! He smiled imagining their heated discussion.

The weather had brightened from the drizzly start and looking around he could see on the horizon to the south west, a dark line that probably would produce a squall before the day was out. Still, that would be no bad thing, as they'd need rain to supplement the water consumed today and the sooner that was collected, the better.

The tied off rope tightened as George applied his jumar clamps to reach the overhang section, which took him about ten minutes. Here, he'd use a combination of an etrier, a waist sling and one jumar to make several gymnastic manoeuvres through the overhang, removing each Friend en-route after he'd passed, reducing rope drag.

Rick took out and focussed his small pocket camera, ready for when George's face first appeared over the lip. He didn't have to wait long, when preceded by a series of violent grunts and a flurry of profanity, he appeared wild eyed and panting.

'Wow!' George gasped, 'that's a nice way to start the day! Good lead mate. Where do you want me?'

They both spent a while getting reorganised, ensuring the ropes ran freely for George to lead through and pulling up the slack from where it ran directly downwards to Hugh, now the Friends had been removed from the overhang crack.

Hugh, out of sight below had been busy at the portaledges, strengthening their security and setting up water catchment spouts on the bottom of the ledge corners. Any rainfall onto the shelters would run-off into collapsible five litre water containers that he'd included with the loads. He'd also rigged a second independent belay line which would be used for the three climbers only whilst they used the shelters and site, particularly when they were horizontal in sleeping bags on the portaledges. Keeping it uncluttered from gear would help them to stay clipped into a secure line, as a constant danger of big wall climbing is becoming over-confident at bivouac sites and taking a fall.

Finishing, he could sense that the rope above was not being used and checking his rig, started to make a jumar ascent carrying the third 200 foot climbing rope and a haulage line. Making good progress, he also assessed the interim belay points, straightening and strengthening as required. At the lower middle stance, still out of view of the two above, he clipped in and rested, allowing his senses to absorb their unique situation.

The views, both down and across Tasermiut Fjord were fantastic, with clouds sweeping in and capturing the mountain tops in a silky embrace. Except for the flysheets of their base camp tents, there was no trace of man anywhere in sight. Hugh spent a few minutes catching his breath and drinking in everything he witnessed, feeling a sense of unique privilege, responsibility and gratitude, that he was able to experience such a view in these special circumstances. The arrival of the first few spots of rain cut him out of his daydream, and he started to propel his jumars rhythmically upwards, placing the soles of his boots to balance out from the vertical rock face towards where Rick was patiently safeguarding George's climbing rope.

George had made good progress up from the changeover stance with Rick and eagerly devoured his chance to lead climb. Tomorrow he'd change over with Hugh, so this would be his last chance in the lead for a couple of days. The main crack still maintained its attraction as their best option and securely absorbed Friends with little difficulty, with just the occasional wired chock being used, to lessen the rope drag.

As the swirling rain cloud enveloped them, George had arrived at an awkward spot where the main crack petered out and it required a traverse twenty feet over to the left, lay-backing up a very insecure looking rising flake to regain another vertical crack system.

The rope drag was now substantial and rather than fight it and risk a fall, George hammered off a couple of final belay stanchions and pulled up and secured the spare rope, before calling to Rick that it was now clear to ascend. Rick was more than glad of the opportunity to move and get the blood circulating in his legs again. En-route, he removed some of George's protection to straighten out the line and make for a freer running rope system.

'The next bit looks a little complicated,' remarked George as he arrived. Getting his breath back, Rick made his own quick appreciation and agreed with George, before commenting, 'It'll be Hugh and I leading tomorrow, so I guess we'd better wait until he gets here for a look.'

'Yes you're right and talk of the devil, here he comes now,' said George.

Hugh jumared up to them displaying a wide grin of satisfaction and made himself secure, before unloading the third climbing rope for the next day.

'That was certainly interesting,' Hugh observed, 'hauling through the overhang should go OK, with someone below to pull it away from the lip.'

'You're right,' replied George. 'Have a look at what tomorrow has to bring.'

Hugh quickly looked at all the possible options before agreeing with their assessment that the rising flake offered the only realistic option. Concentrating hard on working out a series of moves to regain the crack system he said, 'I think with a bit of luck it'll go free style to the corner, from where we should be able to get something in for the etriers. I'm looking forward to giving it a go.'

Leaving most of their gear at the high point, the trio quickly followed each other down the fixed ropes to the portaledge site. It was raining and blowing hard as they sought shelter inside the two man portaledge which were surprisingly snug and weather tight, even if a little cramped.

George soon had some water on the boil for a brew of hot chocolate and within minutes they'd all quickly relaxed in their unique surroundings. The only physical reminder that they were not in a normal tent was the line running from each of their harnesses, through the door zip to a safety belay.

Later George opened up the VHF radio and asked, 'Hello Kevin this is George. How do you read me, over?'

'Loud and clear! How's your day been, over?'

'Good. We've run out two rope lengths, including Rick leading on an A2 overhang midway.'

'Are the portaledges behaving OK?' Kevin queried.

'Better than any of us expected,' George went on. 'Hugh has rigged a water catchment system which seems to be working well in this rain.'

'Excellent! Nothing much from UK to pass on. How does it look for tomorrow?'

'A short little problem to begin with, then it looks straight forward enough to where we can place another bivouac. We'll wait until that's firm before dismantling and moving our present site.'

'Roger to that. What time should we speak in the morning?'

'Should we go for 7am?' asked George.

'7am it is. Have a good night and we'll speak in the morning.'

George asked the other two, 'Fancy a brew?' and seeing their smiles of confirmation busied himself boiling more water. After that they had a state of the art freeze-dried veggie casserole with potatoes and lamb, finishing with a chocolate bar and some dried pieces of fruit. This started a discussion about body waste disposal techniques in their present situation and personal preferences. Agreeing that the far side of the single portaledge provided the optimum hygienic spot in the bivouac site, they all thought it was also a time when extra care had to be taken regarding personal safety, even if it meant someone else providing a separate rope to safeguard the activity.

'A true test of friendship,' laughed George, packing away the stove and the cleaning up the pan, 'and I am sure I'll be the first!'

Once George departed to the single portaledge at about 10.00pm the extra space available became a luxury to be relished. Even though the floor was flat and at right angles, they instinctively placed the head of their sleeping bags inward towards the wall. The combination of insulated flooring, sleeping mat and Ajungilak four seasons sleeping bags gave them an excellent nest to burrow into.

Anticipating night temperatures of just below freezing, the Ajungilak ensured they should get a sound night's sleep. Getting ready for bed would involve removing outer boots and loosening inner boots, taking off warm outer jackets and wrapping them around the outer boots to form a pillow, before, locating the head torch with small nibbles and a water bottle being kept handy.

Then, checking their individual life lines were securely fastened, they could eventually climb into their sleeping bags, taking with them a pee bottle. Settling in and closing the bag gave a real sense of well being, and with only a light wind causing the shelter wall to vibrate, it was not long before they relaxed. Both George and Rick took a sleeping pill and whilst these were taking hold they could both hear Hugh yawning and sighing himself to sleep, before they too slipped off into a deep slumber.

At some point in the night, half asleep, they would each use their respective pee bottles, remembering to ensure the tops were then firmly secured! Before drifting back off to a dreamless sleep.

At these high latitudes the short Arctic night means that they would not find it difficult to wake after their seven plus hours sleep and start the process of getting ready for a days climbing. Having dressed, George moved back into the two man shelter, where his priority one task was firing up the stove to produce steaming mugs of sweet tea whilst the other two remained dormant in their 'scratchers!'

A definite 'morning' person, George had no problem getting breakfast organised and delivered, as it also gave him a chance to assess the weather, how it would affect their day and any other events to be finalised. Whilst tea was being sipped, George opened up the radio link and gave Kevin a check call to report in and get the weather forecast for the day which Kevin had obtained from Eric in *Nanortalik*. Kevin was his usual humourous and helpful self, passing on the couple of emails of encouragement he'd received. The day's weather forecast promised a wet front passing through by mid-afternoon, which was just the encouragement they now needed to get underway, once they'd eaten a bowl of porridge and had another brew.

Hugh would be the lead climber today, so he quickly finished off his breakfast and after getting ready, was first away up the rope to the high point, shortly followed by Rick. Already the trio were adopting a working routine to ensure safety, efficiency and fairness in their division of labour.

The ropes were wet from the night's rain and Hugh found a welcome solitude as he moved up them, paying particular attention to any sign of wear. With only three climbing ropes, this could be a massive problem and attention to detail now would save lots of angst later. They had rope tape and lengths of protective tubing to use should they find abrasion on the rope's outer sheath. Wear here was to be expected and if dealt with quickly enough, it would not affect the inner core and the rope's ultimate strength.

Within thirty minutes Hugh had reached the high point from the day before and started to sort out from the gear on hand, the climbing rope and protection devices he would use. Rick arrived soon after and looked in detail at the main belay points, seeking how they could be improved with use of less gear. Rick got himself well secured onto the wall and using hanging etriers in addition to his harness belay, hoped to enjoy a comfortable but secure stance whilst he readied Hugh's climbing rope for use.

'Well! What do you reckon pal?' Rick enquired looking at the thin flake.

'With a little luck it'll go OK to fifteen feet, where I'll hopefully get a runner in,' replied Hugh ensuring all his gear was where he wanted it to hand for instant use.

'Here goes,' Hugh remarked as he reached up onto the flake and quickly brought his feet up high against the wall, using the pressure on his boots against the pressure of his hands. He quickly reached up again and made another smooth move, then again before he momentarily stopped for an intake of breath.

Layback moves are ones of precision and speed, without any rest. Success depends entirely on speed and fluidity, before arm strength gives way. Hugh sobbed loudly and made another two arm moves, then with a loud grunt like a wounded animal he made a final desperate effort, which got his boot onto a small step below the top of the flake. Pressing down on that he reached behind the flake and jammed in his left fist, before hopping a right boot to where the other had been.

He shuddered with effort as he momentarily rested and took in the surroundings. The immediate priority now was to place protection so that he could rest. Braced for the worst, Rick watched intently, knowing how frantic Hugh was feeling as he searched for somewhere to place either a Friend or wired nut. If he did not get one in soon, he'd fall, with all the possible ramifications that could bring to them all.

For what seemed like an age, which in reality would probably not be more than ten seconds, with his right hand Hugh teased a nut into a crack out of his sight behind the flake. It jammed tight. Clipping in a tape sling, he first gave a gentle and then a harder tug. It held. Finally he clipped the sling into his harness, visibly relaxed and withdrew his jammed left hand, with its bleeding, grazed knuckles.

As the blood flow to his arms resumed, Hugh spotted a useful crack, into which he introduced a thin piton that slipped half way in with no undue pressure. A few sharp taps with his hammer, sank it in to the hilt and whilst it was not overly impressive, in this world without much protection, he'd take anything on offer. Only after clipping another short sling into that and then placing his climbing rope onto it, did he feel secure enough to shout down to Rick, 'That was very nearly a brown pants job.'

To which Rick laughingly replied, 'Great lead mate. Probably your best yet! How does it look now?'

'The crack system starts again and I'll be into it after a couple of moves,' answered Hugh. 'I think your stance is more secure than here, so I'd like to continue and see what we come up with.'

'No problem. Go for it and I'll see you soon.'

As Hugh moved his feet up onto the flake, the pull on the wired nut was in the wrong direction, so it loosened and became non-effective. However, the extra height he gained meant immediate access to the deep two-inch wide crack that appeared to go on forever. For Hugh the next hour of climbing was probably the best he'd enjoyed - ever.

The crack accepted his Friends with a satisfying 'crunch' as the cams bit home and he was able to build up a satisfying rhythm of text book artificial aid climbing. Soon the 200 foot rope was near its end and alerted by a yell from Rick, he doubled up protection for a stance in hanging slings, where Rick could move up to join him.

It had steadily become more overcast and slightly colder during the last few of hours, with a slight increase in wind, not enough to be of concern yet, but with the forecast of a weather front moving in, it would be worth keeping an open mind.

Rick moved up powerfully, carrying the second climbing rope, which he would use to climb through, above Hugh's high point. George let the lead pair clear the portaledges before making an attempt to clear everything away securely and tidy up the site. He also took the opportunity of having another radio chat with Kevin and they relayed a couple of email messages. Hugh's water collection system was working well and he transferred everything to fill up the main containers. Their usage was as expected, with replacing it so easily being a real bonus.

George sensed he would be the first to try out the toilet system whilst sorting their next main meal. Possibly by association he felt his bowel system giving a nudge, as if to say, 'Don't forget about me,' as he looked at the various menus before settling on chicken and sweetcorn. This gave him a couple of minutes to think about the various preparations that he'd have to make.

Sitting in the solo portaledge he re-arranged clothing layers, so that he was only wearing his Helly Hansen Lifa long johns and boots on his lower half, with a fleece on top. Over the fleece he fitted the sleeping harness and sling, which went around the shoulders and chest. Last but not least, he checked that a packet of medicated baby wipes was open and ready for use in his fleece pocket. Exiting the portaledge, he checked the harness sling was clipped into the short traverse rope before moving along it to the far side of the platform, using a jumar clamp for extra security.

Once clear of the platform, he moved down slightly to the full extent of the sling and leaning back against the chest harness and bracing his boot against the wall, quickly hauled down his long johns. As nature took its course, it gave a whole new meaning to the expression 'going' he thought, as his body waste disappeared down the wall. It certainly was not a place to linger.

As quickly as possible he used the baby wipes, hauled up his long johns and recovered quickly to the portaledge, crawling back inside much relieved. After sorting out his clothing for the day he made a flask of hot drink and prepared to re-join the others.

By now the weather was becoming a little bleak and stormy and George mentally worked out that they would probably have no more than two hours of reasonable activity – if they were lucky – before having to get battened down in the portaledges. Moving through the overhang, he could now see Rick smoothly lead climbing, well safeguarded by Hugh.

The sheer vertical crack Rick was ascending had to be a classic example of quality climbing using aid, in particular the Friends cam devices, that really came into their own in such a scenario. The crack soared up spectacularly, with a slight right-hand bias splitting the centre of the face for well over a thousand feet, before it disappeared into the thickening cloud. The dramatic, uncluttered lines beckoned for someone to accept the challenge of making the first ascent. By the time George arrived with Hugh, Rick had led a full 200-foot and was concentrating on establishing a stance for a changeover with Hugh.

Seeing the grey stormy horizon, Hugh was not over optimistic of breaking any new ground today and instead suggested that he take up on the line all of the excess rope and gear, in preparation for the next spell of good weather after the front passed through.

'Yes I think that would be a really wise move,' George remarked. 'I'll leave you this flask of hot drink and scoot off down to get out of the way and start on today's meal.'

'That'll be good,' replied Hugh, getting his kit ready to start the jumar ascent and exclaiming, 'See you later!' as he hauled upwards.

George went down to the portaledge camp using an abseil device known as a 'descendur.' This was a metal figure of 8, around which the rope was placed in such a way, that his controlling right hand could easily increase or decrease the pressure of the rope running around the metal, governing the speed of descent. Like portaledges and Friends, they are one of the simple looking items that have helped to revolutionise big wall climbing.

As George descended, all the security points appeared to be in good condition, but he checked them just the same. Where the rope went over the edge of the overhang it was beginning to show signs of wear on the outer sheath. Binding on some tape, he reminded himself to bring up and fit a split piece of tubing to give it further protection.

The weather front was preceded by an increase in wind velocity which hit the portaledge camp as George arrived. 'This will be a good test,' George remarked to himself checking out the rope anchors and the door zip fastenings. The fabric walls of the portaledges were two skins thick with about an inch separation, the circulating air between them cutting down on condensation. It meant the zip doors could be used independently, allowing some extra security from the elements. Ensuring the water catchment bags were in place, George slipped into the solo portaledge and started heating water, as he anticipated the others would not be far behind.

The stove set-up was pure innovation. Hugh had made a lightweight collapsible aluminium frame that placed the pot squarely above the flame from the gas cooker, without it resting on the cooker itself. The base of the butane propane mix gas canister slotted firmly into a six inch by one inch square block of wood, into the corners of which fitted the four legs of the stand. It was a neat, efficient piece of low-tech engineering, that would make all the difference to living well, rather than just merely surviving, as plenty of hot drinks and food were a major contributing factor on the long haul that was Ketil.

Voices from above soon indicated Hugh and Rick's imminent arrival. Once they had secured their gear and were in their portaledge they were presented with mugs of hot chocolate to wash down a snack of cheese, jam and wholemeal biscuits. George told them he'd christened the loo, describing the system that he'd adopted.

'Let's hope this weather allows us to do the same,' grinned Hugh, 'otherwise it could get just a little interesting!'

'According to Kevin the best estimate Eric can give is that it should have passed through by tomorrow evening,' announced George, 'so I guess we'll have to batten down the hatches until then and conserve our strength.'

'Nothing like a spot of festering to recharge the batteries and yearn to get the Damn thing over,' remarked Rick, 'and at least it'll top up the water stakes.'

They'd all been through bad weather on mountains many times before and they knew, rather like people on a sailing yacht, that the two go hand in glove. The very uniqueness of their situation understandably gave cause for a slight apprehension and as if on cue, the wind power increased, buffeting the tiny shelters incessantly as it roared across the face.

'Cooking in this lot is not going to be possible,' thought George, 'but at least I've managed to fill up our three flasks with hot water.' He slid into his sleeping bag as the temperature dropped and icy sleet tried to invade the shelter. Successful bad weather festering is an art form that only comes with practice, and key to it is a lowering of the pulse and a heightening of positive thought.

Noise is the greatest single enemy, so the ability not to try to identify what each creak and groan means and have complete faith in equipment and preparations, is paramount. Also very helpful was the short duration of darkness in the Arctic summer, as daylight is a welcome friend. Deep sleep is elusive, with prolonged periods of dozing instead, as the subconscious mind is ready to react instantly to a life and death scenario. A sense of comfort was derived from the security lines, outweighing any inconvenience they caused but the feeling of having drifted into deep slumber for hours when it was only for a couple of minutes, was perplexing.

Each one had his proven method of combating the tedium. For George it was an opportunity to record into a rugged dictaphone his thoughts and feelings as events unfolded. These helped him later when writing the relevant chapter of the account. He found it was the small, but personal details that attracted the most attention from his growing readership. Contrary to popular belief they included a growing number of non-climbers, who relished the escapism he was able to provide. 'And you cannot beat being here for that,' he thought, conscious the swaying of the portaledge had increased.

Hugh escaped into the music delivered via a state of the art Sony sports CD walkman. It was the only luxury he permitted himself, with four CDs bringing the best he liked in a particular musical area. They included Welsh male voice choirs, Tina Turner, M People and the latest Classical Brit awards. With the whole lot in a small padded zip case the size of a writing pad, they provided many hours of enjoyment. The earphones cut out sounds of the wind, leaving only the movements of the portaledge itself to indicate what was happening beyond a few millimetres of fabric.

Luckily, Rick had an uncommon skill of being able to doze at the slightest chance, regardless of situation or circumstance. In the current environment nothing was more advantageous. However, even whilst gently napping, he'd wake up alert to any changes in his immediate surroundings.

Patience become more than just an adjective at times like this, with any undue apprehension draining them mentally and physically. Their awareness of each other's strengths and weaknesses, an explicit trust and compatibility, would be fundamental to success in sitting out a storm. Once all possible precautions and preparations are in situ, the mind has to go into neutral, waiting for Nature to finish demonstrating its awesome power.

George rummaged amongst the food bags in his portaledge to sort out three individual snack packs in addition to the flask of hot fruit juice and their own water bottle each which would have to suffice for the duration. He deliberately only put a couple of dried fruit pieces in each, as a bowel movement right now was definitely not on the agenda. The noise of the wind was so high that he had to yell loudly to gain the attention of the other two only four feet away and, confirming they were ready, he partially opened the door zip and quickly passed the food and drink to them.

Then switching on the VHF radio George called Kevin to let him know they were at the camp and asked for any new weather reports. Kevin relayed that Eric still had the front moving through for the next ten to twelve hours, with 60-knot gusts from the south west, followed by a calmer period of three to four days. Confirming that he would keep his radio on, Kevin wished them a safe and comfortable night.

The storm reached its zenith shortly after midnight. The three climbers' world now filled with noise as the wind howled, screamed and bucked at the portaledges. Their excellent design ensured that with the exception of an updraft, the wind pressed them more firmly into the face. The occasional violent updraft gave the floor a ripple effect, pushing into their backs, jolting them awake when they instinctively reached to checking their body harnesses were secure.

'Women and children first!' yelled George to the others as an energetic updraft bounced him into the sitting position. Flicking on his dictaphone he tried to explain what was happening and capture the violence of the night. His main concern was excessive wear on the ropes aloft, as the wind hammered them against the rock, in particular where they ran over an edge, as at the overhangs.

To distract his mind, George broke into a rendition of *Liverpool Lou* and *Maggie May*, which exhausted his repertoire. As the stormy night continued none of them slept, merely dozing until the next buffeting shook them awake. Fortunately the night sky began to brighten about 2.30am and their spirits lifted as the new day dawned. An hour later and the wind had steadily died down to a mere gale force, allowing them an opportunity to relax for the first time for six hours and fall asleep.

It was 9.00am before George awoke, opened up the VHF and gave Kevin a call. 'Good to hear all's well with you and that the portaledges survived their first baptism of fire,' said Kevin. 'This morning's forecast continues to look favourable with a high promising to settle in by mid-afternoon. Over.'

'That's good news indeed. Just what we want to get some height,' said George. 'Anything further for us? Over.'

'Negative,' answered Kevin, 'I'll send the update to everyone and remain on listening watch. Have a good one! Over and out.'

CHAPTER 16

George packed the radio away, then organised the stove and large pot for making breakfast. Once the guys next door were organised, he swapped shelters and got busy in theirs firing up the stove. Hot chocolate was soon on the go, followed by porridge. Moments after eating his, Hugh quickly exited, heading for the airborne toilet, pronouncing it 'unusual' upon his return. George and Rick had been discussing the possible options for the day and suggested they continued for the final rope length, then concentrated on helping Hugh haul up and establishing the next bivouac.

'Sounds mighty fine by me,' Hugh replied. 'You'd better get going so as not to miss too much of the day.'

Packing everything away and getting ready did not take long and soon Rick and George jumared up and away showing little evidence of their sleepless night. After checking the ropes for un-due wear and arriving at the high point, George suggested that Rick may like to lead through as he'd be in support tomorrow. Rick readily agreed.

The crack line to follow could best be described as ideal, soaring upwards to the right of centre of the face, offset at an 85 degree angle to the vertical. Using the Friends at six-foot intervals was perfect, with added protection of the occasional piton placed for good measure.

George shouted up to Rick that he only had 20 feet of rope left, happily coinciding with Rick's arrival at an area that would make an ideal portaledge site. Securing the rope off, Rick called down it was safe to ascend. George swiftly moved up, removing most of the Friends en-route for later use, arriving with a huge grin of satisfaction of a job well done.

Getting his breath back he remarked, 'Superb lead mate. Shall we get busy with the camera?'

After the spot of 'photomania' and a chance to stock up on fluids and snacks, they decided the best option would be if George returned to the overhang section and helped Hugh get the haul bags above that, before the final lift to the new portaledge site for the night.

The next five hours were exhausting as they grappled with the haul bags. As expected the overhang section gave them a struggle, made easier by a crafty diversion George was able to apply, where a line from the bottom of the bag went up at an angle, to lift the base when it was at the lip of the overhang. With a couple of co-ordinated heaves the bag shot past the obstacle and headed upwards on the haulage device.

Rick was also busy, setting up the site security for the portaledges. This entailed the construction of four major points of independent security, each backed up and capable of holding at least two people. It was serious engineering indeed, whilst standing on thin air only!

Setting up the portaledge anew gave very little problems, as they now felt relaxed and confident in its use. By early evening they were installed and George had the brew pan going for some serious re-hydration after the physical day of moving up the two haul bags.

'I don't know about you two, but I am knackered,' offered George, 'I've never hurled so much abuse at such an inert object.'

'I thought we moved them well,' replied Hugh, 'especially when you rigged the special 'engineering' bit to get us through the overhang.'

'Yes I remembered that from a chat about the exact situation with Simo,' said George. 'Now who's for hot orange? Whilst I sort us out a good pog-up!'

The weather was almost perfect, with very little wind, clear skies and now as the sun went down, just a cold nip in the air. Despite no rain being forecast, Hugh had rigged his water catchment scheme, which gently swung around like wind chimes below the two-man portaledge. As they would be in-situ here for at least two nights, there was always a good chance of some rain, despite the forecast.

'Here we are folks, chilli con carne and rice,' George called, 'with fruit, cheese and chocolate to follow.'

'Just what I need to test out my body's waste disposal system,' said Rick laughingly as they spent the next hour eating and drinking their meagre supper. Each had already started to shed a few pounds of body fat, as it's impossible to haul enough food to keep that on. Knowing this would happen they'd deliberately started with some extra weight, and the longer that lasted, the better.

Drinking enough fluids was always a necessary mountaineering discipline, as the human body can go lengthy periods without food, but needs a regular supply of fluids. Drinking plain water is boring, so to encourage rehydration, the effort to include fruit juice and hot chocolate mix powder was always worthwhile.

As he anticipated, after they'd eaten Rick soon beat a hasty departure to swing out over the abyss below George's portaledge for the few seconds necessary to do a body function. Whistling suspended in carefree animation he could hear George on the radio joyfully sending Kevin a censored commentary!

The next day's plan called for George and Hugh to lead climb, with Rick in support - George to lead the first couple of rope lengths, as he would then rotate the following day with Rick. By the time they'd eaten, drunk and cleaned up, it was late evening and no-one needed any persuasion that the next thing on the agenda was a good nine hours horizontal in his sleeping bag. Clutching pee bottles and checking security harnesses they crawled into their warm bags and were soon asleep.

It was Hugh who stirred first the next morning and fired up the stove to produce 'bed tea' for the others. There can be fewer moments of unadulterated luxury for the recumbent mountaineer, than unzipping and reaching out an arm from a battened down sleeping bag, for a steaming mug of tea freshly made tea.

An hour later George, secured by Hugh, led off up the excellent climbing line. The crack absorbed his Friends with a satisfying crunch as he released the cams and they bit solidly into the rock walls. The style of climbing called for fluid motions with minimal exertion, letting the equipment take the strain and not the climber's upper body strength. That at least is the theory and George would be the first to admit that he was too aggressive, expending far too much energy as he gripped and gouged his way upwards. It did not seem long before Hugh yelled out 'twenty feet' and George began establishing a changeover stance for him. As Hugh made his way up, it gave George an opportunity to absorb the enormity of the face and the wild grandeur of its setting.

The sun shone warmly, the light wind gently fanned them and all was at peace - in strong contrast to the previous day when they'd been grimly hanging on and battered relentlessly. Hugh arrived hardly out of breath, having removed most of the Friends from below. After posing quickly for George's camera shot he took over the spare hardware, and with barely a break in momentum carried on leading out the new rope length, humming gently to himself as he did so. Within an hour Rick also arrived with the third climbing rope that he and Hugh would use in the morning.

It was only now that George looked at his watch and seeing it was nearly 4pm remarked, 'I don't believe it. I thought it was only about noon.'

By now Hugh was also at the end of his climbing rope and they could see he was busy making a stance. Once he was secure, George headed off down, leaving Rick to follow when he'd met up with Hugh. At the portaledge his first priority was to open-up the VHF radio and have a chat with Kevin. He passed on the day's progress report and listened as Kevin read out a couple of emails from well wishers including the British Heart Foundation, which he asked Kevin to send a reply.

Business over, they agreed to speak later when the others had arrived back and George concentrated on making them all a hot drink and burrowed into the ration bag to decide on the night meal. It looked like haddock, potatoes and vegetables. 'Rough life for the wicked,' he thought, putting the freeze-dried makings into a pan of warm water to hydrate.

It was the best food he'd eaten on any expedition. Expensive yes, but palatable, filling and easy to prepare. Not like some of the concoctions he'd been forced to eat on previous trips. Quite the worst was some ex-MoD dehydrated pork bars, which years ago a mate serving in the Special Forces had given him. They'd tasted like blocks of concentrated yak dung and even the thought of them brought on an involuntary wretch. Raising a mug of hot orange he said, 'So here's to you Nigel for all the help and advice with the rations.'

Much later, after they were all fed and watered, George asked for opinions on how the climb was going. His companions were both positive and delighted with progress to date, with just a slight reservation of keeping wear and tear on the main ropes under stricter surveillance. Rick suggested that whoever was in support on a daily basis, should make it their number one priority to inspect and repair where necessary.

For his part George was more than happy with progress. They were slightly ahead of schedule, the portaledges had proven their worth during the last blow, climbing gear and ropes were excellent, water procurement and consumption was better than he expected, comms were good and the wall rations were brilliant. Finally he thought they were working very well as a team.

From what they had seen above them today, the crack system looked to continue for another three to four hundred feet, before a sharp traverse left. After that there appeared to be another overhanging section, beyond which they could not see. Finally, George said they were probably about a third of the way and he was looking forward to time in the lead tomorrow with Hugh.

The next couple of days sped by as they continued to systematically make good, steady and safe progress. The weather remained favourable and they'd moved the portaledges up to bivouac number five, just below the new set of overhangs. Their health was good, despite George developing itchy piles and Hugh's skinned knuckles.

One afternoon, a pair of large birds with white tails spent an hour or so circling the face, wheeling in the updrafts and seemingly watching what they were doing, before dropping away to the surface of the fjord. No one was an ornithologist, so they could only guess what species they were observing. All three men were impressed with the sheer majesty and freedom on display, with the birds certainly more at home than they were.

It was Hugh and Rick's turn at the front when the second set of overhangs were reached. They consisted of two separate shelves, thirty feet apart and they could see a crack system going through the first, but could not see what lay above that. So it was a case of climb first, then find out if they'd made the right choice, or not, afterwards. The portaledge position gave them plenty of time to make an analysis of the sequence of moves and a good safe site from which to mount their attempt.

From the moment he awoke, Hugh mentally began getting ready for the task ahead, eating and drinking just enough at breakfast to give him sustenance - but not too much. After morning ablutions and cleaning his teeth, he double-checked ropes, climbing gear, boots and clothing, whilst Rick did a complete check on the main belay point, adjusting as necessary. George made busy with a camera, moving to the optimum spot for angle, light and background, saying, 'This should be the picture of the trip - try to look photogenic please.'

Pulling a face and adjusting his helmet strap, Hugh quickly made the first couple of moves, deft and competent to a position where he had to start swinging free under the overhanging roof. Over twenty feet in depth, surmounting it would demand a great deal of respect, strength, agility and speed. Using Friends and tape slings in the main crack it did not take long to arrive at the roof and sitting in his harness suspended from a well placed corner Friend, he surveyed the possible options. The main crack appeared to narrow almost to a close after fifteen feet, with a possibility shortly after of another starting parallel.

He'd have to get out there to see whether it was a go or not. Running his free hand over the rack of Friends, wired nuts, pitons and tape slings, he concentrated totally on maintaining a sequential programme of balanced moves. Once started on his run, it had to be one continuous fluid movement, without excessive losses of speed and strength.

'Moving now Rick,' he called, which Rick acknowledged, paying out some slack rope in anticipation of Hugh getting underway. For Rick, watching him swing, lift, place, test and secure after each move was like witnessing a world class Olympic athlete perform, as he conscientiously safeguarded the live climbing rope connecting them both.

After placing four protection points in the crack, Hugh rested and let the blood flow back into his arms, whilst he looked for a possible answer to the next ten feet to the edge of the roof. The parallel crack started just above him and, widening slightly, continued past where the main crack closed to the edge and beyond. It would only take pitons initially and possibly later he may get in a wired nut.

He tried his blade and was able to force it into the crack about an inch without much effort. Tapping it home with his hammer, he heard it make a high pitched 'sing' as the metal narrowed and bit deeper into the rock. It would suffice for some weight bearing whilst he quickly placed another further down the crack. Clipping on a short tape, he placed in an etrier and stepping over, gently transferred half his body weight. It held. This gave him the reach he needed to manoeuvre another thin piton into the widening crack and speedily belt it home, before reaching over and clipping in his other etrier and climbing rope.

'Tight,' he cried out to Rick, who strongly levered the climbing rope so that Hugh was held, whilst he changed over the short tapes attached to his harness. Once Hugh had clipped these into the protection, it meant that Rick could relax slightly on the climbing rope, giving Hugh more freedom of movement by letting the harness take the strain of his body weight, allowing time to work out his next move sequence. Selecting a wired nut, he immediately reached into the crack and slid it in, before turning and wedging the chamfered nut into the crack walls.

'Better than nothing,' he thought, swiftly stepping out of an etrier, unclipping and transferring it into the new sling, before placing his foot back for balance whilst reaching over with the climbing rope to clip into the waiting karrabiner. Finally, he transferred cow's tails and the other etrier.

The manoeuvres had taken less than twenty seconds. Rick watched intently, as failure of protection now would have a ripple effect on the smaller pitons, with the transfer of Hugh's weight popping them open like a huge zipper. Hugh rested, gently swinging in his harness, concentrating fully on the next move towards the wider crack, which was tantalisingly close. He anticipated getting a Friend into it but never got to make a placement, as without warning the wired nut jerked out.

For Hugh it all seemed to happen so slowly, with time to think, 'now you're going to fall,' before accelerating down into the first of a series of violent jolts. He screamed involuntary as he saw a bright flash of light, followed by darkness.

His limbs flailed first one way then the other as he plummeted down. This downward motion being accompanied by equally violent ones from the side as his fall was arrested by piece after piece of equipment ripping from the hairline crack. Then just as suddenly as it had started, it stopped. Hugh felt a sickening jerk wrenching into his chest and stomach and was left hanging on the rope.

After a few anxious moments his vision returned and he yelled out. He was hanging upright, but facing outward, just ten feet above the portaledges. The main Friend in the corner before the roof had held. Hugh looked down at the others, who were staring at him.

For some time Hugh's brain refused to function. He simply hung on the rope in a dream-like state, unable to take in what had happened. It was hard to know who was more shocked, for the others looked equally dazed. They stared at him as if he was some apparition in a freak show. Nobody spoke. Hugh wondered if blood was pouring from his ears, or if one of his limbs was sticking out at an incongruous angle. Perhaps they could see something he couldn't feel. Hugh scanned his body, but it all appeared to be intact. As feeling slowly returned, his right elbow hurt.

'Are you all right?' George finally asked.

'I think so,' Hugh's voice sounded cracked.

The worry on the faces of the others dissolved, Rick's buckling into a wry smile that he tried to contain.

'What a spectacular lob!' he exclaimed.

'I am going to have to come down,' Hugh said weakly. 'Can you lower me?'

Through a combination of lowering and down climbing, Hugh

rejoined the others at the bivouac site and was ushered into the por-taledge.

'I've hurt my arm. I don't think I'll be able to go back up and finish the pitch,' Hugh said.

'Don't worry about that,' George assured him. 'What about you arm?'

Hugh felt his right elbow with his left hand. It was swollen, but the pain was not intense, although that could have been due to the state of shock.

'I don't think it's broken,' he pronounced, not altogether convinced by his diagnosis, but not wanting to make a fuss.

'I'd like to stick it in a support sling,' said George, 'and get you to take a couple of Ibrufen tablets to reduce the swelling and tuck you into a sack.'

'That sounds fine by me,' replied Hugh, pleased to relax quivering muscles.

'Then Rick and I will give it another go,' smiled George, unfurling a crepe bandage to fashion a sling.

Once they'd departed, for Hugh it was a chance to re-live the fall and come to terms with the momentous event. He lay thinking that any fall you can 'walk' away from is a real bonus and quietly congratulated him-self. The 'what ifs' of the elbow injury been more severe were not dwelt on. Within an hour the Ibrufen had begun to work and all was well with the world. He dozed for a while and then went out to see how the others were faring. Rick was just passing the site of his fall.

Moving lithely, with a relaxed rhythm hiding an intense concentration, he'd placed a long piton and was hammering it in with sure hard blows that rang out with the metallic 'ting' of being well home. One more move placed Rick level with the overhang sill and he effortlessly reached up above it and located an excellent home for a medium sized Friend. Three minutes later and he swarmed out of sight.

'He made that look easy,' George remarked with a laugh and enquired, 'how are you feeling now?'

'The throbbing has gone but I'll leave it in the sling,' Hugh replied.

'Good to hear,' said George and then asked, 'would you give Kevin a call mate, I've nothing for him.'

'No problem,' said Hugh, reaching into the portaledge for the VHF radio. After speaking with Kevin, he watched as George confirmed with

Rick that he'd tied off the climbing rope and that he could now ascend. En-route, George's aim was to remove most of the lead climber's protection, leaving the climbing rope to run as unhindered as possible to the main belay point above the portaledge. This reduces rope drag and meant they would not be hindered in ascent and descent, with free run-outs from stance to stance. The rope was now hanging direct from the overhanging lip to the corner belay and gave 30 feet of spectacular ascent using jumar clamps - just the photo that George sought.

The new stance Rick located was in a scoop, just below the second overhang. Protection was good, which was just as well, as the overhang looked awesome. A crack system started ten feet into the roof and continued over the lip. The challenge was finding some way of getting into that crack to begin with, as it was completely bare.

After careful study, both Rick and George agreed they would have to use their bolt drill to establish a couple of protection points in the roof, allowing them access to the final overhand crack system. Using the bolt kit was a hard decision to make, as they'd hoped to climb the route completely 'free.' There was no alternative unless they restarted again, which was obviously not an option.

Using the bolt kit was also a time consuming operation. The idea being that a hole is made in the rock, using a hammer and hand drill. Once judged deep enough, a one-way plug would be driven into the hole that secured a bracket, into which a karrabiner would be clipped, allowing security for the climber's rope, harness and etriers. It was your average DIY with a difference!

Dangling by a body harness with feet in etriers and working sideways at arm's length, calls for above average concentration, agility and upperbody strength, combined with an inordinate faith in the equipment. They decided that Rick could have the first go at making the hole, then depending on how he felt, they could change over for the second and again for the third. That was the plan, and they hoped the first hole would be drilled today. First of all they had to return to the portaledge and retrieve the hand drill and bits. This did not take long and it gave George a chance to check out how Hugh was feeling, whilst Rick sorted the kit. Hugh was feeling perky and suggested that he became responsible for preparing the evening meal in their absence, to which George was more than happy to agree.

It was 3pm as they returned back up the rope to the second overhang and thirty minutes later Rick was swinging around on the final belay point, looking more like a demented stone mason than a climber. Hammer, twist and swing, hammer, twist, swing and rest, was the routine, until patience gradually paid off and a hole started to appear - gouged out by the carbon tipped drill bits.

Two hours of this industry produced a hole deep enough to embrace the steel core plug and bracket. It was a tired but triumphant Rick who after tapping it home, clipped in an etrier and did a swing to test its weight bearing capacity. No problem! His face smiled looking down to George. Returning a positive thumb's up, George shouted he was more than happy to live to fight another day and re-join Hugh at the portaledge. Tying off the lead end of the climbing rope, Rick quickly followed him back to where Hugh had prepared a brew of hot sweet tea, their bodies absorbing the liquid like a sponge.

'What's for scran?' asked George, downing his drink with relish.

'Scampi, rice and mixed vegetables,' Hugh replied, opening the pot where the ingredients had been gently re-hydrating for the last couple of hours.

'Sounds pretty good mate - even better when someone else is cooking!' observed Rick, as he made room in the confined space for Hugh to operate.

'Will you be OK to spell Rick tomorrow,' George asked Hugh. 'I'd have a go with the second bolt fix and we reckon it'll probably take at least one more after that to get into the new crack.'

'Yes I am sure the elbow will be fine,' answered Hugh, 'but can we confirm that in the morning?'

The night meal over and as they were clearing everything away, George cleared his throat and asked for their attention, 'Even if he has forgotten, I'd like to remind him that today it is Rick's 38th birthday. Helen asked me to give you this card. I'll miss out on the kisses if you don't mind. But I do happen to have a small flask of Glenfiddich to celebrate this happy event!'

Liberally distributing its contents into their mugs, George proposed a toast to Rick's birthday and their continued success forging the new route on Ketil. Rick, in reply, confirmed that away from home he could not think of a better time and place for his birthday party and how much he was looking forward to toasting their successful completion of the new route.

The good weather pattern held for two days and then slipped into a period of intermittent rain storms, followed by short periods of finer cold weather, before the return of more rain and sleet. The new pattern did not hold them up, but it did mean that they were all beginning to feel the effects of the cold, wet weather, which made them quite lethargic.

When a storm arrived, just as they were about to depart for another full day, it was not a hard decision for George to suggest they sat this one out inside the portaledges and concentrated on serious festering while it blew itself out, as they seemed to be above the last of the overhangs. The portaledge continued to provide good protection from the elements and the only serious problem was the wear of the climbing ropes. Two had been changed over by the thinner haulage ropes, with the support man every day spending hours taping new signs of wear on the outer sleeves.

One benefit of the regular rainfall was that their reserves of water were always topped up, never dipping below a full day's supply. This meant plenty of food being eaten, in fact probably too much and the food stocks were beginning to require rationing to ensure a maximum time on the wall, should it be required.

Once again the large birds paid them a visit and Hugh was able to get them in close by throwing small pieces of cheese up and away, which they spotted and dived to recover in mid-air - spectacular.

After seventeen days the preliminary storm warning from Eric sounded innocuous enough and Kevin passed it on during the morning call. They were at bivouac number nine, with about 1100 feet left to go, the first half of which looked to be OK, directly up a nice looking crack system they had been following for the past three days. After a couple of 200 foot pitches it then curved to the right, which they knew led onto the easier final summit traverse. Their portaledge site was secure as any they'd used so far and their living routines in it had been well honed to ensure a maximum of safety and comfort with a minimum of effort. Rick and Hugh were lead climbing and George was trying hard to position the penultimate camera shot.

Within 30 minutes the storm really hit the mountain and it was only the fact that they were on fixed ropes back to the portaledge that saved them from a really nasty experience. As it was, they got back to its haven of security battered, wet, cold and weary, relishing the protection it afforded from the elements. Fortunately the thermos flasks were full of hot, sweet orange drink, which along with a couple of chocolate bars, served to boost their metabolism. Opening the radio they heard the relief in Kevin's voice as they exchanged pleasantries and George informed him that they were all now in the portaledges.

'Eric has just informed me that the low is deepening,' Kevin reported before going on, 'and that you can expect winds in excess of 60mph with sleet over the next 24 hours. Over.'

'Roger to that,' replied George, 'we are pretty confident the portaledges will hold up OK. We'll be ready for the worst and I'd appreciate to chat every hour or so.'

Adopting a calm, low-key manner George suggested to the others that they got ready for the worst and pack an emergency rucsac each. He'd look after the radio and asked Hugh to do the same with the first aid kit. Each took a hand full of energy bars, a full thermos flask and water bottle, and stuffed them, together with an emergency bivouac bag and head torch, in their own rucsac. Then dressed in outer suits, with hats and gloves deep in pockets immediately to hand, they checked out individual attachments to the external security line.

Half an hour later, just as darkness fell the first serious buffeting hammered in. The screaming wind tore at the portaledges with strength and extraordinary power, causing them all to yell in alarm and desperately clutch their safety lines. The only consolation was that it was even worse outside.

The battering lasted between fifteen and twenty minutes and lapsed for a short spell before returning with a seemingly increased violence. Then, an electrical storm added to the mayhem, with deafening peals of thunder crashing into their ears and jagged bolts of lightening turning the inside the portaledge into daylight. For fifteen minutes they were all at a higher state of tense alertness, expecting a lightening strike to hit the portaledge, attracted by the metals. As quick as it had arrived the electrical storm rolled away to the inland ice.

The south westerly wind direction luckily meant the portaledges were forced even harder into the wall, with just the occasional gust ramming the floor upwards. They each employed a different personal response to the forces of nature unleashed upon them, which served to disorientate the trio as they soaked up the outrage.

Every so often George spoke briefly to Kevin on the radio, moderating his own voice as he listened to Kevin's quiet relaxed north country drawl and flat vowels. Wrapped in sleeping bags, they nodded off in between the bouts of savage gusts rudely shaking them awake. In such situations they knew from experience it was critical to 'switch off' from the present and try to focus onto something benign and non-threatening, if only for a snatched minute or two, until forced back into reality as the vicious noises outside encroached deep into their sub-conscious. Mentally, George constructed a dry stone wall at the cottage. Hugh designed a canal craft driven by cycle pedal power and Rick was making a new route on the local indoor climbing wall.

The dawn arrived without any let up in conditions, but the morning light made the storm seem slightly less sinister. Based on what Eric had told him at mid-night, Kevin said he anticipated the storm's epicentre had passed through them and that they should have some improvement in conditions as the day progressed.

'Glad to hear it,' replied George. 'Now I know how it feels to be in a washing machine on full spin!'

The wind speed did slowly abate, so that by mid-afternoon George was able to contemplate making a hot drink of chocolate for them all, without fear of it all ending up on the floor. This buoyed them up sufficiently for Hugh to disappear outside and check out the portaledges' security anchor points. Wielding strips of tape, Rick administered to the small rips that had appeared overnight in the shelters and to where the fabric stitching showed signs of stress. Two of the four water collection containers were missing, blown away in the storm. Luckily, that and three weary climbers being the only casualties of a traumatic episode.

A few hours later saw them eating royally of a freeze-dried beef casserole, dried fruit and cheese, their first cooked meal in 36 hours. Replete, it was not long before horizontal positions in sleeping bags were adopted and snores drifted onto the breeze, which gently ruffled the shelters.

The next two days passed in a flurry of climbing activity, with each climber taking the lead and making great progress in the excellent weather conditions. With the added incentive of soon running out of food, it was a motivated team that continued to break new ground towards the summit. The excellent crack gave them the best climbing of the expedition, with fantastic exposure as they neared the roof of the face. Looking down it was hard to visualise what they had achieved during nearly three weeks fully committed to the face. To say they were in a rush to finish would be wrong, whereas it would be true that minds were anticipating with delight a walk on level ground, having a hot shower and using the toilet without fear of falling.

As George would remind them, it was not a time to relax, which was aimed principally at himself, knowing how easily he could (and had) become blasé at this stage of a momentous climb. He'd relayed via Kevin for Phoebe to try and get the media pumped up, especially during the two days of storm. In the past he'd found that you could not expect them to follow too closely an event that may take a month or two to success or failure. But they did like a short, sharp drama they could follow for a few days if news elsewhere was slack.

With them, it was always the luck of the draw and at this particular time, the Palestinian West Bank was having one of its periodic convolutions, so little else was making the headlines. However, Phoebe had managed to get a couple of the weekly heavies interested, in particular *The Sunday Telegraph* who were keen to run a full article once they were off the mountain.

Their final portaledge site was just where the crack started to make a curving right hand turn. They knew it was only about three more pitches to the summit so after a quick meal they were asleep, aiming to maximise on the next day's daylight. The following day, Rick set off in fine style and had run out a full 200 feet in little over an hour. George joined him and continued to climb through with the angle of the crack now hovering between 75 and 80 degrees to the vertical.

Hugh had packed up the portaledge site and was already approaching the first stance, ready to haul up the first load upon his arrival. The haul bags' weight was now quite manageable, as most of their edible contents had been devoured and the cooking fuel used. They were determined to the point of obsession that everything possible would be removed from the mountain. So far, they had been unable to remove three pitons and also the three bolts they'd used on the large overhang roof. Everything else was either in the haul bags or being used. At one stage they'd even discussed the ethics of leaving behind their faeces but the fact that it was bio-degradable had stopped their removal! So, leaving behind six pieces of unconnected hardware was marginally acceptable in their mentality.

George was becoming intense on all matters photographic. Having skipped a few days on the ascent, he decided that P for Plenty would be his motto and had the camera active most of the time. Good shots were easy to get, especially as their faces graphically showed the effects of twenty days sustained mountaineering at such a high standard.

It wasn't just the fact that their beards had grown, that they were wind and sun burnt, but more in what the eyes had to say. They screamed out 'I've been to the edge! I've looked over! And I'm back!'

With just one more bivouac on the portaledges, they planned to top out the next day. The weather was reasonable, light winds and only the odd spot of rain. Whilst establishing the site, not to over relax was foremost on everyone's mind, all knowing climbers who had done just that and had paid the ultimate price. Food intake that night was limited to porridge oats with sugar followed by the last few bits of the dried fruit. The only drink they had left was powdered orange juice, which went down extra well, knowing that tomorrow it would be water only.

Later, chatting with Kevin, George passed on their intended schedule and anticipated arrival off the mountain. The final three pitches of the climb went well. The wall gently fell back from the vertical and they were soon able to cease using etriers and free climb instead. The other two construed it so that George was the lead climber of the last pitch, which he savoured indeed.

After arriving at the summit dome and first making sure the rope was securely anchored, he sat down and turning his face to the sky whispered, 'Many thanks God. Just one more favour please? Let us get down safely.'

First Hugh and then finally Rick appeared at the top belay point. It was certainly a moment to savour, as grinning from ear to ear they pummelled each other's backs and shook hands in congratulation. It was the ability to freely walk around that they enjoyed the most, after nearly three weeks of continually being clipped in for safety and the only surface to stand on was etriers. A surreal experience indeed.

After working out his bearings, Hugh suggested that he and George run out their three climbing ropes down the south west ridge, in preparation for the descent, whilst Rick brought up the two haul bags. It was still only early evening, the weather was kind and three hours later found them all together again, wriggling into sleeping and bivouac bags for their first night's sleep on terra firma.

Soon after daybreak, they quickly breakfasted and packed, ready to start the series of twenty or more abseils it would need to get them down to where they could walk off. Bringing the two haulage lines into action they quickly evolved a system whereby Hugh acted as the team donkey, with the two haul bags and his own gear strapped across his back. This allowed George and Rick to operate a system of rope retrieval, then its repeat placement for the next abseil descent.

CHAPTER 17

Two days previously, the man positioned himself upwind of the climbers' base, slightly inland from where the beached Avon RIB was dragged up above the fjord high water mark. Here, the steady south westerly breeze would carry any sounds he made away from the camp occupants.

The man arrived shortly before the Arctic dawn and during the last twenty hours he'd remained hidden and virtually motionless in the camouflaged position of a natural hollow between two broken rocky mounds, patiently observing the small dump half a mile away. He had chosen his position with care, above and to one side of the natural route to Ketil and well out of sight from the main camp, 1000 feet above him and close to the start of their climb.

Only one person had entered his zone of vision and that had been Kevin, the oldest of the climbing team. He'd appeared mid-morning and after rummaging around in some kegs, spent an hour or so striding up and down just above the fjord shoreline, in an area of relatively flat and even ground. He seemed to be counting the paces and after twenty-five or so, stopped and, glancing around, then lined himself up before driving in a stake and setting off again.

Once this was finished, he went off to a hollow on one side about a hundred paces away and spent an hour or more prodding a pole into the earth. Finishing whatever task it was, Kevin disappeared by mid-day to the climbing base below Ketil, above which the other three would be locked in their struggle.

One more hour and it would be dark, allowing the man an opportunity to stand up, move about, stretch and loosen tight, aching muscles, before going over to the area where he'd observed Kevin pacing up and down. Darkness would also give him a chance to eat some prepared dry food and drink. Throughout the day, he'd nibbled small pieces of chocolate, cheese, biscuit and raisins from his deep jacket pocket and sipped from a small water bottle. But he needed more bulk and fluids to swell and fill his stomach, also, a chance to dig a small hole and move his bowels, before burying the faeces.

Stifling a yawn the man closed his eyes for ten seconds to allow the gritty feeling to be relieved by the eyes' natural cleaning system. Following arrival at the site after a walk of two miles from where he beached and hid a sea kayak, the man stripped off a sweat dampened vest and donned dry thermal underwear, followed by two layers of thin fleece garments, then he added a medium weight windproof suit. On his feet, the man removed the leather walking boots and changed socks before pulling on a pair of muklet boots. A balaclava and thermal gloves finished off the protection from the elements, with his clothing and equipment coloured black or dark green and brown.

Another reason the man selected a breezy uphill site was to get away from being plagued by the Arctic gnats and on that score the day had passed without too much hindrance. The weather had also been kind, with only one short front passing through earlier with some sleet and now the air temperature was about +2C. As always the greatest danger had been contesting boredom. By mid-afternoon, with Kevin's departure a couple of hours before, he was finding it difficult to keep his eyes open, when he first sensed, then spotted a superb master of the skies, the white tailed sea eagle.

The first sighting of this amazing creature was a mile away at a thousand feet. The biggest breeding bird in Greenland, some had their nests in Tasermiut Fjord, where six eagles had been seen hovering together. Using a small pair of binoculars the man confirmed identification by the distinctive combination of brownish feathers, long neck with a yellow beak and a pure white tail, plus its enormous size, with a body length of three feet and a wing span of eight.

A bird of prey, the adult requires 500-600 grams (1lb 2oz-1lb 5oz) of food a day. It mainly feeds on carrion or fish and it was the latter that he observed it searching for, when after a hover for more than five minutes at a hundred feet, it suddenly swooped and literally tore a fish out from the sanctuary of the fjord surface waters. Gripping it tightly in its talons, the eagle headed down fjord with its supper.

A breeding pair remain in their territory all year, except in areas where the winters are so harsh that they have to leave. The territory is usually between 20 and 50 square miles for a pair, but may be as large as 160 square miles, depending on availability of food and nest sites. The white tailed sea eagle makes use of a number of barking calls, fairly quiet and unimpressive for the size of the bird. The calls are most likely to be heard during the breeding season, and around the times of migration - particularly during the autumn.

The man planned first to look around the dump and Kevin's area of activity and then, based on what he found, would decide whether he stayed until the following night, or disappeared back to the kayak and headed away down fjord.

Thirty minutes after darkness fell the man descended to the area where Kevin had been pacing. There, with the aid of the bright moonlight he searched for and found the markers Kevin had placed. They did not amount to much and were evenly spaced. They outlined an oblong box shaped area that was about 200 yards long by 60 yards wide. The stakes were metal rods two feet long, with their first six inches embedded into the sparse shale and from each, protruded wire tails fitted with short jack plugs.

In the hollow he quickly found what Kevin had been occupied with. It was a small, narrow bore hole about three feet deep and two inches wide. He had a look around the small dump, which besides containing spare cooking gas containers, a sack of empty cans and bottles, plastic storage kegs and a padlocked case marked 'Medical', had little else of interest. Intrigued by what the markers meant and in particular the narrow bore hole, the man decided to stay until the following night. Returning to his observation site, he ate, drank and, curled up in the foetal position, pulled the hood tight around his balaclava and dozed.

~ ~ ~ ~ ~ ~ ~ ~ ~ ~ ~ ~ ~ ~

After first checking his emails and sending the daily morning message to UK and Nanortalik, Kevin concentrated on recalling all of the seismic details that he'd previously tried committing to memory. He'd checked the explosive and detonators yesterday - now all that remained was to place and connect the geophones on the stakes to the embedded tails and run out the leads to the seismometer. Finally he'd link up the seismometer with the Husky laptop, prepare the charge in the bore hole, before setting it off and check the reading had been successfully recorded.

Eric had informed him by email yesterday evening, that both the yacht *Antarctica* and Jake Norris were expected to arrive at Nanortalik in two days time and following an overnight stop, would then head for Ketil. He had suggested that if convenient it would save them time and money if Kevin could place his bulky storage kegs aboard *Antarctica* for the return trip to Nanortalik, rather than him bringing up another RIB. Kevin thanked him and agreed to the suggestion.

This gave the impetus he needed to get the seismic reading out of the way, as progress on Ketil also meant the lads probably returning down soon. Packing everything he needed into a small rucsac, he set off down to the lower dump and marvelled at the glorious day, with the ever-changing contrast and interplay between the sky, cloud, mountain and sea fjord. It always blew him away and added a spring to his step, so that in no time at all he arrived at the lower dump, hard by the beached Avon RIB.

Humming a favourite tune, he quickly opened the medical box and laid out the explosive charge. This was cylindrical in shape, three inches long and half an inch thick. He would use 'end initiation' for the detonator and using a pencil, made an inch deep hole in the centre of one end that would allow him to slide in the detonator, without any undue pressure. Inserting the detonator was always the most dangerous aspect of handling explosives and he would only complete this final step when all else was laid out and ready to go.

The man blinked his eyes wide open and mentally shrank his body as Kevin swung into view, descending from the upper camp. He watched intently through his small binoculars as Kevin first opened the medical box and then laid out wires, mushroom shaped cones and a sausage shaped section, in brown wrapping. At this, his mind clicked 'explosive' as his brain went into over-drive, linking-up the marker stakes and the big oblong shape, with the bore hole in the hollow. It was only when he spotted the geophones being placed in position on each stake, then connected with wires trailing back first to a box then onto a laptop computer, did he consider it was anything else but an eccentric Brit doing his thing.

In the recess of his memory, the man dragged forward an image of a film, or maybe a magazine article about oil exploration and the use of seismology. Was Kevin doing a seismic survey? What else could it be? Why here? Who for? The unanswered questions rattled through his mind as he actively absorbed the unfolding scene.

Methodically Kevin went about placing the geophones in position, switching each on, before linking them into the seismometer and then the Husky. Finally taking the charge to the bore hole, he carefully fitted the detonator securely into position and gently lowered it down, before slowly introducing soil around it and the firing wire.

With a small piece of wood he gently and slowly 'tamped' the soil down, initially around the charge and then on top of it to the surface. Filling a sandbag with earth and rocks he placed it on top, its weight to contain the explosion. Finally, he took the firing wire away from the bore hole and moved with it 25 yards away behind a rocky outcrop. Systematically he unpacked the small hand generator from his rucsac and connected in the two firing wires. A pause of five seconds to confirm all was set right and he depressed the handle.

Simultaneously a dull thump, immediately followed by a sharp crack rent the air, as the sandbag momentarily lifted. It was all over and Kevin could not resist yelling out a loud 'Yes!'

Kneeling down at the Husky laptop he checked that the seismometer reading had registered in the programme, especially set up for the task. It had indeed. 'Job done!' he thought, striding forward to where thin tendrils of smoke wafted out from the canvas remains, before being blown away. Inspecting his handiwork at the bore hole, he methodically removed all unnatural traces, placing all the wires and equipment back into his rucsac.

The man was concentrating hard on remembering every thing he saw, at the same time trying to keep very still and ensure no sounds were generated, nor attention attracted by an inadvertent glint of sun on his binoculars or watch face. From Kevin's body language he could sense that the results had been favourable, as he watched him gather in all the items he'd laid out earlier. At one stage he caught a word or two of a cheerful song being sung by Kevin, whisked his way on the breeze.

By late morning Kevin had completed his task and sat on the medical kit box facing the man as he spoke into a radio, probably to the climbers on the face. Earlier, the man had scanned the face with his binoculars trying to catch sight of them, but to no avail, as they were now on the final summit ledges and out of view. Finishing his conversation, Kevin made a quick check that everything was packed away at the dump and walked on down to inspect the Avon RIB and its various fuel bags. Happy with what he found and hitching on the rucsac, he strode purposefully away uphill, back to the climbing camp.

The man now had eleven hours to wait in his lair until darkness came and the opportunity to move and return to his sea kayak. What he'd witnessed more than kept his mind busy as lying prone he wracked his brain deciding the options available. One of the rewards for staying so quiet and still arrived for the man a few hours later, when a small herd of musk ox slowly hove into view. He counted eleven all told, as they steadily moved parallel with the fjord shoreline, grazing on the short arctic grasses, sedges and reeds.

This group looked to consist of a dominant bull, three or four females and their young. The bull would have driven off the other adult males to form a harem. The males driven out form bachelor groups or individually roam in search of another group where they might be able to achieve dominant status.

He had been watching intently for a while, when he noticed that another full grown bull had joined the group. ' 'This could get interesting,' the man whispered to himself, as at first the herd bull seemed to take little or no interest in the new comer. It took about an hour for the dominant bull to show his displeasure at the newcomer, when quite suddenly with a series of loud bellows, he ran twenty yards and head butted him at full speed. The newcomer tried to counter, but he'd already lost any impetus and snorting his frustration, loped off into the distance, leaving the dominant bull to circle his harem possessively.

The man thought about what he knew of the musk ox which, because of their instincts of forming a circle in response to danger, had proved very easy prey to hunters armed with rifles. The Inuit populations have utilised musk ox hide, meat and horns for centuries and limited hunting permits were still issued for their sole use. Musk ox hides were traded in Canada until 1917 when the Canadian government first passed protection legislation. The species was once on the brink of extinction, being saved by effective conservation management programmes and the worldwide herd is now estimated at 66,000-85,000 individuals.

Their common name refers to the strong odour emitted by the males during the breeding season, which reaches its peak in mid-August. Gestation is around eight to nine months with a single calf being born anytime from May to June, with the calf being weaned after a year, though it may eat vegetation as quickly as a week after birth.

Musk ox has a very distinct appearance that cannot be confused with any other creature. They have dark brown to black fur that is very cold resistant, the thick guard hairs nearly touch the ground and protect a very dense, woolly inner layer that is shed in the spring. The legs and top of the back are paler than the rest of the body. The neck and shoulders are relatively short, giving it a stocky appearance and both sexes have long curving horns that meet at the centre of the head and grow down the side of the jaws. The male horns are considerably more massive than the female.

Musk ox also has a specialised young protection behaviour pattern. When threatened by wolves, or humans, members of the group circle around the young, facing the predators with their heads down and large adults will usually come out of this circle to chase off the threat.

Watching as they peacefully grazed, the man felt he was a privileged observer of nature's cycle. This also included mankind as an active participant, despite human attempts to destroy their own habitat. The wild urge to demolish nature seemed to isolate modern homo sapiens from all other inhabitants of the planet Earth. He asked himself, what other animal poisons its water and food supplies, then pollutes its own air, enough to threaten its existence?

As the evening light darkened, and seeing no further movement from Kevin, the man carefully made his way to where he'd hidden the sea kayak. The moon was three-quarters full, with only a few scattered clouds and a barely discernible wind.

Locating the site, he quietly watched it from the limits of night visibility for ten minutes to ensure he had not attracted any followers, before returning the kayak to the fjord and embarked for a night paddle south west, towards Nanortalik.

CHAPTER 18

The same afternoon in Nanortalik, Eric watched with interest as the exploration yacht *Antarctica* was busily tied up alongside the wharf. She was an unusual sight for a 102-foot long two-mast schooner, coloured gun metal grey with a slightly battered, rugged working appearance and a large observation perspex bubble forward of the small dog-house. For a yacht she had an exceptionally wide beam, like the vessel *Fram* built in the 1890s for Nansen, the Norwegian explorer, for his epic attempt on the North Pole.

Both were designed for wintering in the Polar seas where, with her retractable keel and rudder, she would be pushed up to ride above any sea ice and not be crushed. *Antarctica* was built in 1991 to French Naval specifications, which included a triple plated aluminium hull. Since then, she had spent her years as a privately funded environmental research vessel, visiting various segments of both the Arctic and Antarctica, linking with the world media to publicise the need to protect these special places. Her permanent crew numbered four, and she could embark another eight crew and/or scientists, media or sponsor representatives for a total sea going complement of twelve.

'Good day mate,' yelled a tall, wiry sailor from the cockpit on *Antarctica*. Eric had decided he was probably the skipper by his aptitude and possession of the wheel as they had docked.

'Good day to you. Eric is my name - and what's yours?'

'Mike,' came the reply. 'Our office told me you would probably meet us and I'll be with you once we are secured.'

Two of the crew vaulted ashore and were busily getting the ropes into position on the wharf mooring bollards. They quickly secured fore and aft, followed by amidships, before turning their attention to establishing a gangway. Once in position Mike switched off the engine and made his way towards Eric, with an open smile and out reached hand.

'Pleased to meet you Eric. It's nice to be here,' he said in a soft Australian accent.

Grasping Mike's knurled hand, Eric warmly replied, 'Welcome to Nanortalik! How's the trip been?'

Smiling in memory Mike replied, 'Mainly good, except for one hairy episode just off northern Newfoundland.'

'What happened there?' Eric enquired.

Taking a deep breath, Mike answered, 'We'd been up the St Laurence as far as Quebec on a media jaunt and were crossing the Gulf of St Lawrence to slip through the Strait of Belle Isle, which separates the island from Newfoundland proper and then into the Labrador Sea and across to here. Jim and I were on early night watch, when without warning the steering failed, just as we are doing twenty knots under a strong following wind. We had all practised for this event - but always in daylight - and we knew it was not going to be easy to deal with that night.

'The channel is about five miles wide and we were running downwind fast, so we had to try to get the yacht to turn into wind by just using the sails before it could turn the other way and crash gybe. We managed to do this just in the nick of time, but it was a shock, as you don't realise just how real it is until you find yourself manning the wheel and turning it as nothing happens!

'It took us a few minutes to get the yacht hove to, where she was more stable and comfortable in the huge sea. Then we had to start dismantling the whole of the back end of the yacht to get access to the steering cable, the likely fault. It took us two hours to fix the steering in the horrible weather. The bulldog clamps had slipped and needed replacing, but the only way to them was head first under the decking. John and Chris managed to get there by being upside down.

'There were still waves crashing right over the yacht while they were performing handstands, so they did a brilliant job in the circumstances.' Mike pausing for breath before continuing, 'My other worry was that we were also running out of time, as we were now sailing back towards the northern coast of Newfoundland which was only four miles away and we could not see anything in the dark. We could have tacked and heaved to in the other direction, but this would have been very much harder for the guys to fix the steering, so it was touch and go whether we would get it fixed in time before we got too close for my liking.

'In the end we came within three miles of the shore, and I would have tacked at two, so we only had probably ten to fifteen minutes left when the job was completed. It took us an hour to rebuild the back end of the yacht and make sure that we were happy with it all before we could think about going down below again!'

'Wow! What a tale!' Eric replied before asking, 'How would you all like to join me for supper tonight at the Seaman's Hostel and enjoy some good local home cooking?'

'That would be most welcome!' Mike replied. 'I was going to ask if there were any spare rooms available for a night, after we have looked at the steering gear again.'

'Yes I thought that might be the case,' said Eric, 'I've asked Nauja to expect you all for at least one. We'll complete the necessary arrival formalities and then when you're ready I'll take you round.'

A couple of hours later Jake Norris was waiting in the hostel foyer for their arrival, introducing himself as they boisterously signed in and sorted out their rooms for the night.

'Once you're organised, join me for a beer in the lounge,' he suggested. Within thirty minutes the five of them were back in the lounge, each busily sinking down a cold Carlsberg beer, luxuriating in being on terra firma again as only a professional sailor knows how.

Mike repeated the story of their mini epic with the broken steering gear, in reply to which, Jake made what he hoped were sufficient conciliatory remarks to show his concern. Eric then joined them and after introducing Nauja suggested that they laid siege of the dining room, to do justice to the splendid supper prepared for them. Needing no further encouragement, the group quickly moved to the adjoining room and under Nauja's guidance settled down to their first real meal since Quebec City, five days earlier. Two hours later, Eric made his farewells and promised to see them off mid-morning.

By now Jake felt he was quite accepted, having explained to Mike in detail what he hoped to achieve with his commissioned article and photographs. Mike was no stranger to Quark Expeditions in Antarctica, having met the Russian ships under charter a number of times at various anchorage sites on the Antarctic Peninsular.

The Quark Expedition leader would usually invite them aboard to give an interest presentation to the assembled passengers, invariably wealthy retired North American and European couples, with a smattering of other nationalities. They would stay onboard for a long hot shower, a scrumptious meal, plus hospitality in the well stocked bar. This was always a good opportunity to 'network' amongst the Quark passengers and spread the word about their mission.

By now everyone was showing signs of tiredness, with first one then another heading sleepily to their rooms, until only Mike and Jake remained, finishing off a final six pack left by Nauja before she also departed with a smiling wave.

The next morning, with breakfast over, the well-rested crew eagerly prepared *Antarctica* for the short visit to Ketil. Fresh bread, eggs, fruit and vegetables were loaded, in addition to the topping up of drinking water and diesel. Jake asked to add slabs of beer and boxes of wine to help them celebrate with the Brits their climbing success.

Eric called by to see them off and confirmed the VHF radio channels, reminding them that Arne, the shepherd at Tasiussaq would also be monitoring. As they swung away under engine power from the wharf, Eric and Nauja waved farewell as dancing 'white tops' were visible in the main fjord.

CHAPTER 19

Once *Antarctica* had cleared the harbour and entered the fjord, Mike asked for the foresail to be set on half reef, which with the following wind and still under engine power, gave them a comfortable ten knots. Even though the fjord was two miles wide, following the catastrophic steering breakdown, he was not taking any chances and stayed firm in the cockpit, keeping a close eye on the depth sounder and all the other instruments.

The available charts were basic and Eric had kindly marked out known and potential danger areas of rocks lurking in shallow waters, which were mainly near Tasiussaq. Mike decided that unless essential, he would avoid venturing there. With a dozen or more swooping sea petrels for company they bobbed along, transfixed by the magnificent vista that evolved as steep mountainsides met flat green ice free sea, with puffy white clouds nosing into snowy peaks.

Jake concentrated on taking head and shoulder photographs of the crew, using the yacht's presence amongst the majestic panorama as an out of focus backdrop. They posed with good naturered humour, as he asked them to organise ropes, operate the sail winches, man the deck steering wheel, or gaze at the ever-changing scenery.

Mugs of coffee were passed around and John confirmed he would soon prepare them a snack lunch of salad rolls, cheese and fruit. The hours passed swiftly and soon they were passing Tasiussaq with a quick radio call to check in with Arne. He was out of the hamlet, busily visiting sick sheep on the mountainside, but carried a mobile VHF radio set with him.

After enquiring if they had enjoyed good hospitality at Nanortalik he went on to say over a crackling link, 'Have a good trip and do give my congratulations to Kevin and the rest of the boys. See you all on the way back!'

They made an anchorage 50 metres off shore from where the Avon RIB was beached and using three separate lines secured *Antarctica* to well driven-in metal stakes ashore, in addition to lowering the drag anchor. Any anchorage in a narrow fjord was never totally safe from the potentially catastrophic and destructive effects of a massive katabatic wind occurring when a sloping ground surface cools during the night. The air in contact with the ground is cooled by radiation, increases in density and flows down hill. The large daily ground temperature change in areas of permanent ice fields and high mountains can generate serious gale force winds in a very short period of time.

Mike and the crew had been subjected to such a blast, just off the Fortuna Glacier on South Georgia Island. Luckily, owing to her sturdy design and build *Antarctica* weathered the storm; even so it was altogether a most terrifying experience for all on board, as she was nearly pushed over onto her side.

Whilst the crew was busily making safe, Kevin arrived and lent a hand until Mike was totally happy they were as secure as possible.

'Good to see you,' Mike exclaimed as he shook Kevin's outstretched hand before asking, 'What news of the team upstairs?'

'They are making excellent progress and will top out this evening, spend the night near the summit and then abseil down the West Ridge tomorrow, hopefully getting down by nightfall,' replied Kevin.

'Come on board and we'll chat there,' invited Mike as he pushed out and held the Zodiac for Kevin to manoeuvre safely into. Scrambling up *Antarctica's* short stern ladder, he was met by Jake who after introducing himself led the way forward to the enclosed dog house, stepping down a short section into the entrance to the galley and main saloon.

This was a warm, well-furnished and spacious area, deliberately designed so that an over-wintering crew on the polar sea ice had enough room to move about in comfort and keep some personal space. Most of the ceiling consisted of a thick perspex dome, which allowed the maximum amount of available light to pass through, a vital aspect for polar winters. For this time of the year, with bright sunlight 20 hours a day, screens had been rigged to cut some of the light out.

Easing himself behind the main table, Kevin accepted a mug of fresh coffee, revelling in being able to sit comfortably, in solid surroundings. Jake introduced himself and whilst Kevin mentally dragged forward details about his background, he asked, 'How's the climbing been going?'

Kevin responded, 'From what I've gathered over the radio they've had their moments - water shortages being their biggest single concern. At one stage they were down to half a litre each, when thank goodness it rained and sleeted for twenty-four hours solid.'

'They should have got some magnificent photography,' Jake suggested.

'Unfortunately it's about the last thing you're thinking about,' laughed Kevin, 'With so much to do every waking minute to maintain safe progress, usually I get to remember once every couple of days, have an orgy of snapping everything in sight and then the camera is tucked safely away until the next time.'

'Hopefully the guys won't mind my doing some head and shoulder shots once they're down and possibly a group shot with Ketil as a backdrop?' Jake asked.

'Give them an hour first to get hydrated and fed, otherwise they might be just a wee bit uncooperative,' laughed Kevin in reply as Mike, John and Chris joined them with steaming mugs of coffee.

'Well that's about as safe as she can be I guess,' remarked Mike, before he continued, 'We are really looking forward to spending a couple of days here, having a walk, stretching the legs and getting some mountain air into the lungs. We'll always keep someone on board to monitor the radio and keep an eye on things - otherwise we are open to all offers you may have for us to help.'

'You can add me to that,' offered Jake.

'That's certainly welcome,' replied Kevin, 'I know the lads will appreciate handing over all the gear once they are down for a carry to base. I should hear on the evening call when they anticipate that will be. I estimate they'll be topping out any time now, getting down by tomorrow night.'

Kevin spent the remainder of the evening very amicably indeed, as they all found common ground as adventurous participants in the rich tapestry of events that life had presented to them. As anticipated, a radio call came through from George just as darkness fell to announce they had cracked the route, were on a large flat summit block the size of a house and walking round unroped, the first time for 20 long days.

'Best wait until we're all down safe before sending any reports to UK,' George quietly said, the emotion of relief recognisable in his voice. 'We'll try and join you as fast as possible. Hugh has already fixed three 200 foot ropes ready for an early start and we have another two more and plenty of hardware to use beyond that.'

'That all sounds pretty positive,' answered Kevin. 'As you will have noticed we have *Antarctica* for company and the lads will be ready to porter everything from the bottom.'

'Aye! She certainly looks a grand sight from here,' replied George, 'please pass my best regards to Mike and his crew and I look forward to meeting everyone tomorrow. Go easy with the rum!'

'Roger to that, I'll try,' said Kevin, 'have a good night's sleep - out.'

'They certainly seem pretty positive,' Mike observed, 'I guess most accidents tend to happen on the way down when everyone's tired, the gear's pretty hammered and a downward momentum exacerbates any slip or drop of gear.'

'Twenty four hours from now it should all be over bar the telling of the tale,' replied Kevin, 'these boys will not take any chances even for the fresh food and wine that you'll be forcing down them.'

'Talking of which,' said Mike 'let's see what the galley can come up with tonight for supper, starting with some leek and potato soup perhaps?'

~ ~

The man had keenly observed the area from the mountainside, in particular the moored yacht for nearly an hour. He'd arrived with the darkness, by which time music, voices and laughter issued from *Antarctica*. There was a little breeze as he made his way slowly and quietly to the beached Avon RIB, where he spent fifty or so minutes carefully substituting a fuel bag with the one carried in his rucsac. Once satisfied it was in position, firmly coupled to the outboard engine's fuel line for immediate use, he slowly and with great deliberation replaced the port side hand-rail with a substitute which was an identical twin, but the new one had a coated copper wire antenna pain-stakingly woven into its fabric, indiscernible to casual inspection.

Offshore, the merriment aboard *Antarctica* declined to low voices and soul music. For the man there was only one minor moment of tension when a crew member appeared, first to urinate overboard, before checking out the anchor cable and mooring lines. Satisfied, he returned below decks and five minutes later most of the cabin lights were dowsed and silence finally reigned.

The man cautiously took the thin wires protruding from both the fuel bag and the handrail cord, binding them securely together before water-proofing the join with tape and placing it out of sight beneath the floor decking. Ensuring all evidence of his presence was removed; he quietly slipped away into the darkness of the night.

~ ~

Kevin awoke just before a quiet wind-less dawn and spent his next five minutes stretching luxuriously in the gently swaying bunk on *Antarctica* whilst running over in his mind the sequence of what would probably be happening today. First he made a check-call on his VHF radio blindly into the ether to ensure George was not waiting to contact him. Hearing nothing in reply, he quickly dressed, visited the heads and wash room for a quick wash and scrub of the teeth, before joining Mike in the galley

'Morning Kevin,' grinned Mike, 'coffee or tea? Have a good sleep?'

'Sure did,' replied Kevin, 'after three weeks in a tent on a sleeping mat the bunk was heaven.'

'Yes I'll bet,' laughed Mike, turning to fill a tea pot and coffee caf-fatiere that he placed on the mess table with mugs, milk and sugar before continuing, 'please help yourself and I'll rustle up some breakfast - will bacon and eggs be OK?'

'Is the Pope a Catholic?' Kevin laughed a retort.

Whilst demolishing their breakfasts, Mike casually suggested that should the team, want he was more than happy that they and their gear came onto *Antarctica* as his guests and travelled back with them to Nanortalik. Kevin considered for a moment to satisfy himself that Mike's offer was not being made under any moral pressure, before read-ily accepting.

'That means I can follow in the RIB and use her for any photography shots you want making by Jake,' suggested Kevin. 'They should be quite startling.'

'I could not help over-hearing the last,' Jake quietly added appearing from below, he slipped behind the mess table before continuing, 'It'll be a real bonus to get some shots of *Antarctica* with the fabulous back drop of the mountains from a sea level perspective.'

Kevin's radio crackled into life with George's voice, confirming having had a sound, restful night and that they had already started the decent. He anticipated they would get off late that evening and whooped agreement when Kevin mentioned Mike's offer of boarding *Antarctica* upon their return. Kevin went on to say that he would now pack up the base camp and back load it all to the shoreline for final packing before loading everything onto the yacht. With cries of 'take care,' and 'see you later,' they rang off.

Any meal taken together by the whole crew on a yacht whilst at anchor is always a unique occurrence, as once she is underway the duty watch on deck can only snack at their stations. Being all together, whilst also entertaining guests brought out their best behaviour and displayed their ability to converse over a whole range of subjects, other than sailing *Antarctica*.

They were of course more than happy to spend every waking moment talking of nothing else, but as a courtesy to both Kevin and Jake encouraged them to take the lead. All well travelled, they quickly found areas of common interest, usually centred on odd happenings in foreign parts when lack of the appropriate language and knowledge of local customs produced hilarious outcomes. Needless to say alcohol consumption and women were invariably involved.

Mike's background was fascinating, as not only was he a yacht skipper and old Antarctica hand, he'd initiated a unique drug rehabilitation project set up as a charity for young Australian people based near Melbourne. He used a yacht, as a floating classroom and those joining the programme on first coming aboard had to surrender all their stash of drugs to Mike's control.

He would issue their individual doses whilst introducing them to the wonders of crewing a yacht in the Southern Ocean, slowly building their trust, confidence and self-esteem, whilst at the same time lessening the dose and gradually carrying out a personalised agreed detoxification programme. Trips would usually last about twenty days and his success rate of turning them away from drug abuse was a staggering 70%. Mike remarked that while dealing with young addicts was quite simple - raising the necessary cash was the difficult bit!

This led them on to discussing the highly complex subject of attracting funding for any adventurous activity and how looking after sponsors' media interests sometimes conflicted with them safely achieving their aim. Concerned that the twists and turns of this conversation could tie him down all day, Kevin asked to be excused so as to dismantle the base camp and ferry it down to the shoreline. Mike, Jim and Chris had some engine maintenance to undertake, but both John and Jake suggested that later they would follow Kevin up the hill and help carry the loads down.

'Many hands make light work,' observed Jake, 'it also gives me a chance to get some wide angle area shots, looking down on Antarctica.'

'That's great,' agreed Kevin as he rose to leave, 'I'll get on my way and meet up with you guys later.'

'I'll run you ashore,' said Mike moving out of the way and following him topside readied the Zodiac before saying, 'Give me a call on Channel 16 if you need anything,' as they motored the short distance to the shingle beach.

After Mike dropped him off, Kevin walked back up to the base camp, where first he set up the satcom and laptop to concoct and send his morning message to the UK. After that, he spoke direct to Eric in Nanortalik explaining the current situation with George and his plan to accept Mike's offer of a lift back to Nanortalik.

'That is good news all round,' Eric replied. 'It'll save you some money and also I have to be here tomorrow to meet a government minister, I'll let Arne know your plan and would ask that you please book-in with him en-route past.'

'Roger to that, and we look forward to thanking you properly for all the assistance when we get back,' replied Kevin.

'My pleasure,' said Eric. 'The office here will monitor your movements back and make the necessary helicopter and flight bookings, as they are beginning to fill up. I take it you will want to spend one night here in Nanortalik?'

'Correct,' Kevin answered, 'passing through too quickly will have a bad negative effect on the lads' re-acclimatisation after all that time on Ketil, plus it would be bad manners not to let Nauja pamper us all again!' Chuckling in reply, Eric said he'd ensure she knew of their appreciation and after reminding him again to contact Arne when passing, he rang off.

For Kevin the next few hours sped past, as he dismantled and packed-up the base camp, keeping an ear open to the VHF radio and one eye on Ketil hoping to catch any glimpses of the team descending. It was a perfect day, with hazy sunshine breaking through, a light sea breeze blowing and no storm clouds in sight.

At mid-day George called and reported all was going well and that they were making excellent progress. He anticipated being down off the face by about 8pm, which would still leave a few of hours of daylight if they were delayed. Lack of water was his only concern, as with the dry weather for the last three days, they were running short again.

Soon after, first Mike then Jake appeared, the latter festooned with cameras, light meters and a small tripod. Kevin flashed up a stove and produced hot water for drinks whilst Jake set up the tripod and searched for his wide angle shots. John meanwhile was sorting the various items of camp gear into equal looking loads and then filling three rucsacs ready for carrying down to the shoreline.

'I guess if we leave soon we'll be down by 5pm,' observed Kevin, 'time then for a short break before getting back up to meet George and the boys coming off.'

'Hopefully there'll still be light left to get some decent head shots,' Jake remarked, 'I can imagine how their faces will be looking and I must capture it.'

'I wouldn't be too demanding if I were you,' mused Kevin. 'The lads have been just a tad stretched for twenty days and may not appreciate a camera lens shoved in their faces. I would suggest you first let me explain who you are and what you are after before even showing one.'

'Thanks for that,' Jake replied. 'Yes I guess my Yankee enthusiasm can get the better of me some days. I'll take my lead from you.'

Kevin next scoured the site to make sure everything was packed and keeping a bag of crushed cans and non-combustible wrappings until last, he ensured no sign of their presence was left. Shortly after, Jake pronounced he'd got the shots he wanted and they loaded up the rucsacs and headed off down towards *Antarctica* where they ferried the gear aboard.

It was not until later in the afternoon, as they made their return journey that Kevin spotted the climbers abseiling down the last few pitches of the south east buttress, adjacent to the main face. Even at a distance he could ascertain a sense of weariness in their steady but sure movements, with no doubt each one concentrating hard, totally conscious that mountaineering accidents usually happen late in the day, as tired climbers made their descent.

Another thirty minutes steady walk brought the reception team to where George, Rick and Hugh would arrive. Hugh was the first down the final abseil, shouting a greeting as he arrived, a wide smile breaking through a wind burnt, bearded face, with eyes that were noticeably sunken and strained. 'Hi guys! Would you have any spare fluids with you please? I'm just a mite dry,' he croaked, reaching forward as Kevin produced one of three flasks he was carrying for them filled with warm fruit juice and sugar.

'Thought you might be,' Kevin said as he watched a grateful Hugh empty the first flask in record time and handing him another added, 'There's plenty more for the others so fill your boots!' Sensing an impatient Jake fiddling with his camera settings he quickly made the introductions and asked if it was OK that he took some close-up shots?

'Not a problem pal,' replied a more relaxed looking Hugh. 'I would suggest that we keep an eye out for George and Rick, as they may well jettison the spare ropes on the last pitch. Ah! here comes Rick now with the haulage bag,' he cried as another climber swung into view carrying a large bulky oblong container on his back. On Rick's arrival they went through the same routine of fluid exchange and introductions, with Jake moving to get his close-ups from as many angles as possible.

A massive cry of 'Below!' rent the air as George let gravity take over the arrival of their spare ropes at the bottom of the buttress. They were noisily followed by George who reached eagerly for the outstretched flask of fluid and drank deeply, before shaking Kevin and Jake's hands and then pronouncing with a grin, 'Gentlemen! We have knocked the bastard off!'

CHAPTER 20

Recovering the gear whilst the trio hydrated, Kevin and John quickly got the loads sorted to give the three climbers the lightest rucsacs. Jake eased the triumphant trio into a tight group and took some excellent posed shots of them together peering and gesticulating at the route and then head on of happy smiling faces, grinning with relief into the lens.

'Don't let them tell you different,' George said to Kevin, 'but that was the hardest climb I've ever done in my life - absolutely mind boggling exposure for three whole weeks. It gives a whole new meaning to being a fly on a wall and we suffered, boy did we suffer!'

'Mainly from George's cooking!' cried Rick, making sure he was out of reach. 'What he does with a dehydrated lamb hotpot defeats any digestive system.'

They continued in the same vein as they shouldered their loads and set off down to *Antarctica* arriving at the Zodiac still with an hour of daylight spare. En-route Kevin brought them up to date on the arrangements he'd made with Mike and Eric, which met with everyone's total approval. He also explained that the satcom was set up onboard ready for them to each make a call home, before tucking into a meal of steak, eggs and salad with fresh fruit to follow.

'Am I right in remembering that UK is three hours ahead of us?' asked George and seeing Kevin's nod, he went on, 'I'll send a quick email for Phoebe to read first thing and follow that up with a voice call tomorrow morning before we sail.'

'Yes I'm sure she will appreciate not being woken in the early hours to hear about your piles,' Hugh bantered cheerfully, 'I'll dive into a shower first and then rejoin the human race.'

'You'll find your spare clothes bag on separate bunks,' Kevin explained as they plodded the last kilometre to the shoreline. 'Mike has already allocated them, so we all have the maximum amount of room to get ourselves sorted.' Approaching the Avon, a figure detached himself from tinkering with the engine and walked to meet them.

It was Mike, with an outstretched hand and a beaming smile, 'Welcome guys and I understand congratulations are in order,' he said shaking each of the climbers' hands as they arrived. 'Stick your gear on the Zodiac and we'll soon have you aboard, where everything is ready for you.'

'Kevin has explained all that you have done and it is much appreciated,' said George as they clambered aboard.

'Our pleasure. It's not everyday we meet a team who have just made a world first and will soon be famous - so relax and enjoy our hospitality!' laughed Mike in reply as they drew up alongside *Antarctica*. 'John and Chris will sort out your bunks and explain the shower and head system. I suggest we all then meet in the galley once you've dumped your gear and I'll have a beer ready!'

Five minutes later found each of them delving into cans of chilled Heineken as Mike went over the safety aspects of living aboard *Antarctica* especially in respect to fire. He explained the sailing plan for the next day and how the crew would like them to become involved with manning the ship during the estimated ten hours transit to Nanortalik.

'Once we get underway,' he explained, 'I'll run through the 'man overboard' drill and I'd ask you to familiarise yourself with the location of the life jackets whilst I get supper on the go. Is steak, eggs, bread and salad OK?'

With a resounding cheer the trio affirmed their agreement and after quickly checking out the life jackets with John, they spent the next two hours in the relative opulence of the mess area under the transparent dome by galley. Here, the bountiful food prepared by Jim, plenty of cold beer, combined with a totally relaxed manner, produced a happy pleasant and calm atmosphere.

Jake quietly snapped away, keeping in his assumed character, without upsetting anyone and it was late in the evening before Kevin eased a weary and slightly inebriated George into the bottom bunk of a cabin they were to share. George managed to get his trainers off before falling back into his bunk and with a long sigh went into a deep slumber, snoring gently with small contented moans. Kevin laid back, checked the passport security pouch with Henry's computer disc was secure around his waist and closing his eyes, congratulated himself on a job well done, before he too slipped off into sleep.

Chris quietly produced mugs of sweet tea at 6am and by 7.30 everyone was washed, breakfasted, working topside or queuing to use the satellite phone to call home. The weather had become overcast with a steady south west wind blowing and some rainy squalls promised later.

Kevin launched and made ready the Avon RIB with assistance from Jake who would accompany him, before checking out the engine was working OK and both lent Chris and John a hand as they disengaged the three shore-lines and anchor stakes. They tied up the RIB alongside the rear ladder and boarded to have a confirmatory chat with Mike, fit dry suits, and grab some snack bars and to fill a flask with coffee for the journey.

'I'll aim to maintain six knots depending on wind speed and direction. Will that be OK with you?' Mike asked Kevin.

'I should think so and I'll travel astern on your port side when Jake does not want any particular shots,' Kevin replied.

'The forecast is pretty much as we have now, so it'll be a good idea to stay within a couple of hundred metres,' said Mike.

'Affirmative to that and we'll see you later,' answered Kevin as he and Jake took their leave whilst Mike made preparations for lifting the drag anchor.

In the RIB, Kevin ran up the twin outboard engines, checked the fuel bag connections and secured their items of gear before getting as comfortable as possible, whilst taking station ahead of *Antarctica* where Jake could get wide angle shots of the anchor lift and setting of foresail, with a forbidding Ketil and threatening inland icecap as a background.

'That will certainly wet any jaded appetite,' Jake laughed confidently as he changed and secured used film before continuing, 'It would be real cute to get a series of her as she sails by. Is it be possible to hold station for a while?'

'Can do!' replied Kevin, skillfully manoeuvring as requested, enjoying fully both the freedom and responsibility that being a RIB coxswain bestows.

The next couple of hours passed quickly, especially for George aboard *Antarctica*. He'd already spoken with Phoebe, soon after she had arisen in a warm and sunny Peak District. It had been wonderful to hear her loving voice telling him how much she'd missed him and could hardly wait for his homecoming. She would relay his immediate post climb report first to the British Heart Foundation and then Reuters for distribution. After which it was on to his literary agent for a separate dialogue, concentrating on what words to use, with what emphasise during any forthcoming interviews prior to arrival back in UK.

Hugh and Rick spent the morning working on the laptop, recording all the key facts of dates, times, heights, the route difficulties and climbing solutions which, because of the constraints they'd been under during the climb, were mainly in their memories. Once a base line was established the details quickly followed, so that by late morning they'd adjourned topside for a welcome break from the small screen. Sheltered by the doghouse it was a perfect day to relax and watch the constantly changing interplay between the sky, yacht, sea, mountain and cloud.

Picking up binoculars Hugh made a sweep around the peaks on the port bow and concentrated on a sight any red blooded ornithologist would give their right arm for. One kilometre away a magnificent pair of large birds slowly circled the fjord, riding the air currents in an effortless display of their natural supremacy to man.

'Wow!' he exclaimed, 'does anyone know what species they are?'

'Yes!' replied Chris, 'they are known as white tailed sea eagles and are breeding here again after nearly becoming extinct a few years ago' he said, going on to explain that the pair were waiting patiently aloft to spot a fish, lured by the brighter waters near the surface. As if by prior arrangement one tipped into a steep dive and before reaching the fjord magically slowed down sufficiently to allow just its outstretched talons to hook into its quarry and gripping tightly carry it away. Its partner continued to maintain a vigil for its reward.

CHAPTER 21

The sea eagle surveyed the two boats in its view below. One a tall, sea going monster with seven humans crawling all over her and the other a smaller oblong shape with only two humans aboard. He saw first the flash of intense light, as a huge angry fireball of orange and yellow flame replaced where the smaller boat had been. As he swooped urgently away, next came a violent blast that hurled him furiously across the sky for two or three seconds, before a massive bang exploded all around. He automatically sped off extremely shaken in the opposite direction, attempting to get as far away as possible from the scene.

As he flew over where the mountainside met the fjord he would normally have seen the human squatting in the broken, rocky ground. But this time, an in-built survival system had closed down all brain aspects not needed for escape from immediate danger.

In the RIB, Kevin was leaning forward to ease a small ache in his lower back muscles when the coded electronic pulse found the copper wire aerial on his right side and sped off down to trigger initiation of the detonator encased in high explosive inside the half full fuel bag. Jake was three feet away on his starboard side, fussing over camera settings, when like Kevin, he too was blown into hundreds of pieces, as the detonation trail smashed into them, before the exploding fuel vapourised most of their remains at temperatures of 750 degrees centigrade.

Mike instinctively turned *Antarctica* hard to starboard as the RIB exploded with a mighty boom. He screamed for the foresail to be lowered and the Zodiac to be launched as he opened up the throttle and made a wide sweep in clear water to ascertain any immediate danger to his vessel. Jim and Chris were nearest to the foresail and had it down and secured in record time, as John used a halyard to haul up and swing the Zodiac from its position at the stern, with its outboard engine and fuel bags already secured inside, ready for an immediate launch.

Jim returned to the doghouse and monitored the radios and instruments, whilst Chris joined John to help launch the Zodiac if required. Circling the blazing molten mass floating on the surface that a moment before had been the RIB, they all knew survival of its two occupants was highly unlikely, especially as they closed in and could see small body bits amongst the debris.

'Nanortalik this is *Antarctica*! We have an emergency! An emergency! Over,' cried Mike into the VHF.

'*Antarctica* this is Nanortalik. We read you loud and clear - what is your emergency? Over,' Eric calmly replied.

Mike went on, 'The Ketil Expedition RIB with Kevin and Jake has just blown up and the chances of any survivors is nil, I repeat nil. Over.'

'Roger to that - what is your position?' requested Eric.

'60 degrees 17 minutes north, 44 degrees 40 minutes west, ten miles up fjord from Tasiussaq,' Mike replied.

'OK to that. I'll scramble a rescue heli and ask you to continue searching until it arrives. Please listen out on VHF Channel 16,' said Eric.

Eric called Yann and after quickly briefing him, they adopted a well-rehearsed emergency routine, with each taking responsibility for certain tasks. Eric spoke with air operations at Narsarsuaq, who diverted a helicopter on a routine supply run direct to Nanortalik, whilst Yann contacted Arne at Tasiussaq requesting him to stand-by.

'Understood,' said Arne, 'I'm on my mobile VHF up the mountainside above base. I'll return immediately to activate our air search and rescue plan.'

'The heli will fuel here, pick-up Eric and head direct to *Antarctica*,' replied Yann, 'can you remain listening out as they might want your assistance.'

Arne responded quickly with, 'Understood, standing by!' It took Arne only 50 minutes to run back down the mountainside to his hut, arriving just as the heli passed by, flying up the fjord towards the yacht.

Aboard *Antarctica* Mike had mustered everyone on deck to the area behind the doghouse, before giving each a specific task. Using the sea anchor, he held position 50 metres to the starboard of where the explosion had taken place. The VHF link was on full volume so that they could all hear Eric's co-ordination messages, whilst going about the mind numbing process of trying to assimilate what had happened.

Now ten minutes after the explosion, the only evidence to be seen of the RIB and its two occupants was small patches of individual flotsam; even these quickly dissipating as the wind and current carried them away. Chris was aloft with binoculars making sweeps of the immediate area and directing John to anything of interest he could see. Jim, in the Zodiac with John, carefully retrieved what bits and pieces he could and placed them inside a waterproof bag.

Rick and Hugh had begun a detailed diary of events, starting from the moment they'd arrived onboard the previous evening. George initially spent fifteen minutes on the satellite phone alerting the team contacts as to what had happened, starting with Kevin's wife Gillian. That conversation was without doubt the most traumatic five minutes of his whole life. Following it, he quietly slipped below and packed up both Kevin and Jake's belongings separately, before re-joining Mike to discuss what further steps needed to be taken before the heli arrived.

'At this moment it looks like that maybe one of them inadvertently lit a cigarette or something,' remarked Mike, 'as I've never known an Avon RIB have fire problems before.'

'Kevin never smoked, did Jake?' George asked.

'Yes,' said Mike, 'not many - probably ten a day.'

Shaking his head George wearily asked, 'What water depth do we have?'

Looking over at the depth gauge Mike replied, 'Well over 100 feet - which will almost certainly rule out finding anything that's sunk.'

At which stage the VHF broke into life as Eric called to say they were now airborne from Nanortalik and should be overhead in fifteen minutes. 'Catch you soon,' he said. Mike mused 'I am not sure what if anything the heli can do - but at least they were very quick off the mark.'

'Yes I would agree, at least they can confirm nothing has been missed by Hugh and Mike,' offered George.

The distinctive 'whoop whoop' sound of a helicopter's blades soon broke into earshot and a few minutes later they had each other in visual and in direct communications. The pilot circled at about 200 feet, with Eric at the open rear door peering down through binoculars. The circuit grew steadily wider, as Eric maintained a running commentary. After fifteen minutes orbiting he asked Mike to call in at Tasiussaq, where he would meet them after being dropped off. Confirming an expected time of arrival for *Antarctica* of 3pm the heli then headed off south.

After taking a short onboard prayer service for everyone at the site of the explosion and conducting a final sweep, Mike got *Antarctica* underway on engine power for Tasiussaq. He spoke at length with his UK office who had mustered all of their resources to deal with the media enquires and confirmed they would contact Jake's next of kin. For the first time since the explosion, the psychologically battered crew and their guests were able to make a hot drink and eat some snacks. Jim swiftly placed the waterproof bag containing the items he'd retrieved from the incident area in a forward freezer containing only packed butter.

George made another update call to Phoebe, who'd already been approached by media representatives to expand on the earlier Reuters news flash. Phoebe had asked a close family friend living near Tetbury to call on Gillian and lend support. She'd found upon arrival a very distraught Gillian and local reporters already staking out the cottage and questioning her neighbours and friends for snippets of old gossip and photographs.

He also placed a short call to Camilla, who relayed both her own and Richard's commiserations for the terrible tragedy, so soon after their epic success on Ketil. So far, George, Hugh and Rick had all been on 'automatic pilot'. It was only now, under engine power as they headed steadily towards Tasiussaq that the full impact of the recent savage activity began to sink-in.

They each knew that by talking out loud, it would help them all in coming to terms with their tragic loss. Rick and Hugh's draft diary of events gave them an excellent medium by which they could build up the incidents of the last 24 hours. Again and again, they went over what each of them had done, seen and thought about doing, since meeting Kevin at the foot of the mountain only twenty hours before. As a therapy it had few equals, as it logically followed they started to think about their future arrival in UK and meeting up with Gillian. George skillfully broached the subject of perhaps setting up an education fund for Kevin's boys and was pleased with their positive response. He was pretty sure such a venture would attract support from Richard D'Ilsey, especially if the team had first initiated the concept.

The small huddle of weathered huts that is Tasiussaq came slowly into view, as Mike eased *Antarctica* into an anchorage opposite the largest building. Here Eric and Arne stood waiting, moving down to the water's edge to help secure the Zodiac's line ashore. With Jim remaining in the boat as coxswain and returning to *Antarctica* only Mike and George hopped onto the beach, there to be greeted by a solemn looking Eric and Arne.

Handshakes over, they retired to the main hut and sat around the table, whilst Arne produced a fresh pot of coffee. Eric expressed his personal regrets at what had happened, saying how he'd built up a good rapport with Kevin on their daily radio conversations over the last month.

Arne also gave his condolences, saying that he also had spoken every couple of days with Kevin and had found him a humourous and relaxed character. He'd also remembered Jake from his initial visit with Eric earlier in the year. Mike produced the log of events and quietly read through each item, with George adding the occasional word of explanation. Eric sat totally absorbed, making the odd note and waited until Mike had finished before he remarked, 'I can understand totally why Kevin was coxswain of the RIB, he'd explained to me his previous military experience and qualifications and I was impressed with his handling skills when we took you up - was Jake onboard the RIB just by chance?'

'No,' said Mike, 'he'd asked if he could, so as to get some extra shots of *Antarctica* from the water line for contrast with those he already had. Kevin and I were happy to accommodate his wishes.'

'Did either of them smoke?' Eric continued.

'Yes! Jake did periodically,' replied Mike, 'about ten a day I would say.'

'Have you any idea what kind of lighter he used,' Eric asked.

'I seem to remember it was a metal Zippo type,' Mike recalled. 'He would sometimes sit flicking it open and then striking a light, time after time almost absentmindedly, as some folk do.'

'Do you know if Kevin ever mentioned the RIB as being unreliable or broken in any way?' queried Eric.

As George negatively shook his head as Mike confirmed, 'Never to me.'

'Gentlemen I think we have all the ingredients for a mystery accident that we'll never solve,' Eric pronounced. 'If I may Mike, I would like to travel back with you to Nanortalik aboard *Antarctica* as I have to submit a report to my boss in Nuuk when I get back and I'll be able to chat over details with you. It'll help cut down how long you will have to stay before I can issue clearance formalities.'

'That is not a problem,' Mike answered, 'what about you Arne?'

Glancing across at Arne, Eric quickly replied, 'I would like Arne to stay here, to visit the site and watch the shorelines over the next couple of days, just in case any more material is washed up. I would also like to take over responsibility for the bag of items picked up from the scene.'

'Be my guest' Mike smiled, standing to shake hands and depart.

CHAPTER 22

Half a world away, as the sun went down at Texas Oil in Houston, Ray Watkins was also shaking hands in the reception area of his salubrious office, saying, 'Henry! Thanks for dropping by. Sit down. Bourbon? OK?'

Henry would have normally relished the attention but on this occasion his whole being was filled with self-loathing, so soon after putting the phone down with Gillian. Hearing her speak of Kevin's death had been highly disturbing and left him with a massive feeling of guilt.

'RW,' he began, 'it would appear we may have sent Kevin to his death whilst on Project Alpha,' and he then continued to expand on what he had just heard.

'The results he sent back - have they been analysed yet?' asked RW.

'Yes,' said Henry, 'and it would appear they show negative indications.'

'Other than Gillian knowing you,' queried RW, 'is our tie-in secure?'

'Affirmative,' answered Henry, 'I've no reason to believe otherwise.'

'So if we care for Gillian properly,' RW said, 'it should remain buried?'

'Certainly,' replied Henry, 'I cannot think of anyone else I'd rather trust.'

'In that case we need to agree a sum and how to arrange payment,' said RW, 'I take it you will go see her and lay the trail so it does not get back here?'

'Yes, that would be the very least I can do,' Henry replied.

'OK,' said RW, 'let's set up a discreet $1m off-shore account for her with indirect monthly interest payments. I am sure you can indicate that we would not be best pleased if she abused our trust in her!'

'Thanks for that RW,' Henry remarked, 'I'll get straight on with it and keep you informed once it's in position.'

Descending the lift Henry's mind was in turmoil as he tried to reconcile recruiting Kevin, with his violent death and RW's cold oil man approach. Whilst he appreciated that a large conglomerate such as Texas

Oil had to employ a ruthless chief executive such as RW, exposure to the realities of a corporate business mind set, still came as a shock. 'Still, at least I can make sure Gillian is properly looked after,' he thought, stepping out of the lift into car park below the building.

~ ~ ~ ~ ~ ~ ~ ~ ~ ~ ~ ~ ~ ~ ~ ~ ~ ~ ~

Antarctica tied up alongside the jetty at Nanortalik at 9pm without any welcoming committee to greet them other than Yann. He waved enthusiastically and shouted the various names of individuals as he recognised them before catching the thrown shorelines, making them fast to the bollards as the crew adjusted the fenders and rope tension. Once Mike was happy with the berthing procedure, Eric was the first down the gangway, clutching various documents and the freezer bag with the rescued items from the blast site.

He'd suggested to Mike and George that it would be in their best interests if everyone stayed the night aboard *Antarctica* whilst he prepared his report for the Government officials in Nuuk for perusal the following morning. Once they'd considered it, he would be in a position to offer some on-shore hospitality.

Waving goodnight Eric departed, as they rigged up a fresh water line, whilst he and Yann headed for their office and a hard slog through the night wrestling with the word processor. At 4am Eric pronounced that he was happy with their draft and suggested they should head home for a few hours rest, shower, clean-up and breakfast, returning at 8.30am to call Nuuk and send off the report.

As everyone was finishing breakfast aboard *Antarctica,* Mike suggested they should expect a couple of days delay whilst officials at Nuuk considered Eric's report. He'd already asked his UK office to keep their agent in Denmark aware of events and George confirmed that Phoebe was in direct contact with the Danish Embassy in London.

'I guess we stand down for a few days and I have every confidence that Eric will get us through the bureaucracy as swiftly as possible,' said Mike before continuing, 'It'll help matters for me to have all your passports and air tickets.'

'No problem there. We'll also get our barrels off, sort out what we rented from Eric and manifest everything that returns by sea,' replied George remarking, 'You must put us down on the cooking and cleaning rota whilst we remain on board.'

'Funny you should say that!' Mike quipped, producing a new list.

Either Eric or Yann paid them frequent visits as the day progressed. Initially they did not have much news to impart, other than to say that a senior investigator had been allocated to the case. Eric expressed an opinion that this was normal, as foreign nationals were involved in a fatal accident.

It gave everyone a chance to totally relax, as time had been removed from their personal control. The satellite phone and email link proved invaluable, as did the opportunity to write up the report on the climb of Ketil, which now seemed almost irrelevant after the tragic loss of Kevin and Jake. Rick quietly suggested after he'd been thinking of a way to commemorate Kevin's death that they named the route 'Roach'. A typical epitaph Kevin would have endorsed and everyone was in agreement. So a part of Greenland is now forever his.

As is to be expected some sections of the media were desperately hunting for a story and began suggesting all sorts of ludicrous angles, in their quest to obtain a useable quote, most of which were fielded by either Phoebe or Mike's office. When one was eventually filtered through to *Antarctica* both George and Mike, well versed in dealing with such enquires, adopted the same approach of maintaining that the tragic and regrettable incident was an act of God.

That evening, Eric paid them his third and final visit of the day, explaining that he'd conversed at length with Karl Anderson at Nuuk, the senior Government official allocated to the incident. He felt fairly confident that they would receive clearance to travel the next day and he asked them to stay aboard *Antarctica* for another night to help safeguard this position. In anticipation, he'd asked Yann to provisionally book three seats out on the afternoon helicopter, that linked-in with the evening flight to Copenhagen.

~ ~ ~ ~ ~ ~ ~ ~ ~ ~ ~ ~ ~ ~ ~ ~ ~ ~

In Houston, Debbie was feeling wretched and in a deep personal quandary about Jake. It had been a nightmare listening to Henry talking to Gillian about her loss of Kevin, with moments when she had wanted to cry out loud 'Hey! Me too.' From what she'd been able to gather listening to Henry and the media reports, Jake had been posing as a freelance travel writer, with no apparent family. A simple case of being in the wrong place at the wrong time, which did not leave her feeling particularly good.

The incident had effected Henry quite badly and he was obviously feeling pretty guilty about recruiting Kevin. She'd overheard him express these thoughts to Gillian, who had calmly suggested that Kevin had been more than happy with the arrangement. She reminded him a couple of times that Kevin would have not gone unless feeling happy with the project and what he'd been asked to do. This did little to help Debbie come to terms with her own loss.

~ ~ ~ ~ ~ ~ ~ ~ ~ ~ ~ ~ ~ ~ ~ ~ ~ ~

Eric's arrival at *Antarctica* shortly after breakfast was greeted with a degree of muted interest, with Mike meeting him at the gangway off the quayside.

'Good morning Mike,' said Eric stepping aboard and shaking his hand.

'Even better if you bring good news,' said Mike in reply, leading the way down the steps into the galley area where the others were waiting expectantly.

'I have just been talking with Karl Anderson in Nuuk,' Eric announced to the assembled group, 'he sends apologies for keeping you waiting yesterday and asks that once each of you make a confidential written statement to me this morning, you are then clear to go about your affairs.'

'Excellent news Eric,' replied Mike, 'can I say on behalf of us all how grateful we are for your able assistance - without it we would still be here next week.'

'Thank you,' smiled Eric, 'it has been a real personal pleasure to have met up with you guys and to have you here in Nanortalik, perhaps when you return it will be in less traumatic circumstances.'

'Hear! Hear!' they said unanimously in reply.

~ ~ ~ ~ ~ ~ ~ ~ ~ ~ ~ ~ ~ ~ ~ ~ ~ ~

With each passing day Debbie became more focused on the loss of Jake. She gently relived their last time together minute by minute. His return from the visit to Nanortalik was a definite milestone in their relationship, as afterwards he'd become an even more loving, happy and likeable person, genuinely relaxed in her company. They even spoke of a possibility of sharing a future together.

The decision came to her a few weeks later one sunny morning whilst driving to work. RW was responsible for Jake's passing from her life - therefore he should suffer. Making the resolution, she then spent many hours formulating a non-attributable plan of action. 'He must undergo a living hell!' she decided resolutely.

The initial part of her plan was to compile a dossier on RW from open sources, such as the internet, trade and local media, at the same time she would get closer to Jill, his PA. As they both belonged to the same weekly yoga class sponsored by Texas Oil, it was not difficult to build on social contact with Jill so that after the class, they would enjoy a light lunch together.

As their casual friendship grew Jill intimated that RW was an easygoing boss to work for. Debbie found also there was plenty of open information about his rise to fame in the oil business, his interests and hobbies. She took every valid opportunity to visit Jill at her work place and it all paid off after a couple of months when Jill had to be an in-patient at a medical clinic for a few days.

Henry was away on business over the same period, so it was easy for Debbie to agree to transfer her phone line over to Jill's office and work from there, ready to respond to requests from RW. By now she knew he was a keen golfer, playing off a twelve handicap at the Rosemount Club on the north western outskirts of Houston, not far from his home.

Laura, his wife kept herself busy on various charity committees and their only child Justin was a third year law student at Austin University. Debbie arrived early the first morning to check out his desktop PC, which revealed nothing useful. On the second afternoon when RW went off for an hour to attend a dignitary welcoming ceremony, she was able to look into his notebook PC, which he'd left open.

'This is gold dust!' she exclaimed with a gasp, opening up the list of his recently visited web sites. There, tucked in with a couple of innocuous others, was one that led to a female escort site offering Spanish and English translations.

'Gotcha!' she breathed, noting down the details and RW's site visiting times. She could hardly wait the remaining hours before returning home to open up her PC and investigate the find. Snacking on pizza, fruit and a glass of Californian red she spent the evening drooling over the site which offered contacts to 'play houses' and to over twenty independent females and ten male escorts, in Houston alone, all promising 'VIP standards'. The site linked to ones that included an on-line sex shop, gay escorts and one offering 'young person encounters'.

Texas' common border with Mexico, with its impoverished peasant class meant that every aspect of human sexual deviation was available at a price to the dollar rich Gringo. Reminding herself not to raise her hopes too high for cornering RW, Debbie mused, 'I may well have to do some field research!'

As she had only one more day working in RW's office before Jill returned on Monday, her main concern now was to get as much detail as possible on his future diary dates. This was easy, as a major aspect of Jill's job was to ensure the diary flowed smoothly, with a support file for every event. She'd already noted his personal details, including family birthdays and anniversary dates, credit card, driving licence, passport and club membership numbers, even when his Cherokee Jeep was next due to be serviced.

The obvious occasion for RW to enjoy additional sexual adventures, was when he took off early twice weekly on Tuesday and Friday afternoon for a round of golf. Her opportunity to confirm his routine came after a month, when once again Henry was away on a Tuesday, allowing her to be already positioned in her car in the underground garage when at 1.30pm, RW departed.

Following up the exit ramp she placed herself 150 yards to his rear, tucked in behind another vehicle and tailed him relatively effortlessly onto the main highway running north west. Fifteen miles from the office he took a right off the highway into an area of discreet detached ranch houses, turning without hesitation straight into and parking beside a large older style single storey house.

As he pulled into the driveway, Debbie carried straight on for a few miles before turning round and heading back past the house, confirming his Jeep was parked alongside. She returned to the main road after memorising the number and road name before finding a quiet spot to park up just short of the junction. Ensuring her doors and windows were locked, she spent a while busily putting make up on and doing her nails, when an hour later RW's distinctive Jeep re-appeared and ventured right onto the freeway towards his golf club. Debbie watched him go and after waiting a couple of minutes, drove back again to confirm the house address as number 1157 Mackintosh Way before returning home, well satisfied with a good afternoon's work.

A useful left over for Debbie from a torrid affair some years previously was her continued friendship with Art Price, a reporter with the *Houston Press*. Still privately owned, the newspaper tried hard to maintain its independence. They'd kept in touch and happily shared the same bed for old time's sake on an occasional basis, knowing it was better to be friends than try to force a relationship that neither wanted full-time.

Debbie phoned him and they agreed to meet for dinner that evening at her place, when he'd bring the wine and she would cook prime sirloin steak his favourite way, served with salad. They were well into the second bottle of an excellent Merlot before Debbie gently broached the subject of finding out the detailed happenings inside of 1157. She eluded that it was for a very good female friend who suspected her husband of dallying there and, before employing a private investigator, wanted to make sure what happened either way.

'Ruby will reimburse any expenses you may have in the line of duty,' chuckled Debbie, 'which reminds me, we still have some unfinished business - bring the bottle through!' she suggested, swaying teasingly towards the bedroom.

A week later Art phoned and insisted they eat out at a new recently opened steakhouse that was getting good reports from his media colleagues. Between courses of what was indeed excellent meat, wine and service, Art described his visit to 1157, gaining entry past a burly doorman after explaining that a friend had given him the address and recommendation.

'It may look pretty basic from the outside, but believe me, inside it is one fancy joint,' he reported. 'The décor is modern classical, with lots of light oak and brass candle sticks burning nice aromatic joss. There is a bar area, where you can talk with the four girls on duty and make your choice, whilst 'Alice' the chief hostess, explains the routine and that you can finalise your bill discreetly on departure.'

'Having had my way with luscious Portia,' reminisced Art, 'I chatted with her about the house and the sort of clients who frequented the place. She was full of praise for how 'Alice' ran a friendly place without any bitchiness and made sure all the girls were looked after. She also mentioned that 'specials' could be arranged for known clients,' he said before he smilingly concluded, 'quite what they are I don't know, but I'm more than happy to find out for you!'

'I'll see if Ruby needs any more information and get back to you. Here is $300 she asked me to give you for your expenses,' said Debbie, querying 'will that be enough?'

'That's fine,' replied Art, beckoning the waiter for their bill and remarking, 'let's put this one down to the hospitality of *Houston Press*!'

Debbie called Art later in the week and confirmed that Ruby definitely did want to know more about the 'specials' at 1157. Chortling with delight, Art suggested that it would be his pleasure and he'd report back. She insisted their next meeting would be again at her place

Subject to what Art confirmed, Debbie had formulated an outline plan of action, which would place RW in the most insidious position possible. It was almost unbearable waiting for Art to phone. When the call eventually come through two evenings later, he sounded very buoyant indeed and agreed to come straight over to her place for a meal whilst telling his story.

Debbie quickly baked some chicken breasts and had just finished tossing a green salad when Art rang the doorbell. Giving her a tight welcome embrace, then opening a bottle of white wine, he sat down and started to describe the 'specials' he'd discovered were supplied at 1157.

'So Ruby could consider that the place is a sanctuary for paedophiles,' stated Debbie, before observing that Ruby would no doubt be most pleased with the new information and in anticipation had already left $500 for his expenses.

'It's not often my hobby pays off so well,' laughed Art, 'why don't we go upstairs with the wine, so I can tell you in detail how Portia and Lana showed me why it was called a 'special!'

Just one more task needed to be completed to finish off the information about RW and that was a photograph of his Jeep parked outside 1157. Working on the premise that he was probably a slave to routine, she waited until the next Tuesday when she knew that RW was in the building before discovering a toothache and sought an afternoon off from a concerned Henry to make an emergency dental visit.

Repeating her previous surveillance routine, shortly after 1.30pm she followed RW out again from the building's underground garage onto the freeway and direct to 1157. Waiting five minutes before returning she quietly made her approach to about twenty yards from where the Jeep was parked, slowly executing a three point turn in the wide driveway, as if making the mistake of approaching the wrong house. On the second turn, using her digital Sony camera which was ready for action in her lap, she quickly framed a shot of both the Jeep and the house number, before smoothly departing without even a backward glance.

Later at her apartment she downloaded the picture onto her PC, printed off a copy and then typed out the letter to RW. It read:

'Mr Ray Watkins, You are a regular visitor at 1157 Mackintosh Way - a well-known house of ill repute. Attached is a photograph of your Jeep taken on a recent visit.

'To ensure this image and details of your calls are not broadcast by CNN three days after its receipt at Rosemount Golf Club on Friday - you are required to confirm Texas Oil's immediate decision to fund the complete trial and a production run of the revolutionary hydrogen engine, currently being investigated in Japan. I will contact you by email on Friday evening to receive your proposal.   Friend of the Universe.'

'That should get him worried,' she thought, attaching the photograph and slipping it into a utility envelope already typed with his name c/o the Rosemount Golf Club. She then drove into Houston and posted it first class at the main down town post office.

'It'll definitely be waiting there when he goes for a round of golf on Friday,' she thought, making a mental note to have a chat with Jill first thing Friday morning to confirm RW's diary.

The days until Friday passed with an excruciating slowness made harder by having to act normally at the office for Henry. On the Friday morning, shortly after 9.30am she rang Jill to confirm RW's availability later that day for a possible meeting with Henry. Jill confirmed RW had a 30 minute slot available just before lunch if required. Waiting a short while Debbie then got back and confirmed it would not be needed after all.

At the end of the working day as Debbie drove home she deliberately mulled over the detail of her next hour. Letting herself in, she made up a cold fruit drink and sat down at her desk with a laptop and a mobile phone. She'd bought the phone a few weeks previously at a discount warehouse sale and was running it on a $10 credit top-up card.

Powering up both she entered the email facility and opened up the message already prepared. Her email address was with one of the free servers that continued to function, which she'd not used before. When registering for both the phone and the internet she'd used a name and address from the telephone directory.

Checking the mobile phone modem was connected and operational, she tapped in RW's personal address and sent the message. RW's reply came through 30 minutes later and as expected it was fiercely negative, demanding that an immediate face to face meeting was set up. Debbie let him wait for over an hour before reiterating her original message, with a reminder that he had no room for negotiation.

The local TV news bulletin later that evening carried an article about the death of Ray Watkins, the prominent CEO of Texas Oil. They showed pictures of his Jeep and a police forensic team in woodland near the north west highway and others taken at the gates of his home. The reporter confirmed that a personal firearm had been found in the Jeep and that the police were not looking for any suspects.

CHAPTER 23

A shortening of daylight hours and a discernible drop in temperatures heralded autumn in Nanortalik. Eric finished off his annual report, which had shown a 20 per cent rise in the number of visitors, for which he was justifiably proud. Unknown to him, Government officials in Nuuk had been following developments in Nanortalik with great interest and had earmarked him for rapid promotion to head of tourism south west, once the present incumbent retired at the end of the year.

They had been doubly impressed with his efficient handling of the Ketil team crisis, which could so easily have become a public relations disaster. Upon his arrived at Nuuk for an annual conference, Eric was quietly offered the job if he was interested. Requesting a few days to consider, so he could consult with Edda, he was extremely pleased that his initiative, forethought and hard work had been recognised. He asked who was being considered as his replacement and was informed either Arne or Yann were both strong possibilities if they applied.

He guessed that Arne would not want the job, preferring the shepherd's solitude to dealing with bureaucracy. Yann was certainly more than capable, if perhaps a little young. However, as day follows night that would soon be rectified.

The following spring, at the opening of the polar bear hunting season in Greenland, four tourist hunters arrived at the Nanortalik Hostel off the afternoon flight. It was not a pretty sight as they noisily booked in, with large gun boxes piled high with their bags in the lobby. They'd obviously watched movies on how an Arctic hunter should be equipped, having enough gear to start a minor military operation. As Nauja helped them to register, their loud excited exclamations seemed to include, 'God Damm!' at least once every sentence.

Later, Arne visiting town for a few days was gently teasing Nauja whilst having his supper. One of the visiting hunters joined him and proceeded to bombard him throughout the meal with comments along the lines of, 'How much my rifle cost... I've told my guide to get me a twelve foot bear... A personal preference for hollow point ammo... Can't wait to get me a musk ox!'

And so it went on relentlessly, right through to the dessert. Over coffee, the tourist hunter finally drew breath before finally addressing Arne, 'My name's Wayne Rogers from Atlanta - what's yours and what are you doing here?'

Arne smiled widely and quietly replied, 'I am 'the man', and I'm visiting here to supply the local bears with weapons, ammo and some training in their use!'

More outdoor books from Hayloft:

Military Mountaineering, A History of Services Mountaineering by Bronco Lane, £25.95 (hardback) or £17.95 (paperback)

Soldiers and Sherpas, A Taste for Adventure by Brummie Stokes, £19.95

2041, The Voyage South by Robert Swan, £8.95

A Dream Come True, The Life & Times of a Lake District National Park Ranger by David Birkett, £8

A Journey of Soles, Walking from Land's End to John o' Groats by Kathy Trimmer, £9.50

The Long Day Done, Mountain Rescue in the Lake District by Jeremy Rowan Robinson, £9.50

Oil, Sand and Politics by Dr Philip Horniblow, £25

Running High, the First Continuous Traverse of the 303 Mountains of Britain and Ireland by Hugh Symonds, £16.99

Two Old Bats and a Delinquent Dog by Fiona Hewitt, £8

The Lake District, the Ultimate Guide by Gordon Readyhough, £25

Odd Corners Around the Howgills by Gareth Hayes, £15

To order any of these books or to request a catalogue of all our titles, please contact:

Hayloft Publishing Ltd, South Stainmore,
Kirkby Stephen, Cumbria, CA17 4DJ.
Tel. 017683 42300 ~ e-mail. books@hayloft.org.uk
www.hayloft.org.uk